SCOTZILLA

Also by Catriona McPherson

Last Ditch mysteries

SCOT FREE *
SCOT AND SODA *
SCOT ON THE ROCKS *
SCOT MIST *
SCOT IN A TRAP *
HOP SCOT *

Dandy Gilver mysteries

AFTER THE ARMISTICE BALL
THE BURRY MAN'S DAY
BURY HER DEEP
THE WINTER GROUND
THE PROPER TREATMENT OF BLOODSTAINS
AN UNSUITABLE DAY FOR A MURDER
A BOTHERSOME NUMBER OF CORPSES
A DEADLY MEASURE OF BRIMSTONE
THE REEK OF RED HERRINGS
THE UNPLEASANTNESS IN THE BALLROOM
A MOST MISLEADING HABIT
A SPOT OF TOIL AND TROUBLE
A STEP SO GRAVE
THE TURNING TIDE
THE MIRROR DANCE
THE WITCHING HOUR

Novels

AS SHE LEFT IT *
THE DAY SHE DIED *
COME TO HARM *
THE CHILD GARDEN
QUIET NEIGHBORS *
THE WEIGHT OF ANGELS
GO TO MY GRAVE
STRANGERS AT THE GATE
A GINGERBREAD HOUSE *
IN PLACE OF FEAR
DEEP BENEATH US *

* *available from Severn House*

SCOTZILLA

Catriona McPherson

SEVERN HOUSE

First world edition published in Great Britain and the USA in 2024
by Severn House, an imprint of Canongate Books Ltd,
14 High Street, Edinburgh EH1 1TE.

severnhouse.com

Copyright © Catriona McPherson, 2024

All rights reserved including the right of reproduction
in whole or in part in any form. The right of Catriona McPherson
to be identified as the author of this work has been asserted in
accordance with the Copyright, Designs & Patents Act 1988.

British Library Cataloguing-in-Publication Data
A CIP catalogue record for this title is available from the British Library.

ISBN-13: 978-1-4483-1284-9 (cased)
ISBN-13: 978-1-4483-1285-6 (e-book)

This is a work of fiction. Names, characters, places and incidents are either the product of the author's imagination or are used fictitiously. Except where actual historical events and characters are being described for the storyline of this novel, all situations in this publication are fictitious and any resemblance to actual persons, living or dead, business establishments, events or locales is purely coincidental.

All Severn House titles are printed on acid-free paper.

Typeset by Palimpsest Book Production Ltd.,
Falkirk, Stirlingshire, Scotland.
Printed and bound in Great Britain by
TJ Books, Padstow, Cornwall.

Praise for the Last Ditch mysteries

"A delightful, humorous cozy"
Booklist on *Hop Scot*

"An engaging plot, eccentric characters, plenty of humor"
Booklist on *Scot in a Trap*

"Darkly amusing . . . McPherson keeps the laughs and the action rolling along"
Publishers Weekly on *Scot in a Trap*

"Wildly funny"
Kirkus Reviews on *Scot in a Trap*

"Clever turns of phrase and witty observations fuel this fast and funny novel"
Publishers Weekly on *Scot Mist*

"Plenty of suspects and mordant humor against a background of pandemic paranoia"
Kirkus Reviews on *Scot Mist*

"The banter among the various characters will draw **Janet Evanovich** fans to this engaging, not-quite-a-locked-room mystery"
Booklist on *Scot Mist*

About the author

Born and raised in West Lothian, **Catriona McPherson** left Edinburgh University with a PhD in Linguistics and worked in academia, as well as banking and public libraries, before taking up full-time writing in 2001. For the last fifteen years she has lived in Northern California with frequent visits home. Among numerous prizes, she has won two of Left Coast Crime's coveted Humorous Lefty Awards for the Last Ditch comedies.

www.catrionamcpherson.com

*In loving memory of my dad,
James Gray McPherson, 1935–2024.
I was as lucky as Lexy.*

Midsummer's Day 2023

I couldn't breathe.
 OK, I could breathe but I couldn't bellow and I really needed to bellow. I needed to howl like a wolf at the full moon, to bay like a . . . What bays? Wolves again? . . . to roar like a bear that's been bitten by a snake that's been whacked with a stick.
 If only I could muster a good lungful of breath and get going. 'I have. Had it,' I said, doing my very best. 'I will. Kill who. Ever. Did this.'
 'Wot wong?' said Hiro. She was two-and-a-half, cute as a button in her flower girl outfit, and didn't need to hear any of what was going to burst out of me like a civilization-ending lava flow, just as soon as I could signal to someone to undo my dress for me.
 'What *is* the matter, Lexy?' said Diego. He was nine and cuter in his ringbearer outfit than it would be kind to tell him, since he reckoned he'd grown out of cute a good few years back. He was also a bit of a jerk to his baby sister sometimes, like right now as he hit all those Ts and hissed all those Ss, to show off his diction. Hiro was very much still getting there.
 I gestured madly over my shoulder with the hand that wasn't holding my posy.
 'What?' said Kathi, my best woman. 'Have you been bitten by something?'
 'No, my God!' said Todd, loud enough to make Hiro step backwards in her little white satin shoes. 'Did you get bitten by a bug in those nasty so-called bathrooms? Did you get stung? Is it still on you? I told you this would happen!' He had been a complete pain in the arse about the wedding venue, right from the word go. It was a hop garden slash microbrewery slash farmer's market with an event space for hire. In Todd's mind though, because of his galactic insect phobia, it was an ant farm slash entomology research

centre slash compost bin, with the nerve to invite people along and charge them for being infested. Frankly, he didn't deserve to be my bridesman, with all the grief he had given me.

'Undo. My dress,' I managed to say. 'And take. Hiro. Away.'

Della instantly twigged why I was asking but she took her matron-of-honour duties very seriously, as she should, and wasn't about to leave me. Instead, she told Diego to remove his little sister and escort her to the far end of the wedding venue, where they could be really helpful and count the koi in the pond. That's how sure she was that I was about to turn the air blue with words her children had never heard before. She would rather they play beside a body of open water.

Once they were gone, Todd unhooked the four little silver eye-thingies holding closed the roll-over top bit of my dress. It had a name and I had learned it, along with a pallet-load of other couture terminology, but there's so much to do when organizing a wedding, that it had slipped my mind. I'd retained 'peplum', because it was useful to be able to tell everyone what I'd never be caught dead in, and I remembered 'bound hemming' because I thought he was a Swedish detective, but the roll-over top bit with the silver thingies? Not a clue. It looked like a polo neck that someone had jammed halfway down my shoulders, but it wasn't called a shoulder-polo. It also looked a bit like a whole-body foreskin, but that's definitely not what the magazine captions would say.

Finally, Todd got past the silver thingies and on to the eight hundred and fifty tiny buttons, unfastening me from the bottom of the shoulder-skin to the top of the sweetheart-shaped seam that joined the straitjacket upper portion of my wedding dress to the trip-hazard skirt bit. Once he was halfway down my ribcage and my lungs were free to expand, I heaved in a mighty breath and explained what was wrong.

'Gimme a Prosecco!'

OK, so I cleared my throat first. Kathi fumbled a foaming glassful from the open bottle in the ice bucket and waggled her eyebrows at Todd to make him open another.

'I've just seen the fucking fairy lights!' I bellowed, after a restorative glug. 'I ordered daisy-style flower fairy lights. I know I did. *You* know I did. I've got a receipt that proves I did. And I'm a reasonable woman. I don't expect the bulb-backs of daisy-style fairy lights to have as many petals as real daisies. I'm not insane. But

I'm not a schmuck either. They need at least five. There should be five fucking . . . lobes . . . on the fucking petals that make the petal-shaped fucking bulb-backs of my carefully chosen and extremely expensive fucking wedding fucking fairy lights. Five!'

'Are there . . . four?' said Kathi. If anyone was ever going to sympathize with me about this, it was Kathi. She's got a very tidy mind. That is to say, she's got a clinical aversion to clutter, mess, dirt, and germs that makes Mrs Hinch, the online Queen of Clean, look like a buried-alive hoarder.

I gave her a hard look but saw no kindness or understanding. Which, OK, might have been because she never wears make-up usually and she might not know how much she could move her face without it starting to slide off, but still.

'Do you know what flowers have four petals?' I growled at her. You can't actually keep bellowing while you drink really fizzy Prosecco. It's painful. 'Alyssum has four petals. Fucking Alyssum! The white bit of the red, white and blue bedding schemes from old British men's front fucking gardens in the fucking fifties!'

'Oh no,' said Todd. I rounded on him. Was that sarcasm? 'Wh-what are the red and blue parts?' he stuttered out.

'Salvia,' I said, hoping my voice was as cold as my heart felt towards him. 'And lobelia.'

Kathi snorted and I swung back.

'So . . . *is* it four?' said Della. 'Because even if it is, you know Lexy, that's pretty. And patriotic too. This country or your country. It would be a problem for me but red, white and . . . Wait, do you mean the problem is the fairy lights are the wrong colours? Or just that the number of sticking-out portions of the bulb-backs remind you of flowers that are white and used to be planted with red and blue flowers in your home country?'

'What do you mean "just"?' I said. I put a hand out to steady myself on the make-up table Todd had set up here in my dressing room because the one supplied by the venue wasn't big enough for his cosmetic cases. Even though I could breathe with my whole lungs now, the mere thought of red, white, and blue lights at my wedding, instead of the 'fevered peach' I had chosen so carefully to match the long-range-weather-forecasted colours of the midsummer sunset, was enough to make me feel as if I might swoon. I worked so hard on those lights. I hated the name – who calls a fairy light 'fevered'? – but in all my researches I couldn't find a better colour so I had been mature and magnanimous, and managed to compromise. And now this!

'There aren't four lobes,' I said. 'Four would be bad enough. There are three.'

I spoke the words into a deathly silence. Todd took a sip of Prosecco. Della twisted her own wedding ring, like she regularly did during wedding discussions, almost as if she was trying to summon her husband, as if she needed someone to protect her. From what?

'So . . .' said Kathi. Todd put a hand out and clutched her arm. He was digging his nails right into the sleeve of her tux. Even though he had a brand-new manicure to think of.

'I'm going to say it, Todd,' Kathi announced. Not loud but steely. 'I should have been saying it every day. We should all have started saying it months ago. Oh yes, it was funny at first but it's not funny now. And yes I know we only have one more day and if we've sucked it up this long we could surely keep on sucking and get through to the end. We're going to be hammered, apart from anything else, and we all know how much drinking has helped us, don't we?' She paused and did a bit of breathing that sounded like something you'd learn in a class. 'But I can't,' she went on. 'I physically can't. Therefore . . . I'm going to say it. And, Todd? You can't stop me. Lexy? Three lobes on the petal-shaped bulb-backers of your flower fairy lights?' She took another huge, trained breath. 'So . . . what?'

I didn't understand at first. I thought she had started to ask, 'So what are we going to do about it?', but then been too upset to keep on talking. It took me a moment or so to realize what, in fact, I had just heard.

'"So . . . what?",' I said. 'So what that my bought-and-paid-for daisies don't have five petals or even four petals? So *what*? Do you know what has three petals?'

I paused, waiting for an answer.

'Hey,' said Todd. 'I just noticed you're all out of fucks.'

'Fucking orchids!' I screamed at him. At all of them. '*Orchids* have three petals. Last-minute, we-don't-really-care-about-you, catch-all, sales-point gift-flowers. *Fucking* orchids. And you know what else?'

'Two petals would make them propeller blades?' said Todd. Kathi snorted again and even Della turned away. What was happening here?

'I'm not finished with three,' I hissed. 'Irises. Irises have three petals.' I wasn't an expert before I started planning a wedding, but there wasn't a flower, colourful bract or notable style of foliage in the natural word that I didn't know about now. 'Fucking pond flowers from fucking ponds, with fucking frogs and fucking fish! I'm supposed to get married under a web of stinking fucking fish lights, am I?'

'Um,' said Kathi. 'You could skip the wedding and just have a party.' Her voice was tremulous, as if she was trying not to laugh.

'Or go through with it as a rehearsal and then have it annulled and do it again with greater botanical accuracy,' said Todd, whinnying a bit down his nose.

'Della?' I said. 'Matron of honour, sensible, caring, grown-up, *normal* Della. What do you think?'

'The ladders they use for the hop harvest are really tall,' she said. 'I had to make sure they were all locked up in case Diego got ideas.'

'What are you wittering on about?' I asked her.

'We could lash a few of them together end to end,' she said, 'then you could climb up and get over yourself.'

I couldn't speak. For a minute, I couldn't *hear* – my ears rang as if someone had let off a shotgun. And I couldn't *see* anything either, except a red mist rising in my eyes. I always thought that was just an expression, that red mist. Never knew it was real.

'Don't cry!' said Todd. 'Lexy, for the love of all that's holy, don't cry. You're wearing your wedding make-up. That eye-look is going to be in all your photographs for the rest of your life. Don't you dare cry!'

I hadn't noticed the door opening. 'No, it's not,' said a voice.

'Taylor, get out!' Kathi said, opening her tux jacket and trying to hide me from my bridegroom.

'I get why she's crying,' Taylor said. 'I get it, baby. I'm so sorry.'

'You do, don't you?' I said, throwing down my posy – it hardly mattered anymore if it got crushed, since my whole wedding lay in ruins. 'I love you so much.'

Behind him, his own wedding crew filed into the dressing room, solemn-faced and silent.

'Look!' I said, gesturing wildly to show them off to *my* so-called attendants. I kind of wished I still had the posy to wave around. I turned back to the doorway. '*This* lot were laughing!'

There was a collective gasp from the newcomers, gusty and satisfying.

'Dude!' said Devin, Taylor's best man, looking at Della with a look he had never worn to look at his beloved wife before. He was punching so far above his weight in their marriage that, even now, years after he gave up weed to win her heart, he still stumbled around with a dopey grin on his face half the time. He was always getting stopped and searched by the over-enthusiastic Cuento PD and it never helped when he tried to explain, 'It's love, my dudes. It's a legal high.'

'Why were you laughing, Todd?' said Roger, Taylor's chief and only groomsman. He's been married to Todd for so long he usually just lets it all wash over him – the schemes, the crazes, the fads, the talent for over-reaction – and also he's a paediatrician, used to being calm and kind to sick little kids and their upset parents, so he can't scold to save his life.

'Does that include you?' said Noleen, Taylor's chief and only groomswoman. She's been married to Kathi for a good long while as well, and loves her bones, but she's a grumpy, menopausal motel owner, who only can't be called a misanthrope because she also hates animals. Her tone of voice withered Kathi like a blowtorch.

'See?' I said. Then I turned my back on all three of my half of the wedding party. 'Thank God, *you're* here,' I said, surging forward towards the other, better half. (I hadn't always thought so. Della, Todd and Kathi were my friends but it wasn't like Devin, Roger and Noleen were Taylor's exactly. They were just the leftover people and it made sense to use them to plug the gaps after I had creamed off what I needed. (I tried to say that to my mother at one point, but she didn't understand. She said she thought the wedding pressure might be 'getting to me'. Weirdo.)) I wondered if it was too late to swap friends for the day. They were mostly all in tuxes apart from Della. I'd soften Taylor up first and then ask him.

'Did you call the cops?' he said, just as I went in for a hug.

I drew back. 'I . . . Well, no. I'm going to get a lawyer to send them a letter on Monday.'

He drew back too. 'What are you talking about?'

'The fairy lights,' I said. 'What are *you* talking about?'

'Well, yeah, the fairy lights. I guess. You saw them? By the cake table there?'

'Exactly,' I said. 'I got a really good close look at them and they are not what I ordered.' I blinked as, from very far away, I felt something approaching. 'Hang on,' I said. 'I got a close look because

they weren't up in the beams and rafters where they should be. There was a string of them hanging down.'
'Hanging . . .?' said Taylor. 'Did you see the end of it?'
'The end of the string?' I said. 'No, it disappeared behind the table-staging.'
'Is that the false wall that we were going to take the cake-cutting photos up against?' said Taylor.
'What do you mean "were going to"?' I said. 'What are you talking about?'
'I'm talking,' Taylor said, very slowly, 'about Sister Sunshine.'
'Sister Sunshine the celebrant?' I said.
'No, Sister Sunshine the dessert topping,' said Taylor. 'Yes, Lexy, our celebrant. Because, like you saw, a string of fairy lights is hanging down. And it disappears behind the . . . table-staging? . . . where the end of it is still wrapped around Sister Sunshine's neck from when it was used to strangle her. I'm really sorry, babe, but no one's getting married here today.'

PART ONE

ONE

January 2023

I was right and not for the first time. I had watched the rest of the Last Ditch Motel residents undergoing a collective brain event over the Christmas we spent in Scotland, starting to talk immigration and visas and mortgages and permanence, and I knew all along it was nothing more than some unseasonably Dickensian weather, the fact that we were living free in my mum and dad's hotel, and the unfamiliar (to them) sensation of being half-cut from the Bailey's on their cornflakes every morning to the last Drambuie instead of mouthwash before bed. Then New Year came along, also not markedly sober, and finally 2023 got underway. The decorations came down like the driving rain, the Scrabble went back in the games cupboard, and the Californians came face to face with the non-holiday telly schedule, discovering that PBS and Britbox select the very best, leaving a hell of a lot of depressingly low-budget make-over shows, as well as quizzes where they didn't know any of the answers, and *Emmerdale*.

So we all came home.

And went back to work.

And I started planning a small, elegant, understated wedding.

But let's stick a pin in that and deal with work first because, in January, our joint business got its best-paying and most interesting assignment in all of its four years of existence.

Let me back up here a minute.

I am a licensed MFT. I was an accredited counsellor back in Scotland before I moved, then I retrained and now I'm all set here in California too. And so I should think, since I have assimilated like a chameleon. Look how I just said 'stick a pin' and 'back up here' and even 'all set'. None of my clients ever has to decipher alien English out of my lips as well as all their other problems. They come in, they sit down and we're cooking with gas.

My business used to be called Lexy Campbell, MFT. Now it's called Trinity for Life, which I still think sounds like a cult but I've got a waiting list so I can't complain. And, like I said, it's no longer a one-woman show. Not since the advent of Todd.

Todd is an anaesthetist. That's how he met Roger, at work. Only with the insect problem – full-blown cleptoparasitosis, which is a delusional disorder with an entry in the DSM-V – the hospital managers were too chicken to let him keep the keys to the drugs cupboard and so he got put on long-term sick leave. That being so very boring, he looked around for a side-hustle and found the one he was born for. He runs Trinity for You, providing wardrobe and grooming make-overs to people, OK women, who've had it with the endless yakking and weeping *I* offer and just want to have fun instead. I don't judge him. Plus he came up with the Trinity name.

What's that? Trinity is a stupid title for a duo?

Meet Kathi. For twelve years now, she has run a laundromat, the Skweeky-Kleen, attached to the Last Ditch Motel, which she co-owns with Noleen. That's her day job, like putting my head on one side, offering tissues and saying 'tell me as much as you feel comfortable sharing' is mine. These days, she's also got a de-cluttering side-gig: Trinity for Home.

Now, Kathi and Todd are a marriage of dysfunction made in the seventh circle of hell, if I'm talking professionally. Her germaphobia is bolstered by his parasitosis and his parasitosis is backed up by her germaphobia and the pair of them will probably die clutching each other one day soon, after an unforeseeable chemical reaction between a new cleaning product and a banned insecticide. I could work on either one of them alone; when they band together, I'm helpless.

But that's only my professional opinion. They're also my friends and when I look at them through *those* spectacles, they're good for each other. They make each other feel safe and they stop either Noleen or Roger going absolutely bat-shit from having to deal with it all. No such luck for me, of course, being one of a threesome where they're the other two but . . .

I might need a rain check (thank you, thank you) on that 'but' actually. I'm sure there is a but, a bright side, a silver lining. Just not to hand.

So there we were, couple of years back – actually three and half but it was pre-pandemic and time went weird, didn't it? – when Todd had his brainwave and Kathi stepped up to the crease.

She started working towards her PI licence and we added a fourth string to the bow: Trinity Investigations (aka Trinity for Trouble). Except I'm not allowed to call it a bow string, because it's like a pebble in Kathi's shoe to have four bits of a Trinity, so I have to say 'a matrix level' when I'm talking to her alone. Todd won't stand for that, because it sets Kathi Muntz PI above him, so when I'm talking to *him* I keep it vague and call Trouble 'the new bit'.

Where were we?

Oh yes, in January, enjoying the mild California winter, with its soft rain filling the reservoirs and its balmy afternoons, making everyone shrug off their cardis as they sat on the pavement patios sipping their lattes.

Wait, though. I haven't said anything about the rest of them. Thing is, Trinity isn't the Ditch, and the Ditch isn't Trinity, but the connections are thick and short. Roger and Noleen have been touched on already, which leaves the Muelenbelts: Della, Devin, Diego and little Hiro. They've got nothing to do with Trinity per se and Todd didn't try to recruit either of them – despite Devin being a computer science graduate and white-hat hacker for the state government, and despite Della being the greeter and booker at a beautician's, which they all call a 'day spa' with the usual height of falutingness. Day spa! Sounds nothing like somewhere you spend twenty minutes getting your pubes ripped out, does it? I still have to stare at things lower than my chin to keep from rolling my eyes sometimes when I hear California bombast. Like the time someone at the health centre tried to screw an emergency appointment out of the receptionist, by saying they'd had 'a possible hantavirus exposure'. I edged away but kept eavesdropping. Turns out they'd seen a mouse.

Where were we? Right! January 2023, back to old clothes and porridge after the feast. I was shovelling my way through the post-holiday bulge in new appointments with people who had decided they hated their families, Todd was going through Cuento's wardrobes like a plague of moths, Kathi was straining the landfills of Beteo County with the usual once-loved furniture, dishes, gadgets and art, newly revealed as loathsome when everyone took their decorations down and tried to cram their Christmas presents and sale bargains into their still-the-same-size houses.

We were perfectly happy and mediumly busy (setting the wedding aside for just a wee bit longer), not looking for a case at all, when Todd came home from the supermarket one day, scooped Kathi up just as she was closing the Skweek and dragged her back to my boat.

Urgh. I should have mentioned I live on a boat. (These catch-ups are really hard.) Yes, my home, and Taylor's too now, is a houseboat moored on the slough after which the motel is named. It's poky and inconvenient and I have to ask Della and Devin to open their bathroom window so I can piggy-back on Devin's souped-up and possibly illegal (I don't ask) Wi-Fi, but I love it. Who lives on a boat? It makes me happy every day.

So there I was, cooking a hot meal for my man coming home, when I felt the deck tilt and settle. Kathi and Todd, I reckoned, and felt a quiet smugness when they appeared in the kitchen doorway. It's not much of a party trick – IDing your friends from their footfall – but it's handy, like an auditory door-cam.

I took the pan off the heat – my kitchen is too small for more than one person when there's oil frying – and followed them back along to the porch.

'We got a case,' said Todd, handing over a cardboard cup of coffee from Swiss Sisters. He still hasn't absorbed the concept of teatime.

'Cool,' I said. 'You happy to take it, Kathi?' Since she's the actual PI, she gets final say.

'Not sure,' she replied. I had known that already from the way she had gone over the seat of her chair with one of the disinfectant wipes from the handipack on her belt before sitting. (One of the reasons I'd love to get my hands on Kathi's psyche is that it's so very clear her concerns come from general stress, not specific threats. She liked Scotland and calmed down a lot there, in the land where people don't rinse their hand-washed dishes and might not shower every day.) 'It's vandalism in the cemetery.'

'Sound like a police matter,' I said. Trinity has, now and then, done work that Cuento PD should have taken care of. Once or twice, we've even done work that Cuento PD were trying to take care of. They hate that, I can tell you. In our defence, we have never hindered them. We've only ever annoyed and humiliated them and I'm profoundly comfortable with both.

'The police aren't interested,' Todd said.

'In the desecration of graves?' I said. 'Wait, though. *Is* it desecration of graves? Or are they vandalizing the bins or the gates or something?'

Kathi shook her head. 'None of the above. They're decorating. Tidying plots, planting flowers, changing water, clipping grass.'

'Bastards,' I said. 'I don't get it. Explain.'

'There's this group called the Sex—' said Kathi.

Todd stood up and scurried inside. 'Call when you're done,' he said, as he passed.

I stared after him. I was often bewildered by one or both of these two best friends (thank God for Della), but I could usually nudge it into a category and work it out.

'Because entomologists from UCC found some new kind of beetle in the cemetery, years back,' Kathi said. 'And so they went on a hunt for more.'

'Right, sexton beetles, graveyard, gotcha,' I said. 'Poor Todd.'

'Right? And to help find the damn things they got a slew of extra volunteers who took to hanging out there, clearing all the crap and generally making themselves useful. It helps to look busy when you lurk in a cemetery. Especially when there are burials going on. Otherwise, you know. Creeper.'

'Right.'

'So they got to know it pretty well and, even when the excitement about the beetles died down – it was a false alarm; some dude in Oregon had already written papers about these critters – they didn't feel right leaving the cemetery to go back to rack and ruin. And so they carried on volunteering and it kind of snowballed from there.'

'Aren't you done yet?' came Todd's voice from along the hallway beyond my living room.

'Just wrapped it up,' Kathi shouted back.

'So, fast forward,' Todd said, breezing back out and immediately taking over. (I don't know how Kathi can stand him.) 'And somehow these . . . volunteers . . . are completely responsible for the upkeep of the entire place. The city doesn't bother anymore because there's nothing for them to do and the bereaved love not paying a maintenance fee. Everybody's happy.'

'Or dead,' I pointed out.

'They do guided walks,' said Kathi. 'Social history of Cuento, women's advancement, the process of integration, and – yes, they admit – weird stuff.'

'Weird stuff?' I said, not liking the sound of that.

'Kinda,' said Kathi. 'They just really love graves.'

'Well then, they should call themselves gravediggers or even vampires,' said Todd. 'Instead of sticking with something outdated, irrelevant and offensive.'

'Why, what do they call themselves?' I said.

'I thought you said you'd wrapped it up.' Todd was on his feet again.

'Put your fingers in your ears,' Kathi said. She turned to me. 'The Sexton Beetles. Because they beetle about the graveyard, doing shit.' She nodded at Todd, who stopped la-la-la-ing and removed his fingers. 'Anyhoo,' Kathi went on, 'they stopped in at the Skweek and asked for help, because someone is . . . trolling them, Todd? Would you say?'

'Or it could be art,' Todd said. 'Performance art.'

'Or guerilla grave-tending,' said Kathi. 'But the Sex— volunteers are not happy.'

'They certainly won't be if you call them *that*,' I pointed out.

'I gave them our standard contract,' Kathi said. 'And they're coming back for a meeting in ten minutes. Do you have any snacks? Any ice?'

'They're coming here?' I said. 'All of them?'

'She never has any ice,' Todd said. 'It's like a mania for avoiding pleasure. It's probably diagnosable. Anyway, there's only four of them.'

'Yes, they're coming here,' Kathi said. 'Since you have the consulting room. I'm sick of meeting clients in coffee shops and pizza joints.'

'So we look into renting an office,' I said, for the eleven thousandth time. 'Or you could use a room in the owners' apartment. Or clear out the back room behind Reception. Or Todd's thing.'

'It's a waste of money to hire an office when you already have one,' Kathi said. Then, as if she was an entirely different person she said the exact opposite, basically. 'And you know I like to keep the owners' apartment clean, Lexy. Why would I pay the occupancy taxes on a motel room to sleep in if I didn't need to keep my apartment clean?'

'I can't answer that,' I said. 'I reject the premise of the question and I don't want to upset you.'

'And we can't have clients traipsing through the check-in space of a motel when they might be upset or in trouble,' she tried next.

'You've asked them to squeeze round the back of the motel on a pretty narrow path and board a houseboat,' I said.

'Also,' said Kathi. 'You told me you thought Todd's thing was nuts.'

'Hey!' said Todd.

Todd's thing *was* nuts. He had seen a documentary about Andy McNab, decided it was sexy to be that mysterious, and tried to persuade Kathi that she should only meet clients online, in deep shadow, and with a voice distorter, pointing out that undercover work was well-nigh impossible for all of us because of how often we'd been on the front page of the *Cuento Voyager*. Like it hadn't been him who put us there, forever calling up the newsroom and flirting his way to a photo shoot. Kathi had asked him how she was supposed to do home make-overs without her face being seen. Todd had tried to float Mardi Gras masks as an option. I pointed out that a Mardi Gras mask and an N95 would be the equivalent of a full-face balaclava and the idea was dropped.

'So, *do* you have snacks?' Kathi said.

'Olives, cheesy things, and cornichons,' I told her.

'Really?'

'No,' I said. How in the name of Jerry Seinfeld can so many American people not recognize sarcasm? 'I'll put on a pot of bad coffee and let them smoke, just like a real PI would. But I truly think you should use the storeroom behind Reception from now on.'

'What about the storeroom at the Skweek?' said Todd. 'It's practically empty.'

'It's not empty. It's *organized*,' Kathi said. 'That's how storerooms should look. And garages and basements and closets, too.'

They were still bickering as I set up the coffee-maker and ransacked my cupboards for biscuits. When the boat dipped, a few minutes later, it felt like exactly the weight of four Sex Volunteers (oh yes, the name had stuck already) and so my beaming smile was nothing to do with welcome. The four of them didn't know that, though, and they beamed back at me.

There were too many of us for my consulting room in the end. It was the original dining room and seven people might have been able to squeeze in round a table once upon a time, but it's got my easy chair and the client's couch in there now as well as my desk, so we stayed in the living room, and must have looked like Act One of a creaky old play, as the introductions were made and the stilted explanations got going.

Not that Todd ever finds a social or business situation awkward. Not he. He dished out coupons for introductory offers to his wardrobe consultations – nothing can ever persuade him how offensive this is – and complimented each of them on some part of their appearance, as if that helped.

'You have knock-out brows,' he said. 'I could take them to the next level.' And: 'With that trim bod you could carry off much crisper tailoring.' And: 'Your face shape isn't nearly so much of a problem with that haircut – well done.' And: 'You wouldn't believe how lucky you are to be starting from absolute zero.'

'Todd has a mental health diagnosis,' I said, as he went back to the kitchen for cream and sugar. It was true. If they chose to join up invisible dots I hadn't put there and assume I meant autism spectrum disorder, that was their look-out. They all smiled at him when he returned.

'But first,' he said, as if he really had just reeled in a few make-over prospects (and the infuriating thing is he probably had), 'to your PI needs. Kathi Muntz, here, is certified, experienced, commended, confidential and completely reliable.'

'Right,' said the one with eyebrows. He was a man probably in his sixties, with salt and pepper hair and one of those classically ugly faces that end up attractive, despite the two zoological wonders crawling over his forehead. His name was Bob Larch and his interest in cemeteries arose out of local history. 'Well, we're less concerned about confidentiality than you might think. We probably need publicity. Isn't that right, Mitch?'

The one that Todd had singled out as having a trim bod nodded. I wouldn't have said 'trim bod'. I'd have said 'built like four bits of knotted string'. 'Crisper tailoring' would make him look like a paper-wrapped straw. 'Mitchell Verducci,' he said. 'No relation.'

I never know who it is people mean they're not related to. Hardly ever. Once, a man called 'De Vito' said it and I was so excited not to be left out that I blurted, 'Danny!' like an idiot and he walked away.

'I'm no local history buff,' Mitchell went on. 'I'm drawn to darkness.'

'Bob is right,' said the 'absolute zero', who of course was absolutely fine-looking. In fact, better than fine-looking, with the carefully protected skin of a savvy Korean woman who could pass for twenty-five but might be fifty, as well as that poker-straight, black-satin hair with not a split end anywhere. She smiled. 'Juni Park,' she said. 'Social and cultural change. Graveyards are treasure troves and this has been both disrespectful and disruptive.'

'"This" being . . .?' said Todd.

'It's hard to explain in a nutshell,' said Juni Park. If she couldn't manage it, then no one could, I thought to myself. She had a moleskin notebook open to a blank page and a slim silver pen in her hand. 'I think,' she went on, 'that we should lay it all out and let you draw your own conclusions. Linda?'

The one Todd reckoned had a terrible face but a corrective hairdo – she looked perfectly unremarkable to me, I must say – wasn't listening, I didn't think. She was staring at my . . . lap? 'Linda Magic,' she said. 'Amateur genealogist and professional wedding planner. That's a beautiful diamond you're wearing and it looks new.'

That's how it began. Nothing to do with me at all really.

TWO

'Did you know people often have weddings in our parkland?' Linda Magic explained.

'Parkland meaning cemetery?' asked Kathi.

'Is that your real name?' said Todd. 'Magic?'

'Ellis Island,' said Linda. 'M-A-J-I-E-K in the old country. But it's perfect for my business, isn't it? I've been married twice and never even considered changing it.'

'It started last summer,' said Juni Park, in a quelling sort of tone. I imagined she'd have to quell Linda Magic as much as I had to quell Todd. 'We thought it was the family the first time it happened and so, although it seemed odd, we ignored it. But let's start with the second incident.'

'Why?' said Kathi.

'The second incident was almost funny,' Juni said. 'It was June, so it was Pride and we noticed that one of the graves had been bedecked with rainbows. Rainbow flags, rainbow streamers, rainbow wind whirlers, and a beautiful posy of rainbow flowers. Petunias, marigolds, bachelor's buttons, pelargonium. It was pretty.'

'It was ugly!' Mitchell said. 'It was outing! Outing isn't pretty.'

'Right, right,' Bob Larch put in. 'I think Juni was saying colourful flowers are pretty. But yes, it was outing and there's nothing pretty about that.'

'Who was outed?' said Kathi.

'Kermit Kellog,' Linda said.

'Who the hell is Kermit Kellog?' said Todd.

'The deceased,' said Linda. 'But it's not an outing if he wasn't gay, is it? What would you call it?'

'A smear,' said Bob Larch. 'Except that makes it sound as if gay is bad,' he added, so fast all the words ran together. He had seen Todd reacting, I think. He certainly saw him sit back and relax.

'Trolling?' said Mitchell Verducci. 'Baiting?'

'Anyway,' Juni said. 'The Kellog family came and cleared the stuff away.'

'Then a few nights later,' said Mitchell, 'although we can't be sure when, the gravestone was lit up with rainbow lasers.'

'Why can't you be sure when?' Kathi said. She was taking copious notes. 'Also, was that his real name? Kermit Kellog?'

'He was old,' Mitchell said. 'Born before the frog. Poor guy.'

'He wasn't born before cornflakes, was he?' I said. 'Or alliteration?'

'Why can't you be sure when?' Kathi said.

'Because it wasn't until six nights later that I did our next moonlight tour and saw it,' said Juni. 'Everyone in the group thought it was us and they were all the way into it, so I styled it out and then told the cops the next morning.'

'But they didn't care,' said Bob. 'I tried myself to work out where the beam was coming from but I was an actuary before I retired and I don't know the first thing about . . .'

'Electrical engineering,' Linda supplied. 'It still lights up now and then, randomly. But we've been too busy dealing with the rest of it.'

'Which is . . .?' said Kathi.

'Dead snakes,' said Bob. 'Creepy dolls, pizza deliveries, a glass harmonica – that got smashed by the donkeys, though – donkeys, goats, and all the little stuff too.'

'Like . . .?' said Todd.

'Inappropriate pebbles,' said Juni.

'*Are* there inappropriate pebbles?' Kathi asked. She had stopped writing.

'There are inappropriate words to spell out in pebble-form,' said Mitch. 'Like—'

'Don't say it!' said Linda.

'And slanderous accusations,' said Bob. 'At least, actually, you can't slander the dead but what else would you call it? There's this sweet gravestone with a married couple buried together and whoever it is that's doing all this laid out "SIBLINGS" in the grass in bits of sea glass. Well, probably tumbled glass. Sea glass doesn't usually turn up in such even pieces.'

'And I take it they weren't?' I said. I really wanted to hear the inappropriate pebble words, but I wouldn't demean myself by asking. I knew Todd would do it for me, if I waited.

'Why haven't we read about any of this in the *Voyager*?' Todd said. Then added, right on cue, 'Especially the slurs. If they're printable.' He waited but nothing came of it. 'I mean, you said yourselves that you needed publicity to get to the bottom of things.

Why not call the *Voyager* every time something happens and get the whole town on it? Citizen sleuthing.'

'Because it's not always donkeys and pizza,' Linda said. 'Sometimes the families . . . Like the first case.' She folded her lips inwards until they were invisible and put her head down. It was the best indication I had ever seen that someone wasn't going to talk. And I sit in a room and ask people to open up about painful stuff for a living.

'*I'll* tell them,' Bob Larch said. 'Poppy Cliveson died at the age of three in 2004. What happened with her is that her grave got covered in graduation paraphernalia when she should have been graduating high school. I thought – we all thought – it was her family. Until her family came to visit her grave and . . .' He broke off and put his arms around his opposite elbows as if trying to hug himself.

'I've never heard a mother cry that way,' said Juni. 'I thought she was going to crack her ribs, the way she was howling.'

'That's terrible,' said Kathi. I had taught her that. At first, she had said that spouting such obvious and useless lines would be patronizing but, after she'd seen me do it and receive grateful smiles and even hands reaching out to hold mine, she was convinced. All four of the Sex Volunteers gave her brave, watery looks and nodded their agreement.

'Has anything else that cruel happened?' said Todd. 'Besides the slurs, I mean.' Circling, always circling.

'There was a noose left for the anniversary of a suicide,' said Juni. 'In fact, we didn't even know it *was* a suicide until we saw the rope and looked it up in the records.'

'Same deal with the box of doughnuts that time,' Mitch put in. 'We knew the guy wasn't a cop. We found out from his widow he was a diabetic.'

'Whole Monopoly board set up on the grave of a bankrupt,' said Bob. 'Apart from anything else, you know, these pranks cost real money sometimes. That's what makes me say it might be some twisted kind of consensual art.'

'Conceptual,' said Juni absently, but she was nodding.

'So will you take the case?' Linda said. 'We can pay.'

'We can offer a discount,' said Kathi, which wasn't like her. 'Since you're volunteers and since this is . . . The cops really won't touch it? Did they say why?'

'Repeatedly,' said Bob, in an icy voice.

'Anyway, it's only at the cemetery that we're volunteers,' said Mitchell. 'Juni's a pharmacist and Linda's a wedding planner. They're loaded. And imagine what a sweet retirement an actual actuary sets up for himself before he makes the jump. Bob could buy and sell all of us in the room.'

'What about you?' said Todd.

'I work part-time in the patent office down in San José,' said Mitchell.

'That's a hell of a commute,' I said.

'I have a little plane out at the Cuento airfield.'

We all tried to work that one out until Juni helped by adding, 'Mitch got interested in patents because his grandpa invented the nasal cannula.'

'But don't listen to him on the topic of wedding planning being a gravy train,' Linda said. 'I am very affordable and usually end up saving my couples money because of my connections.' She beamed at me. 'Do you have a private email where I can send a few links?'

'Oh, I'm not really your demographic,' I said. 'Taylor and I are planning a home-made party with a few close friends.'

She looked at me with an infuriating kindness and said, 'I understand. Second-time around, is it?'

'For me,' I said. 'Not for him.'

'I meant you,' she said. 'I don't agree with the habit of a big first-time splash that Daddy pays for and then the shame-faced little admin session.' I had no idea which bit of 'party with a few close friends' sounded like shame-faced admin, but I had to admire her total lack of tact. It's so rare to find here.

'I went to City Hall first time,' I said. 'My parents paid for nothing. They weren't even there.'

I swear to God, dollar signs flashed up in her eyes like Jesus tears on one of those tilty prayer cards. 'Quite right,' she went on. 'The starter marriage had a starter wedding and now, for the love of your life, your family can push the boat out!'

Do people really say 'starter marriage', I wondered. I said nothing.

'Soul mates!' Linda cried, determined to land what she thought was a big fish. 'That's so rare and so beautiful, you owe it to the world to show everyone.'

'I don't believe in soul mates,' I said. 'And if the world wants romance it can go to the movies. Honestly, Linda, I am not your target market here.'

'What about Branston?' said Todd. I had no clue what he was getting at.

'The groom?' said Linda.

'No!' I yelped, shuddering at the very thought. My 'starter marriage' to Branston Lancer had lasted less than six months and had left me penniless and thousands of miles from home. Still, I'd never regret it. If I hadn't checked into the only motel in Cuento that was open after midnight, the day I left him, I'd never have met the ragtag team of freaks and weirdos who were now my dearest friends. Or indeed Taylor, probably. And, while it was true that I didn't believe in soul mates, I also knew that women as far north of thirty as I was didn't usually have long queues of funny, kind, honest, normal twenty-something men clamouring for them.

'What *about* Branston?' I asked Todd crossly.

'Wouldn't he just choke on his morning smoothie to see a big spread in the *Chronicle* with you and Taylor looking gorgeous?'

'Does the *Chronicle* do wedding spreads?' said Kathi.

'Who cares!' said Todd, leaping to his feet. 'We should be aiming higher: the *Times*, *People Magazine*, *Us Weekly*!'

'Todd,' I said, 'I am neither rich, nor famous, nor gorgeous enough to get into any of those publications, even if I wanted to.'

'Not gorgeous enough?' said Todd. 'When's the wedding? As long as it's not tomorrow, you've got time and more important, you've got me.'

'And is there any pattern to the timing of the incidents?' Kathi said. She had just finished writing the notes on what the Sex Volunteers had told her and was carrying on as if there had been no interruptions. It's the best way of coping with Todd, but it took the rest of us a while to switch gears back again.

'That's part of what *you'll* be telling *us*,' said Bob. 'Surely. We've kept a diary and a picture record, but we weren't looking for patterns. What sort of pattern did you mean anyway?'

'The full moon is the first thing that springs to mind,' Kathi said. 'Cemetery freaks, you know.' It wasn't the most diplomatic thing to say to four new clients who were surely the biggest cemetery freaks within five hundred miles. It went over Mitchell's head: he looked as gormless as ever. Juni? Hard to say: she gave a slow blink that might have been disdain or might have been contact-lens management. Bob, though, brought those outstanding eyebrows down like an auctioneer's hammer and Linda pursed her mouth so hard you could see her lipstick seeping out into her wrinkles in real time.

'We don't encourage the more sensationalistic aspects of cemetery lore,' Juni said. 'We see the cemetery as a sociological and genealogical resource, an important wildlife habitat and a community space.'

'Apart from the ghost walks,' said Mitchell, 'to be fair.'

'We are self-financing,' said Linda, unpursing her mouth enough to speak. 'And, as I know very well from my business, you need to give people what they want. Speaking of which, Lexy, a small home-made party for close friends is a theme I know like the back of my hand.'

She was like the energizer bunny.

'Or it might be significant dates in the lives of the deceased,' said Kathi. She doesn't half plough on too. 'Let's make an appointment for you to turn over your records to us and we'll take it from there.'

Juni Park gave a firm nod, twisted the nib down on her slim silver pen and tucked it in her bag.

'We'll need a key,' Todd said. 'I take it the cemetery is still locked at night? I remember vaulting over that wall many times when I was a teen, but I'd rather walk through an open gate these days.'

'Tell me about it,' said Bob. 'I did a handstand a year back and shredded my rotator cuff like pulled pork at a barbecue.'

Todd scowled, and Bob did have twenty years on him, it was true. 'I meant that my clothing is designer these days and I'd hate to snag it,' he said.

'No offence,' said Bob. 'And thank you.'

'For?' Todd asked.

'Explaining your clothes,' Bob said. 'I was wondering.'

I expected Todd to need a rant after they had left, but he surprised me. 'Lexy,' he said, 'I need to tell you something. I have no intention of trying to get your little event into any magazine, not even *Kings River Life* or *Sactown*, just so you know. I was merely shaking my horns to make that woman back off. She has absolutely no boundaries and that sort usually can't bear to cooperate. See? If she thinks I'm going to be at her elbow the whole time, she might stop bugging you.'

'Right,' I said. 'Yeah, *she* would hate not to be in charge of my wedding, so *you* kindly stepped in so that I wouldn't have *anyone* interfering. Gotcha.'

He beamed at me. Truly, if Jerry Seinfeld was dead he'd be kicking off the coffin lid and coming back to smack people every day.

'I'm gonna head over early tomorrow and pick up the documentation,' Kathi said. 'Todd, can you keep an eye on the Skweek for a half hour, eight to eight thirty? I still have a lot of the holiday linens passing through, so I can't hang an "out" sign or start late.'

'Or,' said Todd, 'I could go on the errand. Lexy, want to come with? Coffee and muffins and a trip to the graveyard?'

'Are you kidding?' I said. 'It's January. My client list is full to busting. I'm jammed from eight till six every day with people who need their hands held while they dump their spouses.'

'You should have asked them to courier the paperwork over,' Todd said.

'Over *where*?' said Kathi. She was going hard on this 'lack of an office' thing.

'We could go after your last client or before your first,' Todd said.

Taylor appeared round the side of the motel before I had to think up an answer. 'Hey,' he said. He took off his phone shop lanyard and slung it in through the open front door as he came up the steps. He tries every night to get it to hang on the coat pegs by the passageway door and, although he has never managed it yet, he still says trying is the best thing about the job. 'Who was that?' he said, jerking his head back-the-way. He must have run into the Sex Volunteers en route.

'A wedding planner,' said Todd, out of sheer badness.

Taylor went very still. We hadn't talked much about the wedding at that point, beyond saying we both wanted to get on with it.

'And an actuary,' said Kathi, for good measure.

Taylor frowned briefly.

'And a guy with a private jet,' said Todd.

Taylor put his finger inside his phone shop uniform collar and yanked it to make more room.

'And a pharmacist,' I said. 'They're winding you up.'

'Trinity clients?' said Taylor, with a laugh that had a bit too much relief in it not to be kind of insulting. 'What's the case that's brought *them* together?'

'Trolls in the cemetery,' Todd said.

Taylor nodded and started untying his phone shop tie and unbuttoning his shirt. He never kept the uniform on, even until he got to our bedroom where the rest of his clothes were. That's how much he hated the place.

'He thinks that's urban slang for something he doesn't care about, doesn't he?' said Kathi, once my betrothed had disappeared inside.

I nodded. Taylor was used to all his colleagues and all his customers not making any sense to him and it led to a kind of cheerful hopelessness about understanding people, which reached right across the board. He once told me straight-faced that simping, stanning and spilling were all moves in what he called 'online video games' – the things other people call MPGs – so he probably thought Trolls in the Cemetery were a band.

'I love you for being such a bird nerd!' I shouted after him.

'OK,' he shouted back.

'I don't love that his answer to "I love you" is "OK",' I said to Todd and Kathi. 'Look, how about if Todd gets the paperwork and we eat together tomorrow night, start to plan the investigation? I need to speak to Taylor about personal stuff tonight.'

'I'm great at personal stuff,' Todd said. 'I should stay. Is it wedding-related? Health issues? Bedroom-based?'

'Finances,' I told him.

'Bo-*ring*!' He got up, kissed me on both cheeks and left, not even waiting for Kathi.

'Just in case you ever wonder,' she said, 'I don't want to know about your health issues or your sex life, Lexy. And the less I hear about the wedding, the happier I'll be too. I'll come to your bachelorette party—'

'Hen do,' I said. I was trying to train them.

'And I'll do one whole day and parts of two others: rehearsal dinner, day of, post-mortem brunch. But that's it.'

'Why do you think you have to say that to me?' I said. 'When did I ever give the faintest hint that I was going to let this thing escalate? I've never even heard of a post-mortem brunch and what's to rehearse? We walk in, say yes, walk out. Don't worry, Kathi.'

'I've seen things,' she said, darkly, then waved at me – her version of double kisses – and headed off to the Skweek to fold. She loves folding. She doesn't even charge for it.

THREE

'Hon?' I said, going to find Taylor. He was in the kitchen, trying to work out what I'd been cooking from the ingredients on the chopping board. 'Bouillabaisse,' I said. 'Cioppino. Fish stew.' I edged up behind him and put my arms around him as he laid into the red pepper. He is the least ticklish person I've ever met. If he put his hands inside my sweatshirt when I was chopping vegetables we'd have to go to A & E and we'd have to find a third, uninjured, party to drive us both. 'You hate that bloody job, don't you?'

'No,' he said. 'I hate that bastering job. I don't know how I ever did it without Scottish swearing.' He paused the chopping and twisted his neck so he could reach my face to kiss it.

'Right,' I said. 'So when are we going to sit down and have a serious discussion about finances, work out what we can do about it?'

He stopped chopping completely and set the knife down.

'I know we've never talked about money,' I said. 'But we're getting married.'

'Exactly,' he said.

'What?'

'It's an expensive business. And then the extra responsibility. And maybe there won't always be just the two of us either.'

'It's not an expensive business marrying me,' I said. 'Look, come and sit down so we can face each other at least, eh?' We got the two skinny chairs out from under my midget table and sat down, him up against the sink and me half out the door, which is the only way the galley on the boat functioned as an 'eat-in' kitchen.

'And what "extra responsibilities" anyway?' I asked. 'It's 2023. I'm not a dependent. I've got a business and I've got Obamacare.' Which cost me an arm and a leg, it was true, and ironically enough didn't cover prosthetics. 'Also, if we're lucky enough ever to be more than the two of us, I don't want a spoiled little snot with designer togs and a jogging stroller. Do you? I want a manky wee toerag in second-hand dungarees who loves nothing more than going to the wetlands with its daddy who knows everything about birds.'

'You can't take babies to wetlands,' Taylor said. 'It's not safe.'

'It's going to live on a boat!' I said. 'It can drown right here at home without your job getting involved.'

'Wait,' said Taylor. 'Do you mean you want to *stay* on the boat? After we're married?'

'Why not?' I said. 'What did I ever say to make you think anything else?'

'I-I just . . . I kinda assumed you'd . . .'

'Start giving a shit about stuff I don't give a shit about?'

'Yeah, totally,' Taylor said. 'I've been looking at little three-bed, two-bath ranches out in the west of town. I was going to surprise you.'

'You certainly were,' I said. 'You were going to buy a house without telling me and then wrap a big red bow round it and drive me out there in a blindfold and carry me over the threshold?'

'I was probably going to have a panic attack and tell you what I was doing and have you put me straight, if I'm honest,' he said.

'I'm glad we got there without the panic attack,' I said. 'Have you ever had one?'

He shook his head. 'You?'

'No, but I've seen plenty and I've driven clients to the hospital because there was no way I could convince them it wasn't a heart attack.' I shuddered. 'And then, this one time, it was.'

Taylor leaned back in his chair and breathed out as if he was blowing smoke towards the ceiling. He didn't smoke.

'So,' I said. 'The way I see it is you're sitting on the proceeds of your mum's house.' He had sold his family home after his mother's death last year, and I knew how much he got for it thanks to Zillow, but I had no idea what he had done, was doing, or intended to do with the proceeds. 'And we don't need to buy a different house because we've got a boat, like I said. And that means you don't need two jobs because I've got one, so . . . what I wanted to talk to you about was what exactly you're waiting for?'

He lowered his head very slowly and stared at me. 'Obamacare.'

'Ah shite,' I said. 'I forgot about that, yeah. You mean we'd have to get it for you too if you left the phone shop and it would sink us?'

'No, no, not that exactly,' he said. 'I have health insurance at the wetlands too. Of course I have.'

'You have?' I had known Taylor for years but he wasn't even

thirty and he hadn't had any health stuff in that time, except for free things like COVID vaccines, so he'd never had to decide which insurer to soak for the likes of a hip replacement or a prostate probe.
'What is it you're getting at?' I asked him.
'Well,' he said, 'if you were willing to give your Obamacare up and come on to mine as my dependent . . . No! Not my dependent. I didn't mean that. Just that I'd be the primary policy holder but you'd be covered just the same – mammograms and pap smears and whatnot – and really it would be better for you than for me because I'd have to do all the paperwork and you could skate. So if you didn't mind—'
'Taylor,' I said, breaking in, since it looked like he was never going to stop. 'Are you telling me I can stop paying my Obamacare premium when we get married?'
'Only if you were willing,' he said. 'Why, how much is it?'
'It's seven hundred dollars a month!' I said. 'Why the hell wouldn't I be willing? Are you kidding me?'
'Because the state plan isn't exactly luxurious,' he said.
'Oh please! I cut my teeth on the NHS. Not luxurious how?'
'You have to go to the UCC hospital in Sacramento for in-patient procedures. You can't choose the hospital you like best.'
I tried to think of a way of telling him how absolutely bonkers it sounded to me that I would ever waste my time choosing a hospital when I was ill, but I failed. In the end, I just wound my hand round like a football rattle to get him to tell me more.
'And you don't get a private room,' he said. 'You share with another person.'
'Oh, the squalor!' I said. 'Are you kidding?'
'And the dental doesn't cover cosmetic . . . Wait. Right. I forgot. OK.' I had bared my cream-coloured, snaggly, British teeth at him. 'And the optical doesn't cover prescription sunglasses.'
'Shit, really?' I said. 'Man that sounded great for a minute there, Taylor. But if I have to use clip-on sun-screens on my specs, if I ever need specs, then I'm just going to keep shelling out seven hundred a month and you stay in a job you hate. OK?'
'Sarky cow,' he said, like Jerry Seinfeld's little helper. I loved this man and I was pretty sure I was going to love him even more when he wasn't grumpy from a job he hated, ten shifts a fortnight.
'So, we're agreed? I'm leaving the Temple of Mammon?'
'Isn't that a New Testament thing?' I said. Taylor wasn't much

of a Jew but he was still a Jew and didn't quote Jesus much as a rule.

'A. That's how much I hate that place,' he said. 'And B. How do you know that?'

'I—' I began, all set to tell him about Christian worship in the state schools and bishops in the government again.

'And C.,' he said, speaking over me, 'answer the damn question, Lex! I can go?'

'Let's write your letter of resignation together right now,' I said. 'And take a stroll into town to leave it on your boss's desk so he sees it first thing tomorrow.'

It was a work of genius, even if I say so myself. Snotty, chilly and terse – we even used a gerund – but we got in such a subtle bit of passive aggression, I reckoned everyone left at the phone shop might feel complimented anyway.

'Read it through,' I said, when we were done.

'"Dear Tobin",' he began. '"I am writing to give you the statutory two weeks' notice of my leaving your enterprise. My last working day will be January twenty-fifth. I have been equally happy selling phones and working beside you and will never forget my time there. Yours regretfully, Taylor Aaronovitch".' He looked up and smiled. '"Regretfully" is true, by the way. I regret not doing it years ago. I could have lived on the state salary if I'd known I was going to meet a sugar . . .' My eyes narrowed. 'Plum fairy.'

The age difference didn't bother me really but I didn't want him to get in the habit of making jokes about it.

'Send it to the printer,' I said. Trinity shared the motel printer these days, since Todd thought it was a waste of money to have more than one and it was good for all of us to stand up and walk to the office to pick up our print-outs, saving our circulation from desk-bound atrophy and/or making all of us think twice about whether we really needed a hard copy.

A couple of times I had wondered whether Noleen read my confidential patient notes during slack times at check-in but she assured me she wasn't interested in a load of rich whiners and their non-problems. We were just about to bust that story wide open.

'Good for you!' she cried out when we arrived at Reception. She was standing in the back office with a sheet of paper, still warm from the printer, in her hand.

'Noleen!' I said. 'I knew it!'

'What?' she said. 'I was in the middle of something. I thought it was mine. You want an envelope and a stamp? I still got the puppies and hearts from last Valentine's Day. I'm saving them for taxes and complaining, but you can have one for this.'

'I'm walking over there and dropping it off,' Taylor said. 'You need anything from downtown? Something from Munchies perhaps?' (Since cannabis was legalized in California, all-night snack emporia have popped up all over the place, especially in college towns like Cuento. Most of them had *veiled* nods towards their expected core customers, but you had to hand it to Munchies.) Noleen let us go without placing any orders and we set off into the night.

The railway skirts the bottom of the town of Cuento on the south of 1st Street before hooking round to head north just beyond G Street, but there's an underpass to the old Muelleverde Road where the Last Ditch Motel sits – literally on the wrong side of the tracks – along with a self-storage facility and absolutely nothing else. On the far side of the underpass are the PD and Swiss Sisters, then downtown begins depressingly enough with the palatial phone shop.

Taylor let himself in using the staff keycode – 0420, obviously – and dismantled the alarm system. He breathed slow and deep as he made his way across the sales floor, looking around as if for the last time.

'Remember you've got two weeks to go,' I said.

'It doesn't count,' said Taylor. 'I'm free. I'll breathe in Ceris's aggressive perfume and Tobin's home-made keto-shake and even Leo's gym bag and it'll be like Ambrosia. I might even try to sell a few phones.'

'Ambrosia?' I said. 'Is that the same as Nirvana?''

'In this case, you betcha,' said Taylor. He was busy positioning the envelope on Tobin's desk, trying to make it stand up against Tobin's only photo frame, which held a picture of himself doing a fake pull-up. (You couldn't see his feet.)

Taylor smacked his hands together, wiping off the phone shop so lavishly he looked like some kind of folk dancer, and grabbed me round the waist, planting a big smoochy kiss on my wide-open, startled mouth.

'Amfulooplu mo wor,' I said, then managed to shake him off. 'Absolutely no way, Taylor. I am not marking this moment up against that desk with you.'

Taylor physically shuddered. I felt it, like a wet dog shaking itself dry. 'If you think I could . . . that's revolting.'

'Good,' I said.

'But let's hurry home.'

I considered this. 'Also good,' I said in the end, and hand-in-hand we scampered back out to the sales floor to reset the alarms and get out of there.

Then I saw something.

'Stop,' I said, pulling Taylor back out of the light cast by an advertising screen that beamed out the joy of a new smartphone into the world twenty-four hours a day.

'What?' Taylor said.

I hugged the wall and made my way, crab-like, to the plate glass windows facing the street. 'Look,' I said.

'What am I looking at?' said Taylor, right beside me.

'The Sex Volunteers,' I said. Taylor put his face right up to the glass and cupped his hands round his eyes for a better view, like anyone would hearing that. He was disappointed, of course, for there on the street, slipping in and out of the shadows as they processed between the lamp posts, were a lanky figure, a stocky figure, a neat figure and a strapping figure. One of the heads was the yellow of blonde hair under sodium lights and one of them was the silvery-blue of jet black hair seen the same way. In short, it was our new clients.

But why would they be out walking around here at this time of night? The cemetery was away over beyond the train tracks off of Turkey Farm Road, at the old town line.

I told all of this to Taylor in a fierce whisper, but he's no Todd. He's not even much of a Kathi. He only shrugged and said, 'Maybe they've been for a drink somewhere.'

'Where?' I demanded. 'If they were going the other way, certainly. But the only drink you can get down where they were coming from is coffee and it's shut. And nobody walks to and from the self-storage, so . . . Aha!'

'Aha?'

'They were at the police station!' I said. 'What a nerve they've got. They told us the police weren't interested.'

'In what?'

'And then they employ us and load Kathi up with a bar exam amount of reading.' I was guessing at this, of course; Todd hadn't even picked it up yet. 'And before their retainer cheque is even written never mind cleared, they're at the cops handing the case right over.'

'Kathi uses Venmo,' Taylor said. 'And slightly less speculation.'

'Let's check,' I said. 'We've got to pass the door anyway.'

'Aw, come on, Lexy,' said Taylor. 'A visit to the cops instead of a trip to heaven in my arms? You gotta be kidding.'

'Happy wife, happy life,' I told him. 'Get used to it.'

I hadn't been at the Cuento PD headquarters late at night since my very first visit all those years back. That had been the Fourth of July and pretty raucous, but this was a random day in January, so I was expecting to be warmly welcomed by a bored dispatch. But I'd forgotten how near the start of the semester at UCC we were and how reliably students chose to celebrate their reunions with mid-week parties. The foyer of the police station was awash with sorors and fraters all dressed in not a great deal, remonstrating with two of my favourite Cuento cops about – I tuned in – the arrest and incarceration of someone they had all come here either to bail out, bust out, or hold a vigil for.

'I do not care who your daddies are,' said Soft Cop, a man whose doughy figure belied his sharp tongue. 'I do not care how you wanted this evening to go. I do not care what kind of pressure your friend is under or what crucial events he had planned for tomorrow. Mr Durkus was naked in the street trying to urinate through a basketball hoop and so he is my guest until after breakfast tomorrow.'

'Ambitious,' said Taylor.

Mills of God, Soft Cop's partner, either overheard or happened to be sweeping the foyer with his trademark leisurely gaze at just that moment. Either way he noticed us and waved.

'Did you just have four non-students in here telling you about crimes in the cemetery?' I said, when I had waded through the crowd of outraged youngsters.

'Did he do it?' said Taylor, at my elbow.

I didn't know what he meant but Mills of God did. He shook his head and addressed Taylor's question first. 'Don't get excited. It was lying down.'

'What?' I said. 'Officer, did' – I applied myself hard –'Juni Park, Bob Larch, Linda Magic and Mitchell Ver . . . a . . . como maybe . . . just leave here?'

'What kind of name is Magic?' said Mills of God.

'Polish. Did they?'

Behind us, the aggrieved students all fell silent and Mills, looking over my shoulder, straightened up and gave a quick nod.

'It's Molly, isn't it?' I said. No one else could get twelve drunk over-achievers to shut up and stop complaining like Sergeant Molly Rankinson.

'Sarge,' I said, turning. 'I thought it was you. It suddenly got cold and all the birds flew off.'

'Your neck's no better then,' she said to Taylor, meaning that he was still engaged to me and I was a pain in it. Her insults were as resourceful as they were oblique and they made mine look crude and lumpen in comparison.

'Does he have a private cell? No one else in there with him?' the ringleader sorority moppet asked Soft Cop.

'He has a single, with a mattress, blanket and pillow all checked for bed bugs and a nice shiny metal toilet to hug when the time comes,' Soft Cop said.

'OK, well then, maybe we should go home and come get him in the morning. Only, can I ask you one thing, Officer?' She batted her expensive eyelashes and drew closer. Soft Cop looked at her like gum on his cat. 'Do you have to call his parents? Maybe they don't need to know.'

'We have no intention of calling any of Mr Durkus's relations,' said Soft Cop, stepping back out of the blast zone of her booze-breath. 'He is an adult. God help us all.'

When the students had shuffled out, dragging their pool slides and slowly lowering their phones from 'filming an outrage' height – which was just a bit below 'lighter app at a concert' height – all the way down to scrolling level, so that they all looked like they were hanging their heads in shame, Molly turned her full attention our way, giving us a stiff-necked stare that we didn't deserve.

'What?' I said.

'Posture,' said Molly. 'Looking at those kids with turtle humps before they're twenty-one makes me stand straighter every day.'

I reared back then too, pulling my shoulders down and tucking my bum under like they always tell you. Soft Cop tried: he threw his shoulders back so that his belly strained and his buttocks jutted. 'Ow,' he said, and slumped back to normal.

'Was it you the Se . . . cemetery people came to see?' I said. At work, I ask a lot of open-ended questions and it's dead useful to know the difference between them and this kind of leading, unfair, inescapable question. I hadn't given Molly the chance to deny they'd been here or claim she didn't know who I was talking about. I am a genius.

'Who are the "se cemetery people"?' she said.

'I thought they had given up on trying to be protected and served by the PD their taxes pay for,' I said. 'They came to Trinity instead, to seek justice and answers. But maybe they decided to give you one last chance?'

Molly turned to Taylor. 'Has she had a stroke? Do you need an ambulance?'

'Why don't you care about the desecration of graves?' I said.

Molly frowned and moved her eyes from side to side very fast. I didn't need to be a body-language expert to work out that she was assembling a lie disguised as a memory. They had only left minutes before.

'Oh yeah,' she said, giving a big stagey finger click. At least, finger clicks are all the same size and the staginess is baked in, but I happened to know this one was bogus. I wished I could raise one eyebrow. I settled for poking my tongue into my cheek.

'Need to borrow a floss wand?' Molly said. 'Yeah, I know who you mean. Those weirdos who love the graveyard? I remember they tried to flex their muscles about what tributes were allowed or something. It didn't go anywhere.'

'That's not . . .' I began, then I considered her words. 'Huh,' I said. 'That's certainly a different take on it.'

'Yeah, it's like they never heard of Susan B. Anthony,' said Molly.

'Or Jim Morrison,' said Soft Cop, hinting at a wild youth.

'Or Babe Ruth,' said Taylor, my old soul in his young body.

'Or Buddy Holly,' said Mills of God, who had obviously always been a square.

They looked expectantly at me.

'Jane Austen,' I said, grandly. I didn't have a clue if her grave got embellished but luckily neither did they. 'There's got to be a limit, though, Moll— Sarge.'

'There *is* a limit,' Molly said. 'As long as nothing is destroyed or removed and no planting is disturbed, then no laws have been broken.'

'You have to flatten grass to lay out slanderous messages in pebbles,' I pointed out. 'And squash worms, maybe.'

'You wanna tell the Guerilla Gardeners of Beteo County that

their Three Sisters Gardens for the needy are illegal because they squashed a worm?' said Molly. She gave me a beat to feel stupid in, then went on. 'And you can't slander the dead. You should know that, Lexy.'

Where the hell did that come from, I wondered. What corpses had I ever not slandered?

'So they had yet another wasted trip?' I said. Molly's brows pinched together just for a second. If I had paid attention, right then at that very moment, things might have turned out different. And better. But I assumed she was as much in control of drawing them down as she was of lifting either one at will, so I concluded that she was annoyed, not puzzled. Hindsight would be a lot more useful if it came along beforehand, eh?

FOUR

'Straight home?' said Taylor, when we were back out in the night air again. 'Or . . .?'

'Or?' I echoed. I liked this new, happier Taylor who didn't work in a phone shop. Of course, he would only get more deeply embroiled in the migratory patterns of North American water birds once he had the chance, but tonight the bit of his soul that had been blackened by consumerism, then bleached by resigning, was all mine.

'I was thinking maybe they were headed to the cemetery,' he said. 'Like, if the visit to the PD was because something's going down tonight, maybe they went back to deal with it themselves? And we could help?'

I had changed my mind: I *loved* this new Taylor. He had never betrayed the slightest interest in Trinity's investigations before. Nor in my practice either, if I'm honest, but I chose to believe that that was because he knew it was confidential.

'Let's do it,' I said. 'It's a nice walk.'

Taylor gave me a puzzled look, but I meant it. For a start, it was January and it wasn't cold. And it was eleven o'clock but the streets weren't alive with the sounds of glass smashing, relationships ending and beer being puked up. In fact, now that Mr Durkus' fan club had gone, there wasn't a single drunk in the whole of downtown; just a dog walker and a kid on a bike delivering cookies.

Also, it was Cuento, and sometimes at night it still made my heart swell to pause at intersections and see the traffic stop to let me cross, to look both ways at the railway line before I strolled right over the tracks without breaking the law, to peer into the windows of houses that looked as if either Buffy Summers, Beaver Cleaver or Darrin and Samantha lived there. Other people might scoff at the lack of architectural variety in Cuento but it thrilled me.

When we got to the big corner where the letters run out and P Street turns into Turkey Farm Road, though, the jaunt started to feel ill-advised. The cemetery gates were tall and ornate and the closer we got to them the more Addams Family vibes they gave off. It was probably funny in the day time. Tonight, what with the bare trees, branches like skeletal hands clutching at the sky, and moonlight shining though them to cast blue shadows everywhere, I started to lose enthusiasm.

'You OK?' Taylor said. I hadn't realized my feet were dragging.

'We've never talked about ghosts,' I said, as the fact struck me.

'What, and you think now is the time to start?' He chuckled and let go of my hand to loop an arm around my shoulders instead. 'It's scary enough without that.'

'So *you* believe in them?' That wasn't going to help me stay rational in the least.

'Of course not,' Taylor said. 'But I believe in the power of all the stories and films and myths and puppets we were all brought up on. I'd have to be a lot butcher than I am to pretend I'm not freaked out right now.'

'Puppets?' I said.

'My mom's mom had a collection of stringed puppets,' he said. 'And when my mom first brought me home, she thought it would be cute to hang them from my bedroom ceiling.'

'Wait? You were three, right? And she decorated your bedroom in a strange new house with a load of hanging puppets?'

'One of *them* was a ghost,' Taylor said. 'But that was OK. The ones that really bothered me were the giant and the old man. The giant because he was the same size as all the other ones and I thought one night he might grow to his real size and squish me like a bug. And the old man had a half-blue face. Looking back, I think it was probably supposed to be stubble but I thought it was mould, so I thought he was real. And Pinocchio freaked me out quite a lot too, because everyone *knew* he could come alive any minute.'

'How did I not know this about you?' I said. 'And how long did they hang there?'

'I pretended to get interested in airplanes,' Taylor said. 'So we could take them down and string up fighter jets instead.' He sighed, lost in memory. Then he sniffed, back again. 'Do *you* believe in ghosts?'

'No,' I said. 'But I believe in my ability to terrify myself beyond all reason. Same as you.'

'What's *your* puppets?' he said.

'Same as everyone else's whose mum wasn't off her rocker,' I said. 'Danny Glick at the upstairs window and the cat that couldn't jump.'

'Jesus, Lexy! Why did you have to bring that up now?'

I laughed and put my arm round his waist, ready to climb over the Gothic gates in mutual messed-up terror. I was looking forward to spending the rest of my life finding out about all the other puppets hanging from Taylor's internal ceiling and slowly building a bank of shared memories, like that time we went walking in the graveyard at nearly midnight. Besides, lashed together by our slightly sweaty and desperate grip on one another, it wasn't too bad. The grass had recently been mown, like always in California where the gardening calendar is a mystery to me, and it smelled of summer and verges and sunshine. There were a lot of flowers around too – jars of them at the older graves and one mound of new wreaths that definitely had some out-of-season orange blossom in the mix. If you tried to think of the gravestones as sculptures and didn't dwell on what lay beneath that oh-so lush and healthy sward, it was halfway to being romantic. Of course it would have been more romantic without some of the most creative recent headstones. The sparkling granite iPhone case was not a thing of beauty and the marble statue of a sow nursing a litter of piglets was just plain peculiar.

Then Taylor stopped dead and gripped me hard enough to make my neck creak. 'There's someone else in here,' he whispered.

'Why are you whispering?' I said. At least I *tried* to say it, but I was whispering too. Which was daft. We had come here looking for someone else, hadn't we?

'Sshhhh,' Taylor whispered. 'Look over there.'

I looked where his shaking finger was pointing, peering to try to see the difference between stone, bark and clothes in the darkness.

'It's an angel,' I whispered back.

'Huh? You believe in *angels*?' he hissed. 'I would have led with that.'

'Shut up!' I said, not whispering quite as softly. 'It's a stone angel on a grave, you moron. Like those ones that hide their faces till you blink and then they're right in your face suddenly.' I turned to see what effect I was having. Then I turned back again as I said, 'It's nothing to fea—uck!'

The angel had disappeared.

'Did you see where it went?' I said, whipping round to check behind us.

'I had my eyes closed, like you said.' His voice wasn't steady.

'Wh—? That's the exact *opposite* of what I said! What's wrong with you?'

'Uh, I'm in a graveyard with ambulatory headstones?' said Taylor. 'Or murderers. There it is again! Oh Jesus! There's two.'

'So what?' I said. 'We were expecting four.' But my heart wasn't in it.

'Look,' Taylor breathed. 'There they go.'

I followed his gaze, but just then there was a gust of wind and the spidery shadows of tree branches danced over the view just long enough for me to lose sight of the figures. When the breeze settled again, they were nowhere to be seen.

'I don't believe in ghosts,' I said, trying to talk at a normal volume and in a normal voice. 'I certainly don't believe in living statues.' I let go of him and shook him off me too. 'Ready?'

'For what?'

'Get 'em!' I yelled and surged forward towards where the angels had been flitting.

'What about murdere—? Lexy, stop! Oh for fuc—' I heard him come crashing after me as together we took on the night.

It was obvious pretty quickly that we weren't dealing with ghosts. They surely don't rustle so much as they sprint and our torch beams would have shone through them instead of glancing off as they ducked and dived, in and out of view. No, the two people we were chasing were definitely living humans, which was great news on several counts: no supernatural powers, for a start. Also, maybe I had caught the culprit and solved the case for the Sex Volunteers; and, finally, I wouldn't have to suffer the indignity of getting whacked by something I didn't believe in.

'They're definitely not your clients,' Taylor said, jogging along beside me as we made for the place – a mausoleum – that we'd seen the figures dodge behind. 'I think they're the trolls. They're all dressed in grey, for one thing, as if they're trying to look like those creepy angels.'

'Only . . .' I stopped. 'That doesn't jibe with everything we heard, does it?'

'Remember I didn't hear it,' Taylor pointed out.

I was pointing my torch at the ground, looking for footprints. 'Well, they usually do things to be found the next day,' I said. 'Vandalism only not quite, hence Molly's lack of interest. Lurking about like vampires is a different MO entirely.'

'Unless,' Taylor said, 'they always dress like that, just in case someone does see them, but they rely on whoever it is freaking out and running away, not screaming like Dan Ackroyd and charging after them.'

'Mel Gibson, please,' I said.

We had reached the mausoleum now, stepping quietly and cautiously all the way round it. There was no one there. I scanned the cemetery beyond and saw nothing moving. Of course, they could be behind any one of the gravestones that stretched away to the far wall. But why would they have stopped running and taken to hiding?

'They might have a gun,' I said, as this occurred to me.

'Nah,' said Taylor. Then: 'Yeah.'

'Nah,' I said. 'Dressing up like statues to make people run away from you doesn't really go with guns, does it?'

'You know, if they *are* hiding behind one of those gravestones, they might be able to hear every word we're saying.'

I held my breath and mimed for Taylor to hold his. 'Nah,' I said again, when I let it go. 'They'd be panting and we'd hear them. They must be quite a way off.' I looked about for a rock or a stick that I could throw like the cowboys always did in the old movies. There was a block of wood right beside the gate in the mausoleum railings. I bent to pick it up but then reconsidered. I know my limits.

'Lob that at something and see if they scatter,' I said to Taylor.

He passed the block from hand to hand, testing the weight, then he wound himself up into that strangely balletic baseball thing and whipped the little object end over end towards a new grave six rows over, where it smashed a vase full of flowers.

Nothing stirred. No one moved. I had just turned to say to Taylor that our prey must have got away, when from right behind us there came a rusty, yawning, creaking sound, growing louder and higher pitched and setting my teeth on edge like fingers on a blackboard, like fork tines on a clean plate.

'*Shi-i-i-t*,' Taylor breathed in a wavering voice. I didn't even have to turn to know what had just happened. The gate in the railings had fallen open. 'That wooden block was a doorstop,' Taylor said in the same, almost non-existent, whisper. 'They're in *there*.'

It's a well-known phenomenon that everyone sitting in the dark in the cinema watching a film believes that the heroine must be some kind of idiot to go poking around in obvious danger instead of scarpering. I knew that. I had been one of those jeering, popcorn-throwing spectators, shouting, 'Gimme a break' and 'Too stupid to live' at the screen. Still, at that moment when any rational person would have taken the chance to leave unmolested, I found myself slipping through the open gate, crunching over the few feet of gravel and laying my hand on the cold, iron knob of the mausoleum door.

'Or,' said Taylor, '*or* we call for help.'

'Call Molly? She doesn't care. She just said that.'

'Call nine one one,' said Taylor. 'Tell them someone is smashing up the cemetery and broke into a vault. They'll come, especially if you don't say who it is that's calling. Or if I call, I mean, because you know . . . the accent.'

'But maybe don't mention the smashing,' I said. 'Because your fingerprints must be on that wedge you hoyed over there. In fact, we should go and get it back before we call *anyone*. Destruction of property, Molly said.'

'We could call Todd and Kathi,' said Taylor, clearly not liking the mention of fingerprints. 'Change the odds? Two against four? Plus let them get in on the swift closing of the case?'

I considered it, then let go of the doorknob. 'OK,' I said. 'I'll call Kathi and you call Todd.'

We speed-dialled and waited for the calls to connect and then our eyes met in the blue glow of our phone screens as Todd's 'Simply the Best' and Kathi's plain old default ringtone sounded from inside.

'I don't believe it!' I said, as both calls were declined and a faint scuffle came through the stone walls. I wrenched the door open and shone my torch down three steep steps into a tiny chamber, lighting up two terrified faces and four hands, palms up and out in surrender.

'We're unarmed,' Todd said. 'But we have money and jewellery. We can't see your faces, so please don't hurt us.'

'I'm throwing my wallet,' said Kathi. 'I'll tell you my PIN. Just please let us go.'

'I already know your PIN,' I said, moving my torch beam so it wasn't shining in their eyes anymore. Taylor clicked his off.

'Lexy?' said Todd.

Kathi let out a sob and barrelled towards me. I truly thought she was coming to hug me until she ploughed into me with one shoulder, knocking me aside and escaping out into the air.

'Dust and mould and rot and fungus,' she said, stripping off her coat and looking as if she was going to unbutton her jeans too.

Todd took it slower. He straightened up and walked smoothly across the gritty stone floor before ascending the three steps like a supermodel.

'Do I have spiders on me?' he said. 'Are there beetles or worms or moths or bats or maggots or crickets or flies or gnats or—'

'You don't have anything on you,' I said. 'No one can afford this kind of storage anymore, Todd. The coffins in there have probably been inert for decades and decades and all the activity they ever saw was over long, long ago.'

It was utter bullshit, of course. Spiders hang out in places undisturbed for centuries and anywhere there's a mousehole there are insects with an appetite for mouse droppings. But I knew that Todd needed to hear it. He had passed through his usual avoidance and over-reaction, travelled right past terror and arrived at a kind of unearthly calm that was either going to protect him forever or make him pop a disc clean out of his back.

'What are you doing here?' Kathi said when she had removed all of her outer clothes and was banging them against the nearest headstone, like a parlourmaid with a carpet slung over a clothesline.

'Not to be clichéd,' I said. 'But "What are *we* doing here?" What are *you* doing here?'

'Getting the lay of the land,' said Todd. 'On the way back from picking up . . . Oh God. We left the paperwork in the torture chamber.'

'I'll get it,' Taylor said. 'Why are you dressed all in grey?' he asked, but then disappeared down the steps without waiting for an answer.

'I'm dressed in grey because it's this season's neutral,' said Todd.

'I'm dressed in black,' said Kathi. It was true, but a combination of germaphobia and free access to a laundromat meant that all her clothes faded quickly. 'What *are* you doing here, Lexy?'

'Following our clients,' I said.

'Shit, are they here?' said Kathi. She looked around herself and then started wriggling back into her jeans. 'This could look unprofessional. Back me up if they see me.'

'They're not here,' I said. 'We saw them walking away from the cop shop – Taylor, are you OK in there? – and we made an educated guess that they might be headed this way, so we came to check.'

'They were at the police?' said Todd.

'Yeah, and Molly denied it,' I said. 'Interesting, eh?'

'Very,' Kathi said. 'Taylor? Why aren't you answering?'

'You know, Lexy,' said Todd. 'I think you should take Linda up on the idea of getting married here. It would be really useful to have a legitimate excuse to hang out without looking suspicious.'

'You're right,' I said. 'It would. And so, if you and Roger want to renew your vows here, have at it. My wedding is not a bird to be killed with half a stone. Taylor?'

'You need to see this,' Taylor said from the crypt.

'I am not going back in there for anything,' said Kathi. 'I'm going home.'

'Have you disturbed stuff?' Todd shouted. 'I'm not coming back in if you've roused things.'

'Not you,' Taylor shouted. 'Lexy.'

'Wait for me, Kathi,' Todd said.

I watched them leave, Kathi shrugging back into her jacket and Todd trotting after her, then I put my torch back on and stepped down into the dank cold of the little stone building, unable to imagine what Taylor might have found there to show to me and me alone.

He was standing facing the back wall. 'Look, Lexy,' he said. 'They were Jewish, the people that built this for themselves.'

'Is that it?' I said. 'I mean, OK. Yeah, good for them. Did you find the paperwork?'

He brandished a square and very sturdy attaché case. I guessed it had been Bob Larch's before he retired.

'Cool,' I said. 'Good then. Let's go.' But he didn't move. 'Taylor?'

'We *could* get married here,' he said, turning to me and taking hold of me with his free arm.

'In a crypt? Are you kidding?'

'It's cozy,' he said, sweeping his arm wide, showing it off.

'It's *crazy*,' I said. '*You're* crazy. I am not getting married in a place my friends are scared to walk into. And we could only fit ten people at the very most. Even if they were willing to sit on coffins. And the family . . . whoever they are . . . would never agree. What's in your head, Taylor?'

'No?' he said.

'Hell no,' I confirmed. 'Did you run into a low-hanging branch out there?'

'Sorry,' he said, shrugging. We headed back outside and he loped off to get the doorstop from among the shattered remains of the vase he had hit.

'Don't cut yourself,' I called after him.

'Good plan!' he called back, all sarcastic, as if he hadn't just said something so stupid he was lucky I wasn't taking him for a brain scan, never mind treating him like he might not be safe around shards.

I didn't say any more about it all the way home, but once we had eaten our fish stew and done the dishes and watched a bit of telly and Taylor was stretching and yawning, I made out like I had suddenly remembered some unanswered emails and went into my office as he headed for the bathroom. When I heard his electric toothbrush humming, I opened Google and typed: 'Sunniest summeriest weddings in California'. I had to nip this in the bud.

Sunny Weddings, Summer Weddings, Sunny Summer Weddings, Dreamy Summer Weddings, Fresh and Flowery Sunny Weddings (which sounded like a salad to me), Sumptuous Summer Weddings ('sumptuous' sounded too purple velvet) . . . I scrolled and scrolled through the first few pages of the twenty-seven million hits. Then I saw it. 'Sister Sunshine: The Sunniest Celebrant in the State.' I clicked. She was a humanist and – from her pictures – a bit of a hippy, whose online gallery was full of flowers and pastel colours and endless dazzling sunshiny tableaux. She worked Sac, Solano, Napa and Beteo Counties, I discovered on her booking page, but her base was right here in Cuento. On a whim, I decided not to fill in the form, but instead to phone her up and leave a message on her voicemail.

'Sister Sunshine!' said her voice, more gravelly than I would have chosen for my own message.

I launched into my spiel.

She interrupted me. 'Sorry, did you say you're not one of my existing clients?'

'Oh my God!' I said. 'I'm so sorry. I didn't think you'd pick up so late. I'll hang up and call back in the morn . . . No, sorry, I'll go online like I'm supposed to and fill in your—'

'Don't apologize,' she said. 'It's your big day and it's exciting. When do you want to get married?'

'Eh? Um, anytime,' I said. 'Well, summertime. Or not the dead of winter or Halloween or anything like that anyway. In the sunshine, basically. That's why I rang *you*.'

'Because I have, just this evening, had the most unexpected cancellation,' she said. 'How does Midsummer's Day sound? June twenty-first.'

'This June?'

'Is free as of tonight, but I'll get snapped up tomorrow. What do you say?'

Taylor's electric toothbrush fell silent.

'Sign me up,' I said to Sister Sunshine. 'Let me know where to bring the deposit in person. I'd like to shake your hand. And obviously this being California, when I say "shake your hand" I mean hug you.'

FIVE

February

I delayed telling my mum because I thought she'd go into instant overdrive. Also, that 'busiest time of the year' thing. Accountants have tax season, farmers have harvest, therapists have January. But, eventually, I could put it off no longer so I poured myself a bucket of wine one late afternoon and phoned home.

'I've got a date for your diary,' I said, when my dad answered.

'It's Lexy,' he replied to the muffled badgering from my mum. 'Lex, I'm putting you on speaker.'

'What's wrong?' my mum said. 'This is a funny time for you to phone.'

'Save the date,' I said. 'Twenty-first of June.'

'It's a Wednesday,' said my dad. 'But you didn't need to phone for that. You could have looked it up.'

'Keith!' said my mum. 'That's not what "save the date" means. Oh Lexy, Midsummer's Day? Lovely! What year?'

'This year,' I said. 'Four months' time.'

'That's impossible,' my mum said. 'We've already got bookings for this June. I can't cancel them for a family thing.'

I took my phone away from my ear and stared at it. Had I ever, at any point, even once, hinted to my mother that I was going to get married in Scotland? I didn't think so. I certainly hadn't breathed a word about expecting to use their hotel as a venue. Of course, it would have been lovely, but it was quite an assumption. Then an even worse thought struck me.

'Mum,' I said. 'Does that mean you can't come?' I felt my lip wobbling and was glad no one was there to see me. As soon as I had the thought, though, I heard the unmistakable sound of Noleen approaching. She swears at the bushes growing round the motel every time she visits me on the boat, as if she herself doesn't own the place. She might even have planted them.

'Can't come to your wedding?' my mum said. 'What soap opera mince is this? Of course, we're coming. Who's going to give you away if we're not there? We'll get a relief manager to run this place for the day. Or the weekend. Where is it you've decided to pay a fortune to hold it like an idiot?'

'Here,' I said.

'Here? Where are you?' said my mum. 'Oh! Have you come over to surprise us? Are you standing outside the door? It's pouring with rain. Oh, Lexy! Keith! She's flown over.' The sound changed as she left the cosy, basement sitting room of the owners' flat and went out into the stone passageway. 'And, if you *did* mean "here", never mind what I said about our guests – it's four months. I'll cancel them tomorrow.' The sound changed again as she opened the big front door. I could hear rain spattering and line interference from the wind.

'Judith!' came my dad's voice from a long way away. 'I think you've picked up the wrong stick, love!'

'Not *there*, Mum,' I said. 'Here. California.' Noleen had arrived on board and I waved her into a seat on the porch. 'So you might need that relief manager for more than a day.'

'Is that your parents?' Noleen said. 'Put it on speaker. Hi, Judith and Keith. I've cleared a block of rooms for the big day. You can have first dibs on a good one.'

The front door over in Scotland closed, cutting off the sound of wind and rain.

'How long have *you* known?' said my mother, as I signalled frantically at Noleen to back-pedal.

'A half hour,' she said, which was a lie. I blew her a kiss. She mimed a puke.

'Well, are you buying your dress over here?' my mum said.

'Um . . . no,' I said. 'Why would I do that?'

'So I can go with you.'

'I'm not sure what I'm wearing yet,' I said. 'I don't want to go over the top like some people.'

'Now look, Lexy,' my mum said. 'This isn't all about you. Your father and I have been looking forward to this since your Christening. And that's another thing. Can you even *get* a Church of Scotland minister over there?'

'Judith!' Maybe my dad was going to be the voice of reason here. 'Remember this is a mixed marriage. They're probably getting a rabbi.'

'We're not getting either,' I said. 'We're having a lovely humanist celebrant who'll be happy to go along with whatever vows we want to make.'

'Oh no,' said my mother. 'It's not going to be one of them, is it?'

'It's going to be great, Mum.'

'Hay bales? Jam jars?'

'Haven't decided yet.'

'Doesn't the venue give you a choice?'

'The venue?' I said. 'You mean here?'

'*Here?*' said Noleen.

'There like right *there*?' said my mum.

'Well, yeah,' I said, to both of them. We had had lockdown here and the 2020 outdoor Thanksgiving and Della and Devin's reception after they got back from the church. Where else would I get married except right here at the Last Ditch Motel?

'Keith, can you get my big diary from the office?'

My dad is such an easy mark. Only the most innocent of innocents wouldn't twig that he was being got rid of, but Keith Campbell just said, 'OK-doke', then I heard his footsteps receding.

'Right, here's the deal,' my mother said. She had even taken the phone off speaker. 'You know we used all of our money and the profits from your granny's house to buy this place and set up the business? Yes? Well, we didn't. We kept a nice little wedge back to pay for your wedding, Lexy. It's very important to your father. So let's agree that, OK, fine, you're getting married over there and we're all staying in that roadside motel you're so glued to.'

'Mum, *you* took *me* off speaker. I didn't take you off speaker.'

'None taken anyway,' Noleen said. 'I like plain-speaking and the Last Ditch is a motel at the side of the road.'

'But,' said my mother, 'you will find a venue. And there will be no hay bales, no jam jars, no burger vans, no string.'

'Strings? Like violins?'

'String!' my mother said. 'Wound round posies of weeds. But since you mention it, there will be no guitars.'

'How about a banjo?' said Noleen. I took it off speaker.

'There will be roses, satin, tablecloths and napkins, crystal glasses, candles in candlesticks and, when your father walks you down the aisle – there *will* be an aisle – you will be wearing a floor-length white dress that you and I choose together when I come over there to go shopping. Agreed? There will not be a penny-piece left in our Lexy's Wedding bank account when we wave you off on honeymoon. That's all I ask.'

'That sounds . . . nice,' I said. I wasn't even kidding. It sounded beautiful. And the thought of going dress shopping with my mum sounded potentially hilarious. It had taken me a year to get used to the insane level of customer service that went along with buying a loaf of bread in California, so Judith Campbell dealing with the kind of women who work in wedding-dress shops was going to be an entertainment second to none.

'Does it have to be just you and me?' I asked her, because I had thought of a way to make it all ten times more hysterical.

'Are you having bridesmaids?'

'Try stopping Todd,' I said. 'Noleen, would you like to be a bridesmaid?'

'I would rather go pony trekking on a hungry alligator,' Noleen said.

'That's what I thought, but would you like to come with me while I choose my dress?'

'I would rather be a bridesmaid,' said Noleen. 'Imma be on Team Taylor. You get Kathi as your bridesmaid. But you have to tell her and my name doesn't need to come up.'

'This is going to be fun,' I said. I was talking to Noleen but my mum, at the other end of the phone, gave a happy sigh.

'It's going to be perfect,' she said. 'Or heads will roll, believe me.'

'Uh, OK,' I said and started making all the goodbye noises it took to get off the phone with my mother. I thought I was going to have to resort to a fake call waiting but in the end Todd called me for real, and my mother only kept me on for long enough to tell me that I had to tell him that if he insisted on being my attendant then he had to fit his outfit around the actual bridesmaids and not be a diva.

'I'll tell him,' I lied, knowing that I would probably have to settle for a dress that toned in with whatever Todd picked out for himself. At that point, while I was still myself, all I thought was that I'd have to be sure and instruct the videographer to capture Todd in all his glory.

So I wasn't *entirely* still me. I had already got to the stage where I assumed there would be a videographer. Oh, it's a subtle and insidious process, right enough.

'What's up?' I asked Todd, when I had finally got off the line from Scotland. 'Oh and hey – while you're here – if I was going to have you as part of my wedding party, what would your title be?'

'Huh?' said Todd. 'Whaddaya mean "if". I'm the bridesman. What are you talking about? But, since you finally *have* started talking about it, I have a few things to discuss with you.'

'Like wh . . .?' I said.

'But not today. Have you seen Noleen?'

'She's right here.'

Noleen clicked her fingers and swore. 'That's right. I was supposed to tell you.'

'Did she tell you?'

'What?' I said. The question would have worked for either of them.

'Something has happened at the cemetery,' said Todd. 'Finally!' It had been bothering him that we hadn't earned a penny since the retainer and the fee for the couple of hours it took for Kathi to make up her notes. 'Do you have time to come with?'

'As long as I'm back for an emergency divorce coaching session at seven,' I said.

'How can you stand to plan a wedding and listen to so many ending at the same time?' Todd said. 'Isn't it depressing? Never mind. Get your pre-pre-wedding-dress-diet ass round here in the next five minutes or we're going without you.'

There was a lot of erroneous information packed into that gratuitous reference to my backside. For a start, I had no intention of going on a diet. My arse was fine. I wasn't planning to wear a fitted dress anyway. But still I found myself selecting a long cardigan to sling on top before going to meet him.

And I was glad of the distraction, if I'm honest, because the other half of what Todd had just said to me was a bit too close for comfort. That very day, I had faced a client who turned up for a first appointment with the crumpled under-eyes and pink philtrum you only get from frequent and sustained bouts of weeping.

'My marriage is over,' she said, as soon as I had got her name, age and credit card details. 'I know it. I've known it for a long time. I just need a little support while I actually do it.'

'That is an admirable amount of self-care,' I said. I can speak California-Therapy-ese like a native. 'And can I say I'm sorry to hear that this is happening to you?' She frowned. Of course, I still make slips. Giving voice to the quaint idea that a marriage ending was a bad thing came straight from Scotland, not from this neck of the woods where I have literally heard people call their marriages 'completed'. Even Gwyneth Paltrow didn't go that far.

'I went in knowing it wasn't a permanent arrangement,' my client said. Her name was Gaynor and I couldn't help myself imbuing her with all the stoic verve of Gloria, even as she started sniffling again.

'Uh-huh,' I said. This was new. Nobody actually went into marriage knowing it was a bust, did they? *Did* they? 'Can you tell me a little more about that?'

'It was mixed, you see,' she said. 'We're from different religions.'

'That doesn't necessarily mean the relationship has to end,' I said. 'What religions are you both?'

'Does that matter?'

The clinical answer was no. The personal answer, as far I was concerned, was . . . of course not! Still, it would have been nice to hear that the two faiths in question weren't Judaism and Christianity like Taylor and me. Except neither one of us was religious, actually, just sort of wishy-washy and sentimental about childhood memories. He had a dreidel; I had a fairy for the top of the tree kind of thing.

'Not as such,' I told Gaynor. 'Just that I would like to gauge the amount of difficulty you might each run into with your faith communities over the dissolution of your marriage.'

'Oh,' she said. 'No nothing like that. We're not super devout or anything. He's Catholic and I'm a Buddhist.'

'Huh,' I said. I had no idea what Buddhism said regarding divorce, and if she didn't think the Catholicism was a stumbling block, I wasn't sure asking would get me an answer. 'And what stage of separation are you at?'

'He chain-sawed through our bed,' she said.

'Wh . . .? Are . . .? Do you feel safe, Gaynor?' I said. 'Did you notify anyone?'

'What?' she said. 'I wasn't *in* it. He did it to get it out of the house without having to remove a window. He had built it right there in the room. Out of driftwood from the beach where we stayed on our honeymoon. So, you know, it wasn't a rage thing or anything. But it struck me as pretty final.'

Me too. 'And clearly it upset you,' I said. 'I can tell you've been crying.'

'What? Oh this?' She pointed to her lip and nose area. 'No, I've been having electrolysis. It stings like crazy but I'm sick of waxing.'

I got through the rest of the session on auto-pilot. This woman was so together she was still removing her moustache even while her relationship fell apart. She was so mature she didn't consider 'ever after' as the given period in which to be 'happy'. She even told me, at the end of the first hour she thought six sessions would probably be plenty.

So, as I say, thank God for Todd, Kathi and the Sex Volunteers, saving me from being alone with my thoughts, because even before we got married the spectre of divorce terrified me. I was all for 'till death' whether or not we actually said it. I had already imagined Taylor and me old and grey together, him pushing my wheelchair, me reading his prescription bottles. Or the other way round if his knees packed in and my eyes gave out. So I was looking forward to the graveyard. I would no doubt see acres of headstones where couples who'd stayed married their whole lives were lying side by side for eternity.

'Did they give you a clue?' I said, sliding into the back seat of Todd's Jeep. Kathi was driving.

'They gave us coordinates,' Todd said. 'And instructions not to disrupt their tour. It's religions of the world today, apparently. Juni Park in charge of describing death rituals, Bob Larch on Beteo County demographics, Linda on leaflets – well, QR codes – and Mitch . . .'

'On darkness?' I said. 'He's such a weirdo. Well, they're all major weirdos but he's creepy with it.'

'I dunno,' Kathi said. 'It's kinda interesting. We asked them how many world religions were represented by the dead of Cuento. Guess what they told us.'

I started counting on my fingers. 'Eleven.'

'Twenty-eight,' said Todd.

'Get lost. There aren't twenty-eight rel . . . Wait, are they counting all the flavours of Christian separately? There can't be twenty-eight any *other* way.'

Kathi started singing 'Wide World' except using, 'Ooh, Lexy, Lexy' instead of the right lyrics.

'What's made *you* so chipper?' I asked. Although Kathi mocked me on the hour every hour whenever we were together, doing it in song was not an everyday occurrence.

'Work!' Kathi said. 'I love February. The bulge of holiday laundry's finished and, once everyone's been paid again and started clearing their credit cards, their thoughts turn to spring cleaning. So I've survived the hungry gap again. You know, the hungry gap you force on me.'

I breathed slowly and told myself not to respond. Kathi kept trying to get me to recommend her surveillance package to clients who thought their spouses were cheating and was deaf to my protests about confidentiality, mental health, ethics and plain old common sense. We hadn't ever had an out-and-out fight about any of it but the insulation was definitely peeled back off the wires and it was best if we didn't touch.

'I mean to say,' she went on. 'You're tee-ing them up for divorce lawyers and that doesn't worry you? Why's it so hard to throw them my way first?'

'I don't want to talk about divorce,' I said. 'I came out to have a nice change.'

'Death?' said Todd. 'Graves?'

'Cemeteries aren't necessarily depressing,' I said. 'Linda Magic used the word "parkland"?'

'Yeah, not for this she didn't,' said Todd darkly.

SIX

Mind you, the cemetery wasn't looking its best. In the grey damp of a typical February tea-time, all the flowers appeared washed out and the pots of water they sat in were cloudy and rank. This, I thought nodding to myself, is northern California's bleak little secret. Los Angeles might bathe in balmy sunshine all year round but up here when the blistering heat finally lets up, the winter months are as soggy and dull as Dundee. Except worse. On two counts.

First, you can't live in California and moan about rain. As the reservoirs and aquifers and wells all refill, and the fish in the delta of the Sacramento river start to flip their tails and think about spawning, as the frogs in the ponds wake up and croak news of their survival, as green things unfurl and rub their eyes like Munchkins in the morning, only the bubbliest of bubbleheads would complain about their hair going frizzy or their car getting mud on the bumpers.

And then there's the other problem: it's not cold. You get clammy inside your raincoat and your wellies stink like the bottom of a rabbit hutch, because there's never a single spike of frost to go with the dark and damp. It's just grey and sweaty like something you'd find in a long-forgotten locker at the gym. Not that the Californians will admit as much. They wear cute bobble hats and matching scarves with pom-poms on the end, mittens even. And skiing jumpers and fur-lined puffer jackets with the fluffy hoods up to flatter their faces. And big butch quilted flannel shirts over long-sleeved vests like lumberjacks. It makes me faint just looking at them. But it's only the equivalent of how Scottish women strip off to their spaghetti straps at the first blink of sunshine in spring, and get through the 'summer' purple and mottled and freezing, all the men in shorts with the goose pimples on their shins making their hairs stand out like they're in soft-focus. What else are you supposed to do, when the fashion-spreads from London and New York have suckered you into buying the wrong clobber for your climate?

Suffice it to say there were numerous ways it was miserable in the cemetery that day, and the fuggy air made me think of typhus and cholera and plague. Or maybe just mosquitoes. Plus, Todd's interpretation of the coordinates took us to the very darkest, dankest corner, at the bottom of a slight slope, overhung with trees and smelling strongly of mushrooms and cat pee.

'It's the grave of a Mr and Mrs Truman,' Todd said. 'Pink marble with gold lettering . . . Here it is!'

We stood in a row and contemplated the headstone, clean and unadorned although a little weathered owing to the years it had stood there. The inscription read:

> Sacred to the memory of
> William Benson Truman 1922–1978
> Beloved husband of Betsy
> And in memory of
> Elizabeth 'Betsy' Truman (Pollock) 1926–2001
> Much loved Mother and Grandmother
> At peace with Christ

Exactly! I thought to myself. Gaynor was clueless. People stayed married all the time. I ignored the fact that the epitaph meant they were both Christians and the fact that William and Elizabeth were two of the WASPiest names imaginable, so they were probably both Anglicans to boot, so they might have hated each other but stuck to it anyway.

'Can you see anything?' Kathi said, after a while.

'Professionally, tons,' I replied. 'But my profession, not yours.' I'm not immune to showing off. 'His memory is sacred, hers isn't. He doesn't get called a father but she gets called a mother, and presumably she didn't remarry and start popping them out after he was gone because she was in her fifties *and* she would have been buried with number two. So I think he was a bit of a pig whose kids hated him, only she was too conventional not to give him the "beloved".'

'*I've* seen it,' said Todd, who's a worse show-off than me. 'And you're wrong, Lexy.'

'Oh?' I said.

But he had shut his mouth like a Kilner jar, clearly meaning to torture me until I either solved it myself or begged him.

'Turn and face the other way a minute, Lex,' said Kathi.

I thought it was a clue so I spun round on my Converse,

grinding one sole into the mud and scanning for whatever I had missed.

'Oh yeah!' said Kathi. 'Well-spotted, Todd. You can turn back now, Lexy.'

She was grinning like the kid on that magazine, the one with the freckles and the tooth missing. Taylor's got a pile of them that he didn't get rid of even when he had to downsize into half a boat. I narrowed my eyes at her but the grin only widened. Why did I have to turn away to let her see whatever it was I couldn't see?

Todd was grinning at me too and, as I scowled back at him, he started to curtsy. At least, that's the closest thing I'd ever seen before to what he was doing, bending both knees out to one side and tilting his head so he was looking at me out of the corner of his eye. Then Kathi did it too, the knees and the head tilt both.

'Stop it,' I said. 'You're creeping me out.'

They kept crouching and grinning and, call me easily led but, before I knew what I was doing, I was at it as well. I bent my legs with my knees clamped together as if I was getting into a sports car in a short skirt and I craned my neck until my chin was pointing right at the Trumans' gravestone. And there it was.

'Bloody Nora!' I said, straightening up and bending down properly, hands on knees and face to the ground. 'What *is* that?'

'Green things,' Todd said. Even when he and Roger lived in their house they had landscapers to look after the outside so he's not much of a gardener.

'No, I mean it's crocuses, obviously,' I said, 'but what does it say?' I walked back and forth in front of the grave trying to get the light to hit at just the right angle to let me read the message that had been planted in the ground and was now coming up.

'Three words,' Kathi said. 'Three letters, six letters, three letters.'

'Symmetrical,' said Todd. 'It could just be a pattern.'

Kathi was in a deep squat with her elbows practically in the grass. It looked like a yoga pose, or maybe a contortionist's starting point. 'The first word is something H-E—'

'T-H-E!' I said. 'It must be "the".'

'R-L-L-L,' said Todd. 'The second word isn't a word. It must be code.'

'That's not an R,' said Kathi. 'It's a K. That top part is just a piece of grass.'

'K-L-L-L-E,' said Todd.

'It can't be three Ls though,' I said. 'The first one is plainer than the other two. K . . . I?'

'K-I-L-L-E . . . R,' said Todd. 'Oh my God!'

'And the last word is . . .' Kathi was practically tied up in a pretzel from the competing demands of getting as close to the budding crocuses as humanly possible, while making sure she didn't actually face-plant into graveyard dirt. 'The last letter might be an N. The first one might an N too.'

'The killer nun!' said Todd. And as soon as he said it, that's all I could see. I didn't understand how I had missed it. THE KILLER NUN.

'Only . . . what nun?' Kathi said. 'They're married, right? So she can't have been a nun. Were they both murdered by a nun?'

'I don't think that *says* "nun",' said Todd, as if he hadn't just shouted the word. 'Look at how the downstrokes are placed. It's not "U" and "N" it's "I" and "M".'

'Nim?' I said, like an idiot.

'Him!' said Kathi. 'And the first word isn't "the". It's "she".'

In a chorus, all three of us said it, 'She killed him!'

'Bingo,' I followed up. 'She killed him.'

'Except she probably didn't,' said Kathi. 'Poppy Cliveson didn't grow up and Kermit Kellog wasn't gay.'

'And you can't slander the dead,' said Todd. 'So there's still no excuse to go bothering Molly. Unless making holes in grass and planting crocus bulbs is criminal damage.'

'Kind of a stretch,' Kathi said. 'I could ask one of the older cops still on the force if there was any gossip about the Trumans back in the day.' Kathi had been cultivating the Cuento PD as part of her PI networking plan for quite a while now and her confident tone as she said this suggested that it was finally working.

'And when you report to our clients,' I said, 'could you give them a bit of briefing on what constitutes an emergency? How fast can crocus grow, for God's sake? Why couldn't it have waited until a more convenient time instead of us being summoned and then told to keep out of their way?'

'That's a thought, actually,' said Todd. 'Can we just leave this message to get clearer and clearer as the spring goes on? I think I'll go to Deuce and get some pansies or something to plant in and around, smudge it a bit so it doesn't stand out.'

'Primroses,' I said. 'Pansy season is finished.'

'Ha!' said Todd. 'You're researching flowers!' There was a note of triumph that would have been over the top if he had caught me watering down drinks or pouring Barefoot wines into Mondavi empties. (Two things I had briefly considered when I had first started looking into the price of an open bar.)

'Get a grip,' I said. 'Why the hell would I be mugging up on winter and spring flowers for a midsummer wedding?'

'Like a bride never wanted out of season?' Todd shot back.

'Try *Gardener's World* one night instead of *Project Runway*,' I said. 'Normal people know when primroses bloom.'

'Shut up the both of you,' Kathi said, in a low voice. 'Look.'

She wasn't pointing and didn't nod. Also, darkness had fallen while we were standing there.

'What am I looking at?' said Todd.

'There's someone there.'

'And it's not you two this time,' I said.

'Where?' said Todd.

'Hiding behind a gravestone two rows bac— No! He's on the mov— Wait! Here she com— Look out!'

Kathi dived in one direction, Todd in the other, and I was left, unprotected and backed up against the Trumans' grave, trampling the offending crocuses underfoot, as a dervish – there is no other word for it – in a full-face, snarling dragon mask that hid everything except its flashing eyes bore down on me, screaming at the top of a very screechy voice, and punched me right in the jaw, making a long scratch across my cheek with the follow-through. Then it spun round and was gone before I could punch it back or get my hand to my phone or do much of anything really except stand there too stunned even to cry. That doesn't explain why neither Kathi nor Todd gave chase, but when I blinked my way back to full brainpower, they were both just standing there.

'OK, well, we can go to Molly with *that*!' Kathi said.

'What the hell *was* that?' said Todd.

'She-she—' I said, still pole-axed.

'She?' said Todd. 'You sure? It's not just that face-scratching seems quite *Drag Race*?'

'Lexy, do you want to go to the ER?' Kathi said.

I took my phone out to examine my face and worked my jaw to see if anything felt broken. 'Nah,' I said. 'It's stinging like hell but it's just a scrape. She must have been wearing a ring, eh? My God, she's taken off enough skin cells to grow a whole new Lexy.'

'I'm kinda sorry I dived out of the way now,' said Todd. 'Imagine a world with two of me!' He gave me a hug and either delayed shock, affection or *that* terrifying thought made me start, at last, to blub like a kid who's dropped her lolly.

'My face!' I wailed. 'I don't want to be an ugly bride!'

Who does, right? When I met the celebrant for our first face-to-face consultation a couple of days later, I saw her clock the scratch – now scabbing over nicely – and count to five on her reddish-brown fingers, calculating the healing time, February to June.

'What's that on your hands?' I said, thinking if I asked a personal question she'd know she could too. Also, I wanted to know before I shook one of them.

She looked down and said, 'Henna? Probably.'

So I settled for an elbow-bump.

Otherwise the meeting went well. Twigs of Joy, Cuento's downtown kava bar, had been her suggestion. It gave me pause for a minute but it was handy for nipping out at lunchtime so I agreed. I had spotted her as soon as I walked in the door. She had white blonde hair down to her bum, and wore a shift, or kaftan, or maybe just sack, that was so loosely woven you'd have been able to see her bra if she'd been wearing one. As things stood her left nipple was being rubbed raw and her right nipple was trapped and made me think of Whac-a-Mole. She must have made this garment herself. She might have woven the threads herself. She might even have made the loom.

'Sister Sunshine?' I said.

'Call me Sunny.' That was a relief.

I sat down on the nearest thing that might be a chair. (Twigs of Joy didn't make a strict distinction between furniture and art. (Or between art and junk.))

'So, midsummer?' I began. 'I haven't got a venue, you know. Well, I *have* got a venue, but I've also got a mother and she's kicking off about it. So I might be looking for a venue.'

'Don't worry about that,' said Sunny. 'It won't be a problem.'

'Really?' I said. 'Cool.'

'At the moment of commitment the universe conspires to assist you,' she added, diluting the comfort considerably. 'Goethe.'

'Gouda?' I said.

'*Goe*-the.'

'Girder?'

'G-O-E-T-H-E!' she said.

'Ah!' I said. 'Goethe. Sorry.' She had cheered me up again despite the adventurous pronunciation. If she was quoting a German philosopher rather than a fridge magnet, I might be in safer hands than I thought. I gave her a bright smile. 'I've never had kava juice before. What do you recommend?'

'You should probably stick to something more conventional if you have to go to work this afternoon,' she said. 'They serve kombucha, kefir and kvass too.'

'How about ktea?' I said, but she didn't laugh. 'So *you're* not on duty later today?'

'I've built up a sturdy tolerance,' she said. 'But no, I have no celebrations today. I'll be immersed in my curator role until sundown.'

'Curator?' I said. More culture, I thought.

'I curate a collection of sharable artefacts and life objects,' she said.

Five years earlier, I would have been stumped but I was practically a native now and I knew what she was telling me: she ran a gift shop.

'So midsummer,' I said again. 'Do you have a set text that you use? Or a menu of them? Or do we work it out together, like a eulogy?'

'There are a few words the state requires me to say,' she told me. 'But the rest is up to you and your partner. What's his, her or their name?'

'His. Taylor,' I said, feeling boring. 'And it looked like you could liaise with caterers and florists and everything, from looking at your website. Is that right?'

'We are a forest,' she said. I waited. 'As the trees twine roots and share energies across countless miles, so I commune with providers of all beauty and bounty in celebration of true love.'

'Excellent,' I said, panicking inside but managing to hide it. 'So we're all set then?'

She put down her jam jar of cloudy liquid. I had decided, after taking a close look at it, not to order anything at all for myself. She reached out and took my hands in hers. They really were very deeply stained with whatever it 'probably' was ground into the lines and around her cuticles.

'Let these words I'm about to say wash over you and through you leaving no residue to taint your joy,' she said.

'OK,' I agreed, bracing myself.

'Please read and sign the contract I am about to give you and keep one copy for yourself. Then transfer the non-refundable deposit within five working days and fill in the contact form on the website page I will set up for your celebration, once the money has cleared into my account.' She squeezed my hands. 'Now let's take some deep cleansing breaths together and recover ourselves.'

I did the breathing to keep her happy, but in truth I was fine. A bit of hard business dealing made me feel like everything was going to work out okay.

'What happened to your face?' she said, once she'd stopped puffing and panting. It was as if the deep breaths hadn't quite managed to send her back to her higher plane.

'I got hit by a . . . woman in a bit of a state,' I said.

'A client?' she asked. She had Googled me.

'A complete stranger,' I said.

'In Cuento?'

'Yeah, in the graveyard. It was unsettling. And I would have said unsettling and graveyards went together, but . . .' I wound down into silence. The Sex Volunteers had been highly offended at the insinuation; even Mitchell.

'Did she do that with her nails?' said Sister Sunshine.

'A ring, I think.'

'And how are you addressing it?' said Sister Sunshine.

'I reported it, obviously,' I said. 'But the cops were fishnet condoms. So I've chalked it up to life's rich tapestry and decided to think about my wedding instead.'

'Still, let me put some salve on it.' She rummaged in a bag made out of a brown version of that same loose-woven cloth. It was like an onion net, with pens and tampons and the handle of a hairbrush poking through the holes. When she found her tube of ointment she pulled it right though the side instead of out the top.

'What is it?' I asked, just as she lunged at me with a big blob of it wobbling on the tip of one henna (I hoped) begrimed finger.

'All completely natural and plant-based,' she said, which was no kind of answer whatsoever, because so is hogweed and hemlock and that kava she was sucking down.

SEVEN

March

Thanks to Sister Sunshine's manky ointment, my face swelled like a pumpkin for a couple of days but once I got over that, it was only sore from being belted for one or two more. The mark was completely gone after a few weeks and, if my mother hadn't been coming over to go dress shopping with me as threatened, I would have forgotten all about it – just one of those peculiar things that might happen to you if you hang out in cemeteries like a nutter.

The culprit wasn't found, which was hardly surprising since my description was enough to make Molly roll her eyes: I had said she 'wore a ring'. Kathi did a bit better, I thought: thirty to forty, between five feet and six feet, wearing jeans and a grey sweatshirt as well as the dragon mask. But Molly rolled her eyes so hard at that I was surprised she didn't have to stand up and go to fetch them from the floor behind her chair. Todd said he thought the sweatshirt was mixed fibre rather than all-cotton and the jeans had been washed with too much softener and Molly only shook her head and assured him that she would be sure and tell the uniforms to rub up against likely suspects to check for static and the smell of meadows.

She didn't care about the planting of crocuses either.

Anyway, the morning my mum was arriving in San Francisco, my face was symmetrical in colour again – no pink stripes – and I was feeling pretty chipper as I saw my last client for three whole days. It was a man, which always makes a nice change although I'd deny saying that if anyone asked me. He had been circling his problem for three sessions, talking a lot about his children and his duties and his 'investment portfolio', which were all code for how much he was dying to leave his wife. If I had been a different kind of therapist I would have given him a cue and let him broach the subject on his preferred terms. But I was sick of coming up against these same terms every time my client was an unhappily married man. Basically, he wanted to do a shitty thing while still looking good. Fine, but he was going to have to do it without me helping him.

I had had a sense that today was the day when he came in and sat down and I was not wrong.

'You haven't asked me about my marriage in any of the sessions yet,' he began. He was all in! He was going to blame *me* for *him* circling the subject.

'Oh, I think we've been talking about little else, Dex,' I said. 'But if you'd like to address it more directly, today, please go ahead.'

'We have been married for twenty years and we have two beautiful children,' he said, like he was a politician and I was a reporter and he was standing on his front porch with his wife grim-faced at his side and his mistress waiting in their little studio flat. 'But the relationship has run its course. And I know everyone is going to think I'm the bad guy if I leave.'

'Not necessarily,' I said.

He sat back with such a gusty sigh of relief you'd think he had been punctured. 'Really? See, the thing is I can't afford to let them stay in the house and still get somewhere big enough for the kids to come and spend time with me. They're a girl and a boy. Perfect family! So everyone is going to have to downsize. And my wife will have to go full-time at work and I'm going to look like a selfish cliché.'

'No, I think the selfish cliché is when you leave your wife for a younger woman,' I said. Having been pleasantly punctured, he now deflated before my very eyes. 'Ah,' I said.

'She's not *much* younger,' he said. 'I'm fifty and she's forty. Is that a big age gap ? Is ten years a significant age gap?'

'How old is your wife?' I asked. I knew *that* would be the age difference that would reach down this poor part-time working, about to be homeless, mother-of-two's throat and pull her guts out to stamp on them. The age difference between *her* and Jessica Rabbit. He was neither here nor there.

I had hit an accidental cricketing six, a fortuitous base-balling home run. He crumpled as if the remaining air was being sucked out him with a Hoover hose, like he was full of summer dresses being packed away for the winter in a house with inadequate storage.

'When I was thirty and my wife was almost forty,' he said, 'it didn't seem like a big deal. But now she's going to be a senior! She's going to be sixty! She has bad knees! I want to live! Does that make me a monster?'

I didn't say anything. Taylor wasn't ten years younger than me but he was more than five and I could imagine him sitting in a therapist's office years from now, close to tears as he told some other professional soother, 'She's got bingo wings! She farts when she laughs! I want to live!'

'Are you judging me?' said Dex.

'No,' I said, with perfect honesty.

It bugged me all the way to the airport that I'd made him happy. But as I sat in International Arrivals watching the big screen, looking at the trail of travel-weary people pushing their carts and dragging their cases, everything fell away except the fizzing inside. I was going to see my mum! In California! I was going to drive her back over the Bay Bridge, on the wrong side of the road! Take her to reunite with all my friends! Show her the motel and my boat! Buy her pizza and silly coffee and watermelons the size of toddlers and tacos from a truck! And see her eyes mist over as she saw me in the perfect confection of a dream of a dress! I had read two months' worth of bridal magazines now and I was really starting to believe that dress existed, somewhere, just for me. I wasn't going crazy or anything; I didn't even try to look at *all* the magazines. I limited myself to the top twenty and I cut the possible pictures out and filed them in plastic sleeves in a ring binder, discarding the rest of the tome. If there were two good dresses on either side of the same page, I usually picked one. That's how nuts I wasn't going. I had only had to buy a second copy of the same issue four times.

There she was!

I leapt to my feet and surged forward to try to be the first face she saw when she came through the doors.

She wasn't looking. She was deep in conversation with another woman dragging a monster suitcase. They stopped ten feet from me and hugged. Then the other woman opened her phone and started punching buttons and my mother cast her eyes around – at last! – and spotted me.

'Lexy!' she said. 'That lady just told me I could have ordered a car in the blink of an eye and you wouldn't have had to take time off to come and get me.'

'If you've got data roaming on your smartphone and a rideshare app,' I said. 'Absolutely.' I hugged her and ignored all the people tutting and tsking as they tried to edge past us. The whole plane had to be Brits; no Americans did such vicious affront so quietly.

'She made it sound much easier than that,' my mum said. 'No

jargon at all. She said text for a lift and someone would come right to the kerb.'

'With a Y,' I said. 'Lyft with a . . . Never mind. Will we go? Do you want a coffee? The tea is undrinkable.'

'Let's hit the road,' my mum said. 'Half my wee case is teabags for you. So straight home, eh?'

'You didn't have to do that,' I said. 'You could have packed stuff you needed.'

'No, but I said to your dad I'd get him some cheap clothes so I need the space in my case to fill with shopping. Lacey off the library van brought back clothes for her whole family when she went to Orlando and they were practically free.'

I would break the news about that particular difference between Florida and California later, I decided. Especially after she nearly fainted when we paid our way out of the airport carpark with no change from a twenty.

Despite the jetlag, she was a rewarding passenger all the way up the road to Cuento, marvelling at the Bay, the hills, the strips of fast-food outlets and car dealerships lining I80 – 'just like the movies!' – and she was agog to see Cuento itself.

'Why are we stopping?' she asked as we made our way through downtown.

'Because it's a stop sign,' I said.

'There's nothing coming, Lexy. Put your foot down; I need a pee.'

'Mum, it's a stop sign. It's like a red traffic light. It doesn't matter if nothing's coming.'

'Why are we stopping again?'

'It's a stop sign. The blocks are short here.'

'Oooh, Korean barbecue!' she said. 'And what's poke?'

'Po-kay.'

'Taqueria! Thai! What's artificial pizza? Does no one cook in this town?'

'Artisanal,' I said.

'What's an up-and-down burger?'

'It's a brand name,' I said. 'Up and Down is a chain.'

'Sounds like food poisoning,' said my mum. Then: 'Wait! I recognize that balcony from FaceTiming in the pandemic. Is that the motel?'

'Welcome,' I said, 'to the Last Ditch. Hey, look!'

The entire crew were out on the forecourt to greet her: Diego and Hiro, who would always associate both my parents with their Best Christmas Ever; as well as Noleen and Kathi; Della and Devin; Todd, of course; but also Roger who was either working an odd shift for him or had taken an honest-to-God afternoon off in Judith Campbell's honour.

'BIENVENIDA A CUENTO' read the banner the children were holding up.

'MOTHER OF THE BRIDE' read the balloons Todd had tied to the railings outside my mum's room. We had chosen carefully where to put her. Technically, all the rooms were the same, except for where the connecting doors were permanently open to make bigger spreads for permanent residents, but I had put my foot down over the question of the room where a murder had been committed one time and the room where, another time, a body had been hidden. I found my gaze travelling over the remaining doors, telling myself not to be silly, assuring myself that things happened in twos.

The reunion greetings were effusive and long-lasting and, when my mum hinted that she had brought presents for Diego and his sister, the entire Muelenbelt family bore her off to her room without me getting a look in.

'Lexy,' she said, over her shoulder, 'I'm going to have a nap. Wake me for dinner, eh?'

'You'd be better to power through till bedtime,' I said.

'You have a nice long nap, Judith,' Todd said, elbowing me in the ribs in a way he probably thought was subtle. 'Dinner isn't till eight. We're going out for sushi.'

I waited for my mum to object but either she had been studying up or she had taken a good tranq for the flight. 'Lovely,' she said. 'I've been wanting to try salmon-skin salad.'

'What is it?' I asked Todd once the door had closed.

'Trooble at tit cemetery,' said Todd. Four years of *Coronation Street* had convinced him he could do a blinding Manchester accent and nothing short of getting pasted by a Gallagher brother was ever going to shift the notion. 'You're lucky Kathi and I were here to say hi to Judith at all. It sounds juicy!'

'If you had made me use half a personal day and then sloped off . . .' said Roger. 'Don't say that to your mom, Lexy. I was happy to welcome her. After the way she welcomed us.'

'Go for a nap,' said Todd. Roger, being a consultant in a

paediatric HDU, was permanently exhausted and could fall asleep on the lip of a volcano.

'I'll join you, Roger,' Noleen said. 'In my own room, I mean.' Noleen wasn't a huge napper but she was an enthusiastic lunchtime drinker and siestas were standard.

'Of course, we understand if you don't want to come, Lexy,' Todd said. 'After the dragon slasher.'

I nodded, then I thought some more. People were in and out of that cemetery all day every day: gardeners, mourners, dog walkers, our little band of enthusiastic weirdos. 'I'll come,' I said. 'Lightning never strikes and all that.'

'What is it this time anyway?' I said, as we made our way through the streets to the familiar gates.

'Skeleton,' said Todd.

I sat up a bit straighter in the back seat.

'How is that left for a PI to deal with?' I said. 'Do the cops know? Have they called forensics?'

'Wait and see,' said Kathi. 'Oh no! Todd, park outside and let's walk in.'

I looked where she was facing and saw that there was a funeral taking place in the cemetery today, a cluster of dark-clothed adults and children all processing behind a sort of cart with a coffin on top, pulled by two men in the national dress of some country I didn't recognize. They looked far too festive for the occasion.

'Do we know where we're supposed to be going this time?' I said. 'What if the coordinates take us to right beside the burial?'

'Linda said hug the wall and walk clockwise round a quarter of the perimeter,' Kathi told me. 'That bunch' – she braced both hands on my shoulders and boosted herself up to see – 'are stopping in the middle.'

The cemetery was big enough that the mourners didn't notice us as we picked our way through the outer ring of gravestones, clambering occasionally, tripping more than once when we encountered those flat slabs that are supposed to make the sexton's life so easy. Before too long, we arrived at the site of the latest incident.

'Is it real?' I said, peering at the skeleton.

'You should know,' said Kathi. 'You're the last one of us to have seen a skeleton.'

I shuddered at the memory then scrutinized what lay on the tufty grass of the grave in front of us. It was yellow-ish overall and grey-ish in places, like a smoker's smile. Speaking of smiles, it seemed to have some teeth missing from its grisly grin. And speaking of things missing, it only had one leg.

'Well?' said Todd. '*Is* it real? Should I Google it?'

'Google it,' I said. 'I haven't got a clue.'

Todd quirked a look at me. 'I'd have thought it would be a memorable sight for you, Lexy.'

'It was but the thing is I don't think I've ever seen a fake one except the real cheapos from Party Town. Have you found the rest of it?' I pointed at the single foot. Then I looked a little closer. The other leg didn't stop at a joint. It was sawn through. And the raw ends of the . . . bone . . . didn't look like the snarls and puckers you get when you cut plastic. They looked . . .

'How would you describe the look of that cut edge?' I said.

'Spongy and porous?' said Kathi.

I bent closer. 'Anything but,' I said. 'Ragged and splintery.'

'And a darker colour in the middle?' said Kathi. I glanced up and saw that she was reading off her phone. 'So it's real then,' she went on. 'And the funny thing is—'

I spluttered. 'You don't think *this* is the funny thing?' I said. 'Call the cops! For God's sake, this is getting ridiculous! We can't just trot along here every few weeks to see what the latest is.'

'Calm down, Lexy,' said Todd. 'Bob Larch emailed us a copy of the receipt. It was right here under a rock. He said he would have left it but there's rain in the forecast. We're supposed to swing by and pick up the original when we're finished here.'

'Receipt?' I said. 'What are you talking about?'

'Whoever left the skeleton left it too. It was purchased from . . . where was it, Kathi?'

'Moose's Spooks and Pranks, Stanley, Idaho. So you know what Molly or whoever would we say if we called the cops? They already know people are doing tacky things to graves and they don't care.'

'But it's a real skeleton!' I said.

'It's not illegal to own a skeleton in California,' said Kathi. 'Or buy and sell one in Idaho either. Bet you can't guess what three states – only three! – *have* outlawed it.'

'What is wrong with this country!' I said, looking around myself as if another Scot might happen by and join me in being gobsmacked. 'Don't cheat!' I added, because Todd was checking out *his* phone now.

'I'm not looking up states,' he said. 'I'm looking up the UK. And guess what: it's not illegal there either.'

'What is wrong with this *world*?' I said.

'Tennessee, Georgia and Louisiana,' Kathi said. 'Bummer for the NOLA Mardi Gras, huh? And Lexy? We're not.'

I blinked a couple of times trying to thread my way back through the exchange to pick up the loose end. 'Not what?' I said, after I'd given up.

'We're not waiting around to see what happens and coming to stare at it when it does. We've been reinterviewing relatives, grilling local history buffs – mostly the Sex Volunteers but others too – and just about going cross-eyed in the library looking back through old *Voyagers* online.'

'Oh,' I said. 'Sorry. Why didn't you farm some of it out to me?'

Todd did that fake sneeze thing that's supposed to hide a rude comment, and it worked this time. I had no idea what he said except that it ended with 'zilla'. Kathi smirked. 'Oh, you're busy with other things,' she said. 'And some of it's easier when I can say I'm a licensed PI.'

'But if it's recently deceased people, wouldn't a licensed MFT help too?' I said. 'How do you explain Todd being there?'

'No one has complained,' Todd said. 'It's always nice to see pretty people. It cheers things up. That's why everyone loves going to the movies.'

'So, what have you and your beautiful assistant here learned while you've been trying to crack the case without me?' I said.

'Big fat zero,' Kathi said. 'If it was every night or even every week, we could do a stake-out but we can't sit out here all night every night on the off chance.' She put her phone away, then took it back out and started snapping photos of the non-crime scene.

I read the headstone, not really expecting inspiration to strike.

In Everlasting Memory of our Beloved Son
MAX LAVELLE
1986–2017

'Uff,' I said. 'That's really sad.'

'And really sick!' said Kathi. 'Max Lavelle died of gangrenous blood poisoning after neglecting a foot injury.'

'Oh my God! The *climber*?' said Todd. 'I remember that. He was a local kid. I went to school with him. I almost went to his memorial service.'

'Almost?' I said.

'He was both a climber and an asshole,' said Todd. 'He made my life a misery in high school and I didn't trust myself not to stand up and say so.'

'But you didn't troll his grave, right?' said Kathi. 'So, asshole or no asshole, we need to deal with this.'

'I still can't believe the cops won't,' I said. 'This *must* be a crime. Littering? Improper disposal of bio-waste? Something!'

'When you put it that way,' Todd said. 'Maybe if the parents complain? Do the parents know? Oh God, do we have to tell them?'

'Speaking of parents,' I said. 'As well as the fact that I've managed not to be attacked yet this time and I don't want to push it, I'm going to head back and check in on mine. She'll be up all night if she sleeps too long now and guess who she'll be texting.'

I left them to decide what to do about the skeleton and started to walk home. I fully intended to wake my mum, like I'd told them, but Sister Sunshine's curated collection was on the way.

EIGHT

It wasn't a curated collection, as I had known as soon as she started waffling on about it. It was, indeed, a wee shop full of over-priced pretty things. On the upside, she didn't make any of them herself (or get them from wherever she got her clothes) and it smelled lovely from the dried herbs and candles everywhere. I had thought it seemed a bit much overall when I first clapped eyes on it a couple of months back, but it was growing on me. It made me feel excited about the big day because, with all the lace and printed linen arranged on pale spindly furniture, it was a bridal dream – even decorated for Easter like it was today. Last month, for Valentine's Day, it had been the only shop in the whole of Cuento with nothing red. Sister Sunshine had allowed a few items of a slightly deeper shade of blush pink into the window, but offset them with lemon and celadon.

'Lexy!' she said, when I stepped inside, swinging that long bell of pale hair over one shoulder with a massive swoop of her upper body. 'What a lovely surprise!' She beamed at me.

It occurred to me, and not for the first time, that I had no idea how old she was. She never wore make-up but she had obviously stayed out of the sun, despite her name, and her white skin was so unlined she looked like a bleached Barbie. 'Lexy is one of my summer brides,' she added to the woman who was standing at the counter waiting for Sister Sunshine to finish wrapping a small item in tissue paper.

'Congratulations,' said the woman. 'It's a lot of work but it'll be worth it.'

I tried to smile but I felt a strange clenching in my guts at her words, like the time I ate a whole bag of cherries that were nice and tart because they weren't quite ripe. The truth was, I hadn't done anything very much about my wedding yet, beyond name the date and lock in Sister Sunshine. Or maybe she was the main thing; she could certainly read me like a large-print book.

'Breathe,' she said to me now. 'Your mom's coming soon, right?'
'She's here.'
'So you'll pick out a dress and we'll settle the venue, then food

and flowers and you're done. It's a party for forty people, Lexy. It's all going to be fine.'

'It might be thirty,' I said. 'I don't know yet.'

'You don't have a guest list?' said the customer. She was starting to annoy me.

'My fiancé's colleagues are proving hard to pin down,' I said. Taylor hadn't invited anyone from the phone shop, even before he resigned, but he had asked every single last ornithologist at the wetlands reserve and they were all humming and hawing, for all the world as if they had a stack of invitations piling up around them and were trying to choose between my wedding, Sundance, South by Southwest and Coachella.

It was at that very moment that my phone rang. I checked the number meaning to ignore whoever it was, but who it was was Taylor. 'What's up?' I asked him.

'Steve and Steve and Toby and Jamal and Paulie have all accepted the invitations,' he said. 'Plus one.'

'Plus one?' I said. 'Or plus five?'

'Yeah plus one each so that's ten,' said Taylor.

'How come?' I asked him. 'That's weird. Why would five ornithol . . .?' Even as I started to frame the question, though, I could hear the answer clanging in my head. And it also explained why Taylor had been oh-so-very breezy about us not having done anything much yet, for our midsummer nuptials. He had even said it wouldn't be the end of the world if we had to put it off until later in the year.

'Did you just get a calendar update?' I said.

'What?' said Taylor, in a time-honoured although never successful bid to avoid answering.

'Colleagues in Alaska or South Africa or the Antarctic send you an update, did they?'

He said nothing. But his silence put its hand on a Bible, swore an oath and told me *everything*. I dinked the button to end the call. I couldn't believe it. Except of course that it was bloody typical and I couldn't believe I hadn't busted him before today. The reason none of his fellow twitchy bird nuts had confirmed attendance at our wedding was the same reason Taylor was so keen to move it to a different date. There had been news in the air of a migration, a swerving off-course, a delay or acceleration in the yearly plans of some little brown bird that went tweet-tweet, but was a slightly different shade of brown or went tweet-tweet in a slightly different key from all the others, and the combined might of the Cuento and Contracosta County Wetlands Reserve had lost their collective shit at the possibility that they might clap eyes on the amazing sight.

'I'll look in again later,' I managed to say to Sister Sunshine, then I stalked off through the streets to the underpass.

Except I was so angry that I found myself taking a swerve into the police station forecourt when I saw Molly out front heading towards her car.

'How can it not be a crime to mutilate a skeleton and leave it on someone's grave as a prank?' I said.

'What?' said Molly, as well she might.

'Remember Max Lavelle? The climber who didn't see to his burst foot and died of stupidity? Someone put a legless skeleton on his grave and I don't understand how the hell, in a country where you can't take your top off on the beach or dry your washing in the garden, it's not a crime against the deceased, the Lavelle family and the city of Cuento.'

'Legless?' Molly said. 'Like half a skeleton?'

'No, a skeleton with a bit of one leg missing like if Max had gone to the doctor instead of breaking his mother's heart.'

'The skeleton of a one-legged man?' Molly said.

'No, the skeleton of a man with one leg bone sawn through. Fascinating as you seem to find this, can we go back to why it isn't a crime?'

'Of course it's a crime!' Molly said. 'Who told you different? Are you OK, Lexy?'

'Me? I'm fine,' I said. '*What* crime?'

'Health and Safety Code seven oh *fiiiive* . . . something. Mutilation of human remains.'

'A crime against the skeleton? That's nuts. This whole country is barking mad.'

'That's why you've settled in so nicely,' said Molly.

'I have not!' I said. 'And today I don't need to.' Because there was another one, another sane Scottish person very close by, who would be on Team Lexy in any dispute in the world. I left Molly and went to wake her.

She made short shrift of Taylor and his divided loyalties. She said to forget all about him and get on with our solemn task, as brides had been doing since Queen Victoria first decided she'd probably wear the white dress for her big day.

It was the best time I had ever spent with my mum since I came down with chicken pox at the age of five and we watched videos of every single episode of *Dallas* and *Dynasty*, side by side on the couch, while she fed me snacks I couldn't feed to myself because I had mittens on to stop me scratching.

Only this time I think it was fun for her too. She loved the wedding boutique in Sacramento, adored the fact that we had the run of the place by appointment, with no other customers allowed to walk in, and wanted to have the absolute babies of the boutique owner, a man so gay he made Todd look like John Wayne.

Della, my mum and me were all in from the outset, lying back in the sumptuous armchairs, sipping from the icy flutes of champagne, spearing up white chocolate coated raspberries and cubes of chicken on little cocktails sticks. We weren't allowed to touch the food with our fingers because of the dresses, of course.

But what really touched me was how deep Kathi dug to find the bright side of a day she might not have chosen if the other options were driving down I5 to Kern County or a migraine. She was wearing a peach linen shirt, borrowed from Todd, and a pair of white Bermuda shorts, also borrowed from Todd, as well as a pair of peach ballet flats.

'Ballet flats?' I had said, when I first saw her. 'You didn't have to do that, Kathi.'

'I've seen her toes,' said Todd. 'She sure did.'

And speaking of Todd, he had borrowed a JCB and dug deeper still. He greeted the boutique owner, name of Spence, with effusive praise for 'his beautiful store' and 'the excellent wine' and, with only one glint in his eyes as he sat down, submitted to letting someone else run the show. Later in the day, he would get some of his own back by laughing off the suggestion that Spence might have anything to do with Todd's own clothes for my wedding day, firing designer names like poison darts until Spence shut up and went back to flattering the ladies. But until then he was a pussycat, and I appreciated it deeply.

He even tried on a dress. Spence was a genius at this game. If I had known what a blast it would be in his little boutique I would have combined the dress-choosing and the hen do, no question. He kept comedy dresses – battery-powered, man-sized, Princess Diana,

Reality TV – and made sure that all the others in the wedding party were dressed in white before the serious business of me and my choice got underway.

Then he tied a chiffon scarf over my hair – not that *my* hair needed this much care – swathed me in a silk wrap over my underwear – he had told me what to put on for the day: a flesh-coloured three-way bra and plain cami knickers both of which I had to order – and rolled out a rack of possibles for us all to get stuck into.

I'm glad Spence was so adroit with spinning that three-way bra. I wouldn't have had a prayer and the rest of them were hammered. First I went strapless for a boned crinoline that showed off my lack of tattoos and stopped me from breathing. Then he snapped my straps to halter for a shoulder-conscious, mermaid-hemmed thing bristling with crystals. I felt like a fish finger. Then he put the bra on business setting and ran me through all the lengths of sleeves and heights of neck, combined with all the lengths of trains and widths of skirts. Then, finally, with a sparkle in his eyes, he laid one final dress over his arm like a wine waiter with an excellent vintage.

'Silk organza by Givenchy,' he breathed, sounding like a perfume advert, and held it closer. I reached out and felt the slip of the fabric under my fingertips, saw the shimmer as he moved it this and that in the perfect boutique lighting, and even bent down to sniff. It smelled like vanilla and happiness.

'Won't you get sweaty, Lexy?' my mum said. 'All that stuff bunched in your armpits.'

'Try it on,' said Spence, 'It's quicker than explaining.'

So I followed him back to the fitting room, which was bigger than my bedroom on the boat and had a better carpet, and waited for him to detach my straps and turn my bra into a hold-up again. Then he unbuttoned the seven hundred and eighty pearl buttons down the back, because this dress had nothing so vile and gross as a zip, and slipped it over my head. The hem fell to the floor with a smooth shushing noise that sounded like Sean Connery saying 'wishes' and the bodice settled snugly against my rib cage. As Spence bent behind me and started in on those buttons again, I waited to feel constrained, or hot, or itchy, or daft. But as I took breath after breath and felt only the perfect snug cuddle of the satin lining holding me and watched the perfect cheeky amount of swell at the top as I inhaled and the perfect elegant hint of gape as I exhaled, I had to blink to stop tears from falling on the snowy miracle of it. Spence adjusted the swirl of silk that crossed my upper arms and chest like a . . . well, like a rubber ring in a swimming pool, but nicer than that sounds . . . and said, 'How are your armpits?'

I caught his eye in the mirror and we both burst out laughing. Because of course there was nothing 'bunched' anywhere. The bodice was cut away deep and airy under the rubber ring section and I'd have to sweat like a Sumo wrestler who made his own deodorant out of leaves for a droplet ever to get there.

'What's this bit called?' I asked Spence.

'Bardot, sub-category rolled, sub-sub-category simple,' he said.

Maybe I would have laughed once but that day I nodded with all the solemnity his genius deserved and went to show my family.

Of course my mum cried. She was jet-lagged and she'd had a skinful of free champagne (and I was her only daughter and she'd nearly given up), and Della cried too because she's already started a secret little savings account for Hiro's wedding, as well as the two accounts Devin knows about for the kids' education. And if Todd hadn't cried, I'd have checked his pulse. He cries when a contestant has had to miss a round of a reality show because they're ill and no one gets sent home in the end. But here's how perfect my dress was: Kathi cried. I watched a tear roll down her right cheek, then I watched one roll down her left cheek. So far it could have been a reaction to the room spray Spence had chosen. Then she sniffed, but that could have been the white pepper on the cubes of chicken. But *then* she said, 'Oh Lexy. You look like a duchess!'

It was her highest praise, Kathi being more of a Meghan fan than a Catherine fan. For her, duchess beat princess any day.

It took a surprisingly long time to choose shoes, a veil and a headdress. It took a completely unbelievable amount of time to choose stockings, a contraption to hold them up – in my opinion, a shoo-in for least comfortable garment ever invented, including sports bras – a blue garter and a bra. I didn't even know there were such things as bridal bras. And since most bras are white anyway, I still didn't understand what feature of the one I coughed up for made it 'bridal', except the depth of the coughing. It was one hundred and eighty dollars. Plus tax.

Eventually, though, starving despite the snacks – because you can't get a square meal on a cocktail stick – and starting to be hungover because we had all eventually stopped drinking champagne and moved on to sparkling spring water – we reeled out of Spence's kingdom and straight into the nearest eatery, which happened to be a posh Mexican taverna full of politicos from the Capitol and priced on what I was going to call 'bridal scale' for the rest of my life, after those seventy dollar white stockings.

'Thanks, Mum,' I said, lifting a tankard of lager towards her. She had asked for a sherry, but, even when she asked Kathi to pronounce it so the waitress understood, she got a blank look. So she was having tequila. I hoped so anyway. She was away at the other end of the table and it might have been mescal. Certainly Todd had a wicked grin on his face that I couldn't otherwise account for.

'Oh, darling,' she said, lifting her glass back at me and slopping out a good belt of whatever was in it on to the tablecloth.

Della ordered for all of us, talking very fast and serious to the waiter, and soon the table started to fill with little dishes of jewel-coloured bits and bobs and a croque-en-bouche of tortilla chips.

'This looks like a drowned mouse,' my mum said, picking up a stuffed poblano chilli by the stalk. 'My favourite!' she declared, then lowered it into her mouth and chewed with her eyes shut. My God, she was drunk!

She had set the tone for the night. Todd had the idea of everyone giving the speech they couldn't possibly give at the actual wedding and I had to start drinking again to get through it without punching someone. He selected the tale of the first time I had farted in front of them all, standing on the balcony at the motel. It wasn't even a tale; it was just the most embarrassed he could make me. Kathi then reminded him that before I knew he was half-Mexican I had thought – and said! – that he 'had a tan'. My mum was sitting on a bottomless store of material, of course, starting with me leaving my bikini bottom floating on the surface the first time I ever dived into a swimming pool. I had been trying to make a boy notice me. I succeeded. She ran through my brief career as a vegan, which ended when I ate two burgers after closing time one Friday night and then threw them both up on the late bus. She shared the fact that I had walked in on her and my dad having sex when I was three and, because they had frozen in place, I didn't know anything was going on so I climbed in beside them and stuck my thumb in my mouth, meaning to stay all night. They just had to wait, getting cramp, until I fell asleep. Thank God I had no memory of *that* one.

When it came round to Della's turn, I reckoned I was safe. She's kind and she's mature. Also she was sober, because she was driving. But maybe the good Mexican food, unadulterated by enormities of Texas origin, had filled her with *joie de vivre* and a side of malice from the chillies because she let me down hard.

'One word,' she said. 'Bran.'

There was a moment of silence, then the whole manky lot of them hooted and cackled like a chimps' tea party at the zoo.

'You married a golfing dentist!' said my mum.

'Who never stopped banging his ex-wife!' said Kathi.

'And he remarried her a half hour after you divorced him!' said Todd.

I turned to Della. 'Your turn,' I said.

'I'm not going to laugh at you for that,' she said. 'Diego's biological father was no catch either. Instead, I'm going to tell you something I've never told anyone. Just before Branston remarried Brandee after you and him split up, he came in for a waxing.'

'Ewwwww,' said Todd. 'Of what?'

'The works,' Della said, with a shudder.

She had meant to be kind, sharing his secrets, but it didn't surprise me. Bran waxed 'the works' during our brief marriage too, which I had always thought was a monumental waste of time and agony. Because, not to be crude, but no woman ever looked at a scrotum and thought 'that would be just dreamy if only it was bald'. We hadn't been together long enough for him to start bugging me about my cactus legs and the natural wonder at the top of them, thankfully. And Taylor didn't care, also thankfully. Spence had cared a lot, it turned out earlier that day when he was showing me undies, but my third lot of thankfulness went to the fact that Spence had no power to persuade me.

'Anyway,' Della said. Oh? She wasn't finished? 'He had a massage and a wrap and he was so relaxed he was practically asleep and I had told Stacey – the wax technician? – who he was and what he'd done, so while he was out of it she ripped off both his eyebrows for him.'

I inhaled a crumb of tortilla chip and had to cough it back out before I could start laughing. 'Didn't he sue?' I said. Bran was the type who'd sue anyone for anything.

'She said he'd told her to do it. Then he said why would he ask her to remove his eyebrows. And she said the same reason he had dyed his own teeth blue with a laser and dyed his entire body orange with a spray tan. She's fierce.'

'She sounds it. So he just slunk away?'

'Yep,' said Della. 'With no eyebrow hair but two pure white ghost brows in his spray tan. I've been saving that up to tell you on a special occasion, Lexy, and it didn't seem right to talk about your first husband at your new wedding or your bachelorette, even. But tonight was ideal.'

'You are a wonderful matron of honour,' I told her. 'You can choose your dress first and this other pair of toerags will have to fit in around you.'

Della smiled and Todd opened his mouth to argue but before he could speak, sirens split the night air and we noticed all the waiting staff and half the customers clustered at the front of the restaurant looking out into the street.

'Fire!' someone shouted.

'Oh my God!' said another. 'Right across the street.'

We scraped our chairs back and surged forward. Right enough, just before the fire engines and police vans drew up and blocked our view, we could all see smoke pouring out of the door of Spence's beautiful boutique and flames licking at the hems of the dresses in each of the windows.

NINE

April

I would have expected the procession of committed divorcers to be over by springtime, what with the rain stopping and the trees coming out in blossom. My eleven o'clock today actually lived out to the west of town and had had to drive to my consulting room through orchards full of almond trees gently scattering their petals into her convertible on a light breeze, but she arrived as adamant as ever that she wasn't interested in mediation, in a short break, in a slap on the legs, or in a sober look at her post-break-up finances.

I do sometimes struggle with the requirement not to judge my clients when they're being numpties. Or maybe, again, this was hitting me too close to home. I plunged in before that thought could take hold, asking Maura if she could tell me clearly why she was leaving her husband, selling their home and their joint carpet-cleaning business, losing all contact with the stepchildren she said she adored, and probably never seeing her sister-in-law again even though she had described the woman as her closest friend.

'Easy,' she said. 'We have nothing in common. I didn't think it mattered. It didn't matter, in the early years when there was passion. But passion fades. That's when companionship gets to be so important.'

This woman was forty-four and speaking like an old woman sitting on a step in a black dress.

'You must have something in common,' I said. 'What are your interests? Let's start with you.'

'I like Thai food, romantic comedies, folk music, travel to foreign cities and paddle-boarding,' she said.

'And your husband?'

'Barbecue, documentaries, jazz and hiking. And not even hiking. Camping! And not camping at camps. Camping in the wild! He likes looking for mushrooms in forests. He doesn't even collect them. He takes photographs of them.'

'Huh,' I said. She hadn't mentioned any of this before. She had spoken about how he liked to have sex at night and she couldn't get to sleep after but he wasn't interested in the morning. I had suggested happy hour and she'd looked at me as if I'd recommended a swing. She had touched on how he seemed to think it was OK to 'use' the toilet in their master bath while she was in the shower. 'If you know what I mean,' she said, lowering her brows. But that seemed like the kind of thing that could be handled. I asked her if she 'used' that toilet when he was in the shower, because maybe that was how to persuade him it was gross. He didn't know the meaning of the word 'gross', she had assured me. He ate all that barbecue and never flossed.

But what she was telling me today was more serious than the bombshell that people are annoying, even if you love them. What she was telling me today was . . . just like if someone who liked pizza, thrillers, P!nk, staying at home and maybe going for a walk sometimes married someone who liked deli sandwiches, horror flicks, classical music and – oh my God, yes! – hiking and camping, and the only difference was that he took photographs of birds instead of fungus. What she was telling me was that some couples were doomed from the start. But we were completely different. We compromised. Taylor sat through and choked down and submitted and sacrificed and so did I. I had spent an entire symphony with sauerkraut indigestion from a Reuben the last time we had a weekend in San Francisco.

'Oh, we used to,' Maura said, when I suggested gritting her teeth and nutting out a documentary in exchange for a romcom, maybe once a month. 'We did it for years. It only helps the hate come along quicker. And anyway, I can't stand going out in public with him. He dresses like he's camping even when he's not.'

I couldn't smile at that and I didn't ask any follow-up questions either. I found Taylor's terrible dress sense endearing and I didn't want to hear that Maura used to feel that way too.

'Well, the most important thing is the children,' I said. 'Your stepchildren. They can't be expected to give you up after you've been in their lives so long.'

'Not a chance,' said Maura. 'The ex has grudged every minute I spent with them even while I was married to their dad. She'll never let me see them again. I wasn't married before. I don't know if I ever told you that. I had no idea what I was getting into. I don't think it ever works when one of you is a first-timer and the other brings baggage. Do you?'

* * *

'You know something,' I said to Taylor that night as we drove to the ritzy suburb north of Sacramento where Spence the wedding-fashion guru had his palatial home. (I hadn't seen it yet, but I'd clocked the size of the house plots on Google Maps when I punched in the directions and they were humungous, with lots of blue rectangles in the back gardens.)

'You've changed your mind about tempting fate?' he said. 'You want to go on your own?'

'I'm not tempting fate,' I said. 'You're not going to see the dress. It's going to be in the kind of garment bag that could withstand a nuclear attack.'

'OK.' He was craning over his left shoulder, checking for traffic before he joined the freeway, so I couldn't see the look that went with the tone.

'Why? Do you not want to come?' I said. This wasn't the topic earmarked for our two-hour round trip, but maybe it should be. 'Only, I thought we hadn't spent much time together recently and this would be nice. I thought we could listen to a talking book.'

'Which one?' said Taylor, making my stomach drop. 'One of yours or one of mine?'

No, no, no, I screamed inside my head. Not this too. I had planned to address the unequal baggage problem today, not the nothing-in-common doomscape. 'Let's choose one together!' I said, sounding giddy even to myself. 'I've got an Audible credit burning a hole in my phone.'

'Sheh, right,' Taylor said. 'Where do our reading tastes overlap, Lexy?'

'Shakespeare's sonnets?' I said. '*Charlotte's Web*? Maybe there's a classic neither of us has ever tried that we could get through together.' I was thinking of *Anna Karenina*.

'That's an idea,' said Taylor. 'How about *Moby Dick*?'

'But that's not what I was going say anyway,' I said, so hastily I tripped over the words. 'Maybe we could talk about the thing I *was* going to say.'

'O-*kay*,' said Taylor, making me smile. Inside him, alarms were going off and emergency protocols were coming into play. He was such a *guy*. 'What is it?' His knuckles had actually whitened as he gripped the steering wheel.

'Just this,' I said. 'You've never told me about any of your exes.'

Because that was the brainwave I had had while concentrating on how to reject, or at least suppress, the thought Maura had put in my head. I had had one six-month close-to-fake marriage. Maybe I wasn't the one with the baggage after all. Taylor already had adoption and the death of his only parent in his past, to rack up against my still-married-to-each-other biologicals. Maybe he was the one with a trail of carnage in his love life too.

It's useful to say unexpected things when the person you're saying them to is driving; there's no way to hide a knee-jerk that makes a car lurch. Taylor kept driving at a smooth seventy without a hitch, suggesting no excess baggage he wasn't willing to let me help him carry.

'What do you want to know?'

'Is there too much to just give me a quick catch-up?'

'Lost my virginity to Daphne Lassen on a high-school trip to Oregon at seventeen. She dumped me on the bus home. Um, spent two years with Lori Mattas at college before one of us got round to dumping the other. Her, me. Then a dry spell. Then came the summer of three at once, but that was misplaced excitement about getting my dream job. I kept taking girls to the blind to show them the birds and they kept not believing that's why we were there. Daphne Peters lasted about eighteen months, but she kept dragging me over to jewellers' windows pretending she was looking at bracelet charms. And she had children's names picked out. When I didn't move fast enough she got someone else more willing. Or less able to resist. Then there was Mo at the phone shop. But like literally at the phone shop. In the stock room. It wasn't really a relationship. And then you.'

'Seven?' I said. 'And two Daphnes? That's got to be pretty rare.'

Result, I was thinking. I hadn't got the long and sorry history of broken hearts and festering wounds I had been hoping for, but I'd found out that Taylor, my Taylor, was not a dumper. He was a dumpee. Him and Daphne number two had wasted months of their youth waiting for the other one to do the dumping and Taylor had worn her down. He had even let himself get distracted from his precious birds that summer, because he was so easily led by the women in his life. I, as the woman in his life now and going forward, was laughing.

So, strangely enough, was Spence when we got to his palace of kitsch in the hills above the city. He had been in touch the day after the fire to tell me not to worry because 'A' he was insured to the hilt and 'B' the stock in the shop was only samples – with the actual dresses for sale stored in a much cheaper part of town where he could afford the square footage – and finally 'C' my order details were in the cloud and unaffected by that night's calamities. Still, I didn't quite believe his cheerfulness till I saw it with my own eyes.

'Oh honey!' he said, as I offered condolences. He had swept open the double doors of his mansion and wafted Taylor and me through a cathedral-height hallway to a sunroom tacked on the back. It was full of tropical plants and humid as a foggy day in hell, so I wasn't best pleased to see a black garment bag hanging over a hook meant for a birdcage. It better not be getting damp in there. 'No biggie, believe me. I was outgrowing that premises *and* that neighbourhood. Old Sac? With the taffy stores and the tourists? Puh-lease! And besides, there were so many firefighters that night, I didn't know whose arms to faint into first.'

'Did they find out what caused it?' Taylor said.

'Arson,' said Spence, calmly, making me splutter and making Taylor do an actual double-take, like you don't often see in real life.

'Wh-what?' I said.

'Oh yeah,' Spence said. 'Homophobic hate crime. It started with a Molotov cocktail thrown through a back window and someone left a text telling me that the fire was punishment for pandering to abominations that undermined marriage.'

'Wow,' I said. 'Did they catch them?'

'Not a chance,' Spence said. 'No fingerprints and a burner phone. *C'est la vie*. And let's not dwell on it. I will come back bigger, better and more fabulous than ever. Gay will find a way!'

'I'm sorry I'm marrying a woman,' said Taylor. 'Feel like I'm letting you down.'

'I don't mind,' said Spence. Then he put out a hand as if he was stopping traffic. 'As long as you don't go into detail.'

So, all in all, we were both in reflective moods on the way back down the hill into Sacramento and then in the long snake of slow traffic across the causeway to Cuento. When my phone rang and Sister Sunshine's smiling face showed on the screen, I answered at once, determined to say yes to whatever she was suggesting. So many people in this world couldn't get married to the ones they loved; I needed to stop being snotty about the bells and whistles on my wedding and just throw myself into the current, let myself be carried downstream, over the rapids and out to sea.

'Great news!' she said. 'I have secured the perfect venue for you for Midsummer's Day. They're holding it for twenty-four hours. Can you come and see it?'

'Of course!' I said. The wild note in my voice made Taylor flinch and I tensed as the car spurted forward towards the back bumper of the car in front.

'I think you should come now to see what it looks like at night and then come back in the morning to see what it looks like in the sunshine, that way you can be sure that both your ceremony and your party will be right for you.'

I felt myself start to lose interest in that much faff, but I reminded myself yet again of the couples whose weddings were only recently legal and of the backlash still playing out – in arson! – and I said, 'Of course!' again, managing to sound just as enthusiastic.

Taylor's phone was going as well now, but his was linked to the car so the ring blared out from the dashboard and he dinked a button on the steering wheel to answer.

'Where's Lexy?' It was Todd.

'She's here,' said Taylor, 'but she's on the phone.'

'Well, tell her to come to the gr— Who's she on the phone to?'

'It's wedding stuff,' said Taylor. He had so far refused to utter the words 'Sister Sunshine'.

'Well, tell her to forget the wedding for once and come to Ground Zero, asap,' said Todd, then hung up the phone.

'Who was that?' said Sister Sunshine, because of course she had heard every word.

'No one,' I assured her. 'Where's the venue?'

'Way over on the east side of town, off Turkey Farm Road,' she said. 'Don't worry. It's not a turkey farm. It's a . . . Well, it's easier for you to see it than for me to try to explain it. Look for the sign that says "The Garden".'

'Is it a garden?' I said.

'Yes! Isn't that perfect?' said Sister Sunshine.

It sounded pretty perfect, but also quite easy to explain. I was glad we weren't on speaker because Taylor would have snorted his uvula off if he had heard her. 'See you in fifteen minutes,' I said.

'Where to?' said Taylor, once I'd hung up.

'Turkey Farm Road.'

He glanced at me. 'You're going to the cemetery? It sounded like you were saying yes to *her*.'

'I was,' I said. 'The venue is there too. If Todd sees us and thinks I've dropped everything but then we drive right past and leave him in the dust, that's fine by me.'

Taylor was quiet for a moment or two, then he said, 'I know weddings can get . . . fraught. But I thought that was more . . . like if the vendors or the guests or . . . I didn't think you and Todd would . . .'

'I know!' I said. 'I don't know what's wrong with him either. Why's he acting like *I'm* being weird, right?'

'Is-is that what you heard me say?' said Taylor.

'What?' I asked.

'Nothing.'

As always, the traffic speeded up again once we were off the delta causeway. It's one of the great mysteries of Beteo County: there are no junctions, there's no traffic leaving, no traffic joining and yet there's a slowdown on the causeway every day. They can't all be birdwatchers looking for exotica on the floodplain. That's just why Taylor never gets frustrated like the rest of us. He loves the slowdowns. He wears his binoculars when he drives to Sacramento, in case of an actual stoppage.

'What am I looking for?' he said, when we peeled off the interstate at the eastern edge of Cuento and wiggled our way on to Turkey Farm Road.

'The Garden,' I said.

'The hop garden? Hey! That actually would be pretty cool.'

'What? Why? What?' I said. I was fine with him knowing where our wedding was going to be before I did. Absolutely fine with it. Only it was so unlike him.

'But we're not going to pass the cemetery coming at it from here. In fact . . .' He was punching bits of the dashboard screen, until the map came up. 'Yeah, look. It's right next door.'

I'm not great with maps. I could see the cemetery because it had 'Cuento Cemetery and Arboretum' printed right there in the middle of the green bit. And I could see that there was another green bit beside it, but before I could zoom in to see any closer, or work out how to turn to satellite or street view, we were there. Taylor swung off the road through a gateway topped off by a big rickety double gallows made of planks. There was – as far as I could tell – a rusty iron version of the McDonald's golden arches nailed to the apex. This did not look promising.

Sister Sunshine was waiting beside her tricycle in a car park made of bark chips, the spaces delineated by logs lying on the ground. This looked very bad. So did she. She was wearing the spring version of those loose-woven wool garments she had cut around in all winter; the same but linen, and even more see-through although I wouldn't have said that was possible.

'Is that a burger sign on the gallows?' I said, pointing back to the iron shape.

'Gallows?' said Sister Sunshine. 'That's a ranch gate, Lexy. And the sign is a Lazy B. The Garden was called The Lazy B Hop Garden under its last ownership but the new people changed it because people were calling it the Lazy Bastard.'

This was terrible.

'I remember that,' said Taylor. 'Then they tried The Hip, Hop Garden but blues and folk bands stopped booking. So it's just The Garden now?'

'But it's still a *working* hop garden,' said Sister Sunshine. 'And microbrewery. As well as performance space and event venue. Look!'

She waved toward the far end of the car park where the last blink of the setting sun was shining through a web of tall straggling ropes with bits of vegetation hanging off them. 'It looks like someone's drying their fishing nets,' I said.

'I never thought of that!' said Sister Sunshine in a voice of wonder. 'What a beautiful mind you have, Lexy.'

I gave her a good look, checking, but she meant it.

'OK,' I said. 'So, this is it?'

'Come and see,' said Sister Sunshine. 'You'll come through this gate and along the board walk between the hop vines. These can be decorated according to your wishes. And speaking of wishes – here's a well! – and on into the ceremony space.'

She ushered us ahead of her into an open-sided barn, furnished with a selection of mismatched charity shop couches and armchairs. It would have made a funky student union but my mum was going to blow her stack when she saw it. There was a bar set under the hayloft, and the shelves behind it were full of jars.

'Are those the glasses?' I said. 'Can we bring our own instead?'

'I would have thought so,' said Sister Sunshine. 'But why?'

'And is it always this quiet?' I said. 'Why is there no one here?'

'It's closed on Mondays,' said Sunny. 'Out of season. It's busy all summer and at the weekends.'

'People can't get enough of sour beer in jam jars, eh?'

'If you don't like it,' Lex,' said Taylor.

'*You* love it, don't you?' I said.

'I love you!' he said.

'I love love!' said Sunny.

I hated both of them but I thought it was probably best to say nothing. I turned to face the other way.

On the open side of the barn, out in the garden proper, there was a low stage with a backdrop in the shape of a wheel, with painted wooden segments depicting the seasons of the agricultural year. Or maybe the stages of brewing ale, it was hard to tell.

'Over there there's a wading pond,' said Sister Sunshine. 'A maze. A labyrinth. And the bes—'

'Aren't they the same thing?' I said.

'A labyrinth is a meditative path,' she said. 'A maze is a puzzle. And the best thing of all is that at midsummer, the sun will set right behind the mandala and shine through. I don't know when you were thinking of exchanging vows but it's going to be pretty special.'

'That actually does sound quite pretty,' I said. 'Can we bring our own chairs? And caterers? Wait where's the dance floor? And the toilets? If it's portaloos, I'm out right now.'

It wasn't portaloos. There were cubicles with proper flush toilets and, outside them, there were long copper troughs with old brass taps hanging over them on long pipes, like something from a steampunk abattoir. On the other hand, there wasn't actually a dance floor. The bit of packed dirt in front of the stage was where Taylor and I were supposed to do our first waltz.

I frowned. Is it really a wedding if there's not a shiny dance floor for kids to skid up and down on in their socks? Is the marriage legal if no one gets over-birled in a Strip the Willow, skites through the aunties and goes down like a sack of spuds?

And actually that was a thought. Out of all the wedding guests there would be a total of three who knew how to *do* a Strip the Willow. Or a Dashing White Sergeant or Military Two-Step. I could probably get Todd to learn the Gay Gordons.

'Could we rent a dance floor?' I said.

'Definitely,' said Sunny. 'You can rent anything you need for the wedding of your dreams.'

'Can I rent a groom who knows Scottish country dances?' I said, half-kidding.

'And a DJ who's got ceilidh music on his playlist?' How could I not have thought of this before? *Of course* I should be getting married at home, where people knew how to dance the dances of my ancestors!

Taylor was watching me closely and now put out a hand in my direction. I thought he was inviting Sister Sunshine to marvel at the spoiled and unmannerly woman he had found himself engaged to. I didn't get it until he started humming something that sounded like a cross between 'My Old Man's a Dustman' and the theme tune from *The Big Bang Theory*. Hardly daring to hope it was true, I put my hand in his, and stepped out into the middle of the dirt. Still humming, he led me through two perfect rounds of the St Bernard's Waltz, then let go, stepped back and bowed.

'It was going to be a surprise,' he said. 'But you looked so sad. We've all learned them and we've gotten a band.'

'A ceilidh band?'

'Well, they're probably more Appalachian than most ceilidh bands, but they're learning.'

'And they're free on Midsummer's Day?'

'I think they're free most days,' said Taylor. Then he grabbed me and dipped me so that I was looking through the gaps of the driftwood circle upside down as the very last winks of sunset snuffed out and left the three of us in the soft grey of near dark.

'I love it!' I said, as Taylor hauled me upright again and my blood rearranged itself. 'I'm going to jam so many fairy lights and votive candles and satin swags and pedestal bouquets in here it's going to look like someone puked Disneyland. Thank you, Sunny, for finding me such a special place.'

She beamed so hard she'd have made a pretty decent display if she'd been standing behind the mandala. 'It's wonderful to have a client with vision,' she said, pointing to something beside her. It looked like a massive multi-sectional noticeboard, the kind of thing you find in an information centre that makes you feel guilty if you don't pretend to read it. But it had a bolt of pale yellow silk – well, rayon, probably – thrown over it so I'd been trying not to think about what it might be. If the jam jars and rafters and hop-holding-up ropes were on display then God knows what The Garden thought it had to throw a tarp over.

'I did prepare a little mood board in case it was needed,' Sister Sunshine said, twitching the yellow silk off the frame like a magician. I stepped closer. Sketches and swatches and scraps of ribbon and snatches of poetry jostled for space on three metres of pinboard.

'My God, there's yards of it!' Taylor said. 'And isn't it pretty? If our wedding looks like this I'll be the luckiest man in the world. Twice over,' he added hurriedly.

'This is . . . Yeah . . . thanks,' I said. Truth is I felt a wriggle like Christmas morning in my belly, the beginnings of believing it was really going to be a dream come true.

Then a blood-curdling scream and a heart-stopping bellow rent the air, both at the same split second, and the sound of pounding footsteps on a board walkway thumped like the tread of a giant roaring, '*Fi-Fie-Fo-Fum.*'

All three of us turned and watched as a masked figure all in black – tattered black that streamed in their wake like ribbons – galloped towards us on enormous clumping feet. It was coming straight for us, for me!

'Again?' I said. 'Seriously?'

Then, with another ear-splitting screech, it pointed a shiny black finger beyond me and instead of stopping to put its hands round my neck, it sped up and swept straight past.

It brushed close enough for me to reach out and snatch at its garments, finding myself with a rustling fistful, then it took off towards the car park, vaulting the perimeter fence and disappearing into the fields where the night swallowed it.

TEN

'What the *hell*?' I said. 'What is going *on*?' I opened my fist. 'And what's *this*?' It was like crepe paper but it was definitely fabric, crinkled and musty, frayed where I had torn it from the rest.

'Was that the same person?' said Taylor. 'In a different mask?'

'Bigger, I think.' The truth was, I didn't know.

'Should we go see who shouted?' said Taylor.

He didn't sound very keen. And I understood. Night had fallen so quickly that suddenly the cosy little conversation nooks inside the barn looked like caves and the hop vines on their ropes were like the legs of giant insects whose bodies were lost in the darkness above us. I was fishing out my phone to switch the torch on when the sound of more footsteps came to our ears.

'There's two of them,' I said.

'But they sound smaller, at least,' said Taylor. 'You two go and—Oh.'

I looked round and saw what he had just seen. Sister Sunshine had vanished.

'Let's both tackle the smaller one together,' I said, as two figures started to take shape, coming towards us out of the gloom. 'There's one that looks pretty tiny. Not the front one. The one that's not twinkling.'

As I said it, I was thinking to myself, why is that figure twinkling? And, in the second or two it took to form the thought, as the running figures got closer still, I started to laugh. The front figure was twinkling because it was wearing diamond ear-studs that winked with every step, and had a diamond pendant bouncing on its chest, diamond tennis bracelets jouncing around on its pumping arms, and a belly-jewel that showed whenever its crop top rode up. In other words, it was Todd. And, behind him, 'the smaller one' was Kathi. My God, how our plan would have gone wrong if we hadn't recognized her! Kathi could put Taylor and me down without even trying.

'Did you catch him?' said Todd, slowing as he saw us and stopping to put his hands on his knees and bend over to catch his breath.

'Yeah, we caught him,' I said. 'Now, guess where we hid him?'

'Did you get a good look at least?' said Kathi, pulling up. A much more sensible question in my view. 'Is it the same one as last time? Must be, huh? Only, we thought it was taller.'

'And bulkier,' I agreed. 'Although that might have been its . . . cloak, would you say?'

'Did it hit you again?' said Todd.

'I just said I didn't think it was the same . . .'

'Banshee,' said Kathi. 'We're going with "banshee".'

'The Sex Volunteers got a tip-off,' said Todd. Taylor reacted to the name but didn't say anything. 'An anonymous call saying there was a banshee nesting in a tree at the cemetery and that it had peed on a grave underneath.'

There was so much wrong with that sentence, I didn't know where to start.

'What's a banshee?' said Taylor. I will never understand him if we both live to be ninety-nine together like the Carters. *That's* what he had to know?

'Irish harbinger of death,' said Kathi. 'I looked it up on the drive over.'

'But they're women,' I said. 'That thing was a man, surely.'

'Plus women can't pee out of trees,' said Todd. 'And did you see the size of it?'

'Nice assumption,' said Kathi. 'Right, Lex?'

'Damn straight,' I said, out of solidarity, although the truth was I had never tried and wouldn't know where to start. 'I managed to rip off a bit of his her their clothes.' I held out the scrap of fabric and Kathi, while careful not to touch it of course, bent low and scrutinized it by the light of her phone.

'This is antique,' she said. 'Bombazine, I reckon.'

'What's bombazine?' said Taylor. He wanted to know everything *but* what a sex volunteer was.

'It was used for Victorian mourning dress,' said Kathi. 'Ugh, it's filthy.'

'Like it was worn by someone who just dug themselves out of a grave?' said Todd.

'It's pretty,' I said. 'It's like taffeta but it's more sumptuous.'

'How is that relevant?' said Todd. I stared. What was *his* problem? 'Say something about the case,' he demanded.

I thought back to his last contribution.

'Spirits don't urinate,' I said.

'Or dig,' said Taylor.

'OK, *corpses* don't urinate,' I said. 'Jeez!'

'Maybe the urination was incidental,' said Todd. 'From being up the tree too long. Maybe they were waiting up the tree until it was time to do the real prank. I can't believe you didn't catch him. It looked to me like he was headed straight for you.'

'He was,' I said. 'On a plumbline. Then he changed his mind or something. My God, his hands were creepy.'

'What? What about them?' Kathi said. 'We didn't get that close a look.'

'They were black,' I said.

Todd gasped. 'Racist much?'

'Piss off,' I said. 'I don't mean they were the hands of a Black person. I mean they were black. Pure jet black and dead shiny, like a Black W—'

'Wallet!' said Taylor. 'Like a black leather wallet. Right, Lexy?'

I couldn't believe I had been just about to name a spider. Where was my head these days?

'Really?' said Todd. 'Hands covered in black leather made you think of a wallet? Instead of perhaps . . . oh, I don't know . . . gloves?'

'Of course!' I said. 'He had gloves on! And who wears gloves in April?'

'Oh, get in the game, Lexy,' said Kathi. 'It was our perp. And he brushed right by you and you let him get away.'

'I let him get away too,' Taylor said. 'I was too busy thinking about protecting the women. And one of the women didn't need protecting anyway. She's really vanished, Lexy. She's not just hiding till the danger passed.'

'Who?' said Todd.

'Who do you think?' muttered Kathi. I had no idea what she was getting at. '*And* we're right back at square one.'

'Were there any clues on the grave?' I said, since they were so dead set on picking this to death instead of leaving me in peace to look up suppliers of pastel bombazine.

'Are there *ever* any clues on the fricking grave?' Todd yelped. 'We have cross-referenced and de-coded and shuffled and sorted and practically dried and *smoked* the information on the gravestones and there are no patterns anywhere.'

'*I* haven't looked yet,' I said, ignoring the glares. 'How about if we pick up a couple of pizzas and reconvene on deck, like the old days? I miss you, you two. Now that you're so busy with whatever it is you're doing that makes you ghost me all the time.'

'Now that—' Kathi said.

'*We're* so—' Todd added.

'*They're* ghosting *you*, are they?' said Taylor, taking the prize for getting a whole sentence out.

'What do you mean?' I said, turning to leave. Odie's Ovens didn't stay open too late mid-week until they clicked over to summer hours.

'Don't get any of that primavera shit this time,' Kathi called after me. 'Pepperoni and extra cheese. Stuffed crust.'

I thought about turning back and explaining, for the ninth time, that I had my final fitting soon and I couldn't afford to lose or gain any weight before midsummer or my dress wouldn't look right. She knew that. She understood, too, that I didn't want to be having fittings week after week while I ramped up to D-day. It was enough to still have her outfit to organize, and Todd's, Della's and Hiro's too, as well as trying to stay calm about leaving Noleen's, Roger's, Devin's and Diego's in Taylor's hands. My friends were not usually so obtuse as they had got recently.

Noleen came out of Reception as we all pulled up.

'Party on the yacht!' Kathi shouted over.

'Meeting to discuss confidential Trinity business,' I said, but I was wasting my time. Noleen had already flipped the sign on the door telling impromptu guests to call her mobile and Diego had heard us too. He came to the door of Della and Devin's room in his grown-up pyjamas – no feet, buttons down the front – hand-in-hand with Hiro, whose PJs had feet, ears and a cotton tail on the back.

'Can we come?' he said. 'Pleeeaaaaase!' He turned back into the room. 'Mama, can we go? Pleeeeeaaaaase.'

'Half an hour and then I'm coming to get you,' came back Devin's voice. He still sounded strange to me when he tried on his paternal rule-maker hat. The children squealed and scampered across to be picked up and carried over the jaggy undergrowth. Diego was getting heavy, but I would give myself a hernia before I gave up carrying him. He would stop wanting to have anything to do with embarrassing adults soon enough.

'You go on ahead,' said Noleen. 'I'll mix the Margaritas. Lexy, you got any snacks? What am I saying? I'll fix some snacks.'

Roger pulled in through the gates, fresh from a shift. He stepped down out of his car, stretched, beamed and took Diego out of my arms, swinging him up to sit on his shoulders. How he could face another kid after dealing with them all day was beyond me. Or maybe seeing two more was exactly what he needed, so long as it was this two. Diego is a picture of wellbeing, glossy curls, rosy cheeks, glittering teeth and that wiry little bod that some boys have, made for vaulting gates, scrambling up trees and dangling from rope swings. It's wasted on a scholar like him, really. And Hiro gives new meaning to the phrase 'rude health' since in her case it's verging on the obscene.

When we got to the boat, he squatted down deep to let Diego hop off and straightened, groaning. 'I need to build in some gym time,' he said. 'So, what's the occasion?'

He wasn't being snarky. There isn't a snarky bone in Roger's body, but it was true that our get-togethers had been few and far between of late.

'Confab about the cemetery case,' I said. 'With drinks and nibbles.'

'Not the wedding?' said Roger.

There was a strange frisson of sound and movement from the rest of them. I caught it out of the corner of my eye and definitely heard something, as if Taylor, Todd and Kathi had all started to speak but then suppressed it. Weird.

'No, not the wedding, but I'm glad you mentioned it.' I turned to Taylor just in time to see the tail end of some frantic signalling between the three of them. 'What's going on with you?' I said. Then I held up a hand. 'Never mind. Taylor, did you lock the car?'

'I always lock the car,' he said, which was true. It's really annoying when I nip out to get something from the glove box.

'Yes, but my dress is in it,' I said. 'Would you mind going back round to double-check?'

'Not at all,' Taylor said and disappeared. I could hear him talking to himself as he thrashed his way through the bushes, but I couldn't hear what he was saying.

'So,' I said, settling down. 'You really couldn't find any patterns? You really can't make any kind of picture?'

'Lexy,' said Hiro. 'Can you draw me a picture so I can colour?

'I'll draw you a picture,' said Diego. 'Lexy? Do you have any paper?'

'You draw scary monsters,' said Hiro. 'Lexy draws me pretty princesses.'

'I'll draw you a princess,' said Diego, rummaging in the drawer where I had pointed. He turned round with two coloured pencils sticking out from under his top lip. 'With big princess fangs! Rwaarrrghhh!' They set off to run round and round the outside of the boat from prow to stern, like they always did. The railings were sturdy and the water was shallow. I didn't worry about them.

'Stop!' came Noleen's voice, from the steps at the porch end. 'Do not run past and bump into me while I am carrying this pitcher and this platter.' Diego and Hiro stopped running but kept giggling. 'Reach into Gramma Nolly's pockets – carefully! – one on each side.'

She bummed open the living room door and rolled in, carrying a brimming glass jug and a plate that would have held a turkey, but was loaded with cheese and crackers and little pickled gherkins.

'What did you give them?' said Roger, who sometimes takes a while, after he gets home, to stop thinking like a paediatrician and remember he's a beloved uncle.

'Sour Patch and Go-Gurts,' said Noleen.

'Jesus,' said Roger. 'Pour me a drink.'

'No patterns, no pictures, no rhyme, no reason beyond sheer nastiness,' Todd said, when he had taken a glug of margarita. 'Kathi?'

'I agree,' Kathi said. 'It's hard to believe that they still haven't broken any laws, but it's true.'

'What about the skeleton in the end?' I asked. How had I not followed up on that after Molly had enlightened me?

'It came from the store with a leg missing,' Kathi said. 'The person died with a leg missing. I phoned the freaks in Oregon who had him – it – on the inventory and they confirmed. So. No unauthorized mutilation of a corpse, I'm sorry to say. We did think we had them on hate crimes, last month, because we found ground steak at the grave of a woman called Puja Gupta and bacon at the grave of a man called Hamza Nabhan, but it was no go.'

'What?' said Roger and me in unison.

'How can that not be?' I carried on.

'Surely that falls within the purview of hate crime legislation!' Roger carried on. He is much more articulate than I am.

'Aren't you shocked?' I asked Taylor, who hadn't reacted.

'I already knew,' he said. 'I've been keeping up with it. I've had a lot of time on my hands.'

I frowned. Was he complaining about missing the phone shop?

'Anyway,' said Kathi. 'Turns out the ground steak was Impossible Burger and the bacon was turkey. Halal turkey too – we found the wrapper in the garbage can by the cemetery gate.'

'But the intent was so disrespectful,' I said.

'Well,' said Todd. 'I spoke to the Guptas and they said that the intent obviously wasn't personal and in fact the prankster had gone out of their way to avoid disrespect by not using beef. I couldn't track down anyone in the Nabhan family, but I asked at the mosque and the imam said pretty much the same. He said the person doing all these things deserved our pity but not our attention. He's a pretty cool dude.'

'The only other remote possibility of getting them is animal cruelty,' Kathi said. 'Remember the Sex Volunteers told us about the goats and the donkey way back at the beginning? Well, when I read their notes, apparently the donkey was wearing a bridle and it was actually tied to the gravestone in question with a rope. It was a family called Hiller, a whole pile of them. And . . .' She stopped and crunched her face up in a way I knew meant she was trying not to laugh. 'It's not funny,' she said. 'And not relevant to my point.' She took a deep breath. 'And the goats – three little pygmy goats – were tied to a stake driven into the grass.'

'Well, there you go then,' I said.

'But it's not illegal to tie a poor little baby goat to a stake,' said Todd.

'They weren't babies, they were just small, but yeah it's legal,' Kathi said. 'You'd be slapped with a fine if you did it to a dog but what do you know? No dogs were ever used in these . . . I can't call them pranks. In these . . . dick games.'

'Just goats and donkeys?' I said.

'And a snake,' said Kathi. 'But it was dead.'

'Is it legal to kill snakes?' I said.

'Rattlers, sure,' said Kathi. 'Anyway, this one was roadkill. Great big flat part in the middle. And it had been frozen and thawed.'

'Were the snake and goats funny like the donkey?' I said.

Kathi and Todd shared a look and now both of them were biting their cheeks. 'The goats *were* funny,' Todd said. 'It was driving us nuts trying to work out why Les Quinn got goats and the Hiller family a donkey. So we looked in the *Voyager* archives and oh my God, Lexy. If there are human beings anywhere in the world who look more goatish and donkey-ey, then they must work in a circus.'

'Asinine and caprine,' said Roger. I genuinely thought he was passing judgement on Todd's sense of humour, until I caught up.

'So . . . was the snake person a contortionist?'

'A realtor,' said Todd. 'Debbie Yount, the grand matriarch of Yount Realty.'

'Which is typical,' Kathi said. 'Most of them make some kind of sense if you reach for it. The dolls were left on the grave of a woman – a Professor Ernst – who had a glass eye; Monopoly for Larry Whatshisname who went bankrupt a bunch of times.' She nodded at the sheaf of paper I was holding, a print-out of the master spreadsheet with all the names in alphabetical order, in date order, in Kathi's own order of ick. 'The only one that we couldn't get to make any kind of sense at all was the glass harmonica. Right, Todd?'

'What's a glass harmonica?' I said. 'A musical instrument?'

'Kinda,' Noleen said. 'It's just glasses with water in them that sound like someone's murdering cats. And what? It was set up on someone's grave?'

'Inside a little mausoleum,' said Todd. 'Oh, what was the name . . . something beginning with Z.' I flipped to the end of the alphabetical listing bit of the spreadsheet. 'No,' Todd went on. 'First name Z, last name . . . Bullock or something, is it?'

I flipped back to the start. 'Boulley,' I said. 'Zita Boulley. Not a musician?'

'She was a schoolteacher,' Kathi said. 'Died young in the seventies. We couldn't find any family, so we couldn't check if maybe she was a lush, you know? A drunk.'

'What did she die of?' I said. 'Because wasn't there some kind of . . . ohhh, what am I trying to claw to the top of my brain?'

'Seizures,' said Roger. 'There's folklore that glass harmonicas cause seizures.'

'Right!' I said. 'What did Zita Boulley die of?'

'Car crash,' said Todd. 'Which might have been caused by a seizure, I guess. Kathi, was there anything in her autopsy report?'

Kathi cast her eyes up and started clicking through her mental rolodex.

'You've accessed autopsy reports?' I said. 'Wow.'

'Lexy, we have been flat out and ready to kick the cat over this case,' Kathi said. 'But it was winter in Idaho when Zita went off the road. Her death was put down to black ice.'

'And therefore the glass harmonica remains a mystery,' I said. I kept flipping back and forward. 'Hey!' I said, as I remembered. 'Did you ever find out about the inappropriate pebbles?'

Todd and Kathi nodded.

'Well?'

'Read it for yourself,' Kathi said. 'I don't want to say it. The name's D'Ambrosi.'

I went to turn the page to where the pranks were described, then stopped. 'Do I want to read it?' Todd shuddered. Kathi swallowed. I froze.

'Allow me,' said Roger. He leaned forward and took the sheets out of my hands. 'D'Ambrosi, D'Ambrosi, D'Ambrosi,' he said, running a finger up and down the column. Then he stopped and read for a moment, before handing it back. 'Right,' he said. 'Well, it's rare but it's not unheard of. And actually, not wanting to let go of the body of a beloved partner is not really true necro—'

'No!' shouted Noleen, Taylor and me.

More to distract myself than anything else, I went back to the list of names, starting on the second page, well past the Ds. 'This is a very well-organized list, Kathi,' I said. 'Very orderly. Very neat.'

'Are you trying to be funny?' Noleen asked. Kathi drives her nuts but she doesn't care for anyone else teasing.

'No!' I said. 'I mean it. She's got . . . Hang on.'

'Don't mess with us, Lexy,' Todd said. 'If you've seen something, spit it out.'

'There's an O'Brien,' I said. 'Monopoly man. And those D'Ambrosis.' I shuddered. 'And Mr and Mrs McKerran, with the slanderous crocuses.'

'So?' said Todd.

'It was just that, you know, if it was Ireland, or Italy, or Scotland,' I said, 'there would be more. I've never had enough pages under M in an address book in my life.'

'Pages, Grandma?' said Todd, but Kathi hushed him.

'And even here,' I went on, 'shouldn't there be bulges? Ss and Ts, maybe? Still Ms even if they're not Mcs and Macs? You know?'

'Go on,' Todd said.

'Well, there aren't,' I said. 'Anson, Boulley, poor little Poppy

Cliveson. And you've put D'Ambrosi under D, not A. And O'Brien under O, not B.'

'That's where they go,' Kathi said. 'Isn't it?'

'Oh for sure,' I said. 'I'm not saying it's wrong, I'm just saying there aren't any other Ds or Os. There's Prof Ernst, no F yet, but G for Gupta, H for Hiller, Pauletta Ireland with an I. Why did she have pizzas delivered?'

'Morbid obesity,' Kathi said, 'Stick to the point.'

'The point is there's exactly one for each letter,' I said. 'I can't believe you didn't notice.'

'I can't believe it either,' Kathi said. 'I mean, I did notice but it seemed fine. I like things tidy.'

'Babe,' said Noleen. 'We know you like things tidy but if it's interfering with your work . . .'

Todd had grabbed the sheets from out of my hands. 'Kermit Kellog,' he said. 'Max Lavelle, the McKerrans, that Nabhan guy, then O'Brien. My God, Lexy you're right!'

It should have been music to my ears but I didn't stop to enjoy it. 'There's no zed,' I said.

'No what?' said Noleen.

'Oh for God's sake! No zee! Is there? I didn't see one when I was looking for Zita Boulley.'

'It's kind of an unusual initial,' said Kathi. 'Maybe Zita Boulley counts for both.'

'Is there an X last name?' said Roger. 'Speaking of unusual initials?'

'No,' said Todd. 'But, Kathi, wasn't there a . . . Yes! The Reyes who got the noose had the first name Xavier.' I must have looked blank. 'Oh for God's sake right back at you,' said Todd. 'Ex-eh-vee-er, Lexy!'

'So they cheated on the hard letters?' I said. 'Quitters.'

'No, they're not,' said Kathi. 'They're not quitters. We're wrong.'

'You sure?' said Noleen. 'It sounds pretty solid to me.'

'Yeah but, like you said, there's no F either. They haven't finished yet. Unless . . .'

'Oh!' said Todd. 'Of course!'

'But for the rest of us?' I said, knowing I sounded irritable but unable to help myself.

'Well, because we caught the banshee in the act,' said Todd. 'And chased her him them and then found you and we came back here, we didn't actually get the chance to look at the grave.'

'Which, you know, at that point we didn't think mattered,' Kathi said. 'Because we hadn't managed to find a pattern. But now, after what you noticed, Lexy, if we're right about Xavier and Zita doing a double-shift then I bet the gravestone that got peed on tonight, from out of the tree, is someone beginning with F!'

'Which would at least mean that they were finished,' I said. 'So, even if we haven't solved it and caught them yet, there won't be the same time pressure, so we'll be able to focus a bit more. There's only two months to go.'

'Till what?' said Roger.

I laughed and, after a pause, the rest of them joined in but it was the phoniest laughter I'd heard since I forgot to tell them all, at our first shared Christmas, that cracker jokes aren't meant to be funny. I beamed around. Clearly they had found it rude for Roger to make out he'd forgotten my wedding, even in jest.

'So, will we wait till morning or go now?' said Todd. 'Is anyone sober enough to drive?'

'I've had two sips,' said Taylor. His glass was sitting empty on the table by his elbow but, when I pointed at it, he said, 'You drank it, Lex.'

'Why didn't you tell me?'

'Didn't want to . . . um . . .'

Todd said, 'So let's go!' at the same time as Kathi said, 'Poke the bear'.

How many years of living in California would it take before I got all the expressions. I thought I knew that one, but clearly not.

I beamed at them all again. Maybe I *had* drunk two cocktails by mistake, but I wasn't going to miss the trip to the cemetery and the triumph of finding that F name on the headstone.

'Huh,' I said, staring at it twenty minutes later. We had made great time through the empty streets and, since we had a key provided by the Sex Volunteers, we didn't have to clamber over the wall. And Todd and Kathi had perfect recall of where they had been earlier, mostly because the climbable ash tree the banshee had perched in was visible from the gate. We all trained our torches on the engraved words and read them together: 'Vellanda Argyle, 1922–2000. What a gal.'

'Well, shit,' Kathi said. 'We already got an A,' said Kathi. 'Anson.'

'Maybe Anson is an alias,' I said. 'Maybe Anson was in the witness protection programme.'

'Anson was the diabetic with the doughnuts,' said Todd. 'He has family all over Beteo County. They run a winery.'

'Or maybe Argyle is a stage name,' I tried next. 'Who the hell puts "What a gal" on a gravestone?'

'Why not?' said Kathi. 'You ever hear what Noleen wants on hers?'

'Any ideas, Todd?' I asked. 'Todd?' He was no longer standing beside us. He had backed away a couple of rows and was staring at the tree. 'Todd?' I said again.

'You know the Sex Volunteers didn't specify a grave,' he said. 'They specified a tree. And I reckon that tree is closer to the grave on the right than the one on the left that we've been looking at.'

'Hallelujah!' said Kathi. 'What's the one on the right say, Lexy?'

I scuttled over since I was nearer. 'Jane Doe,' I read. 'Died December 1989.'

'Do we have a D?' said Todd.

'Duh,' said Kathi. 'D'Ambrosi. Inappropriate pebbles.'

'Unless he's A after all and this is the D.'

'We just said we had an A!' said Kathi. 'This garbage is frying my brain.'

'If you would shut up for one minute,' said Todd, 'I have the solution.' He cleared his throat, never one to let a big moment look small. 'Obviously, this lady's not really called Jane Doe. Obviously, her name begins with F. So, the cycle of pranks is complete. And, just as obviously, the prankster knows the identity of this Jane F. Doe. That, my friends, is a lead.'

'Possible,' Kathi said.

Hoo boy, he didn't like that. 'Let me explain, Kathi,' he said, in the voice that means he's wishing her full name was Katherine, so he could call her it now. I know that impulse; I had teachers at school who called me Alexandra when I was being a snotrag to them and, no matter how many times I said my name was 'Leagsaidh', they wouldn't stop. 'All the other pranks have been done when no one was around, done in stealth, done so that only the results were public,' Todd went on. 'Then, when we came to look at the crocuses that time, we interrupted the prankster in the act.'

'Yeah, my face interrupted her ring!'

'And maybe he, she, or lets go with they, liked it. And they decided that the last prank would be a performance. Another performance, planned this time.'

'If it's the same dragon slash banshee,' I said. 'And I got the closest look at both of them and I don't think it was.'

'Outfits add volume,' said Todd. 'Look at puffer coats. And shoulder pads. And!' He tried to make it sound grand, but we know him too well and could tell that the sudden increase in volume was excitement because he had only just thought of it. 'The banshee had been waiting for quite some time. Maybe he was even starting to think no one was going to find him.'

'What makes you say that?' I said.

'Ah,' said Kathi, 'because he needed a pee and he hadn't brought a bottle?'

'So, that would mean that pissing on the grave of this Jane F. Doe wasn't the prank,' I said. 'Wasn't the actual point? So . . . it was being here and being seen and risking getting caught that was supposed to constitute the "thing" this time? Which . . . Huh. Yeah, that is different from all the others, isn't it?'

'Like a grand finale,' Kathi said.

'Or,' said Todd, 'the other twenty-five were a run-up to this, and this is the real case.'

'Twenty-three,' I said.

'Hell of a drum roll,' said Kathi. 'Twenty-three nasty little appetizers to get our attention and then the punchline?'

'While you're untangling that metaphor,' said Todd, 'I offer you this: the other twenty-three were either just plain mean – like the noose and the doughnuts – or they were wild accusations and insinuations and there was no reason to think that any of them were true – the incest and the murders and the nec—'

'We've got it!' said Kathi.

'But this one? Jane Doe? This is a legitimate puzzle. Who was she? Why did no one claim her body?'

'That's pretty common,' said Kathi. 'It's a cold world.'

'Yeah, but someone paid for a burial and a gravestone,' said Todd. 'How common is that?'

ELEVEN

May

And then all of a sudden the wedding was next month and there were ten million to-do lists each with ten billion tasks on it and I could really have done without Molly. But I was nothing if conscientious so I went to file another report. Finally.

'This happened last month?' she said, working her eyebrows.

'I've been busy,' I told her. 'Is it too late? I thought the statute of limitations was for courts, not cops.'

'Because if that's the "incident" you're referring to, Mrs Muntz and Dr Kroger already tried, immediately afterward.'

'Tried?' I said. 'And why the scare quotes?'

'Because nothing happened,' said Molly. 'Someone ran past you? Err nerr. Hand me my smelling salts.'

'Someone hid up a tree in a cemetery and peed on a grave underneath,' I said. 'Isn't public urination a crime?'

'Peeing against a tree in the dark of night isn't public.'

'From *out* of a tree, *against* a gravestone.'

'I'm not saying the dude shouldn't have whistled to make sure he wasn't disturbed mid-flow, but . . . Nah.'

'Why don't you care about any of this?' I said, scrutinizing her. 'It's like you're laughing. What are you laughing at?'

'Did I make an appointment?' she said. 'Did I ask you to poke around in my brain and charge my health insurance?'

'You're not denying it,' I said.

She didn't answer.

It was a gross mischaracterization of the therapeutic relationship, which is fundamentally rooted in caring. For instance, the way I had made extra sure to give my valued clients lots of warning about the upcoming interruption to service. Not all of them understood, mind you. A couple of them got pretty snippy, as if the six weeks of wedding preparation that lay ahead of me should play second fiddle to their weekly visits to explore anxiety, depression and lingering trauma. It was especially hard to take with the lingering trauma crew. I mean! If you've been screwed up since you were a toddler, another month and half is hardly going to make a difference. Still, only one of them actually tried to lay a guilt trip on me.

'OK,' she said, when I told her I would be available again in early July. 'Well, maybe it's a sign. I'll use my therapy fees to pay a lawyer instead.'

'What kind of lawyer?' I asked. I supposed it was only a matter of time before someone in this crazy country sued me, but she didn't seem the type.

'Divorce, of course,' she said. 'I probably should have gone straight there a year ago and not spent all these hours flogging a dead horse here with you. No offence.'

'None taken,' I said, which was technically true. I wasn't hurt that she regretted her therapy – some you win, some you lose – but I was dispirited to find myself in yet another discussion about the end of a marriage so shortly before the start of my own. 'But, if I can ask this, why? I thought your concerns were more about your job and your own personal direction?'

'Yeah, but my marriage is in the shitter,' she said. 'I was practising self-care in addressing my work life first instead of being a cliché.'

Again, I found myself wishing I had stayed in Scotland where I'd get people who said things like 'upset', 'knackered' and 'a bit sad now and then' instead of a stream of the pre-diagnosed who, hand-in-hand with Dr Google, had decided they were 'subject to mood swings', 'experiencing chronic fatigue' and 'cycling through periods of low mood'.

'Tell me about your marriage,' I said now, like I had some kind of death wish. 'What went wrong?'

'Money,' she said.

I felt a great whoosh of relief, since I'd been braced for another sob story I'd have to work not to relate to Taylor and me. We were good on money, though. There wasn't a whisker between us financially, either in terms of hard numbers or philosophy. I owned a ramshackle boat, Taylor had the proceeds of an old-fashioned house. He worked for the state. I worked for myself. Both of us were deeply and profoundly 'doing OK'. And neither one of us gave two hoots about whether that ever changed. I didn't want a Lexus; he didn't want a stock portfolio. He liked to have a few bucks left at the end of the month; I liked to pay off my small credit card fairly regularly. We were good.

'The problem is,' my client went on, bringing me back from a flight into smugness that almost amounted to a daydream, 'we don't have a lot of money and neither of us has enough oomph to change that. You know?' I said nothing. 'If one of us earned a lot or cared a little, then that one could drag us both up the scale some. And yeah, sure, when we got hitched we reckoned it was cool or romantic or something not to care about material wealth. But, I tell you, it grinds you down in the end. It torpedoes your self-respect and your admiration for each other and everything just gets so bitter, and so exhausting. Ugh.'

'Huh,' I said, which isn't the most impressive clinical response to such a well-thought-out take. 'Well,' I added, not shifting the needle much, 'it sounds to me, as if actually one of you *does* care. *You* care. So, maybe, instead of . . .' I stopped myself before I committed the therapeutic sin of giving advice. 'Have you ever considered whether,' I said, back on track, 'instead of divorcing, you could be the one who "drags both", like you said?'

'Not a chance,' she said. 'It was me who encouraged him to give up a good job on the management track to pursue his "passion". What an idiot. I can't crack the whip now when I made the mess, can I?'

What do you say to that? I had no idea and I still don't. I can't remember what I did say, only that after the end of the session I was suddenly desperate to go and hang out with Todd and Kathi, talk about my wedding to people who loved me and were interested and believed that Taylor and I would make it, like them. There's nothing like happily married friends to stop you fretting about the divorce rate as you hurtle towards taking your own vows.

Of course, just when I needed my besties I couldn't find them anywhere. Devin was taking care of the laundromat for Kathi and Todd wasn't answering his phone. So I went to chat to Sister Sunshine instead. I had a lot to tell her.

She was in the curated collection, wrapping purchases for a customer who stood at the counter and made no attempt to leave or step away when I approached. People are so self-centred sometimes.

'Have you made a decision about the chairs?' Sunny said.

That wasn't what I had come to talk about but the truth was we didn't think much of the seat pads on the dining chairs from the hire place and I had been trying to choose between re-covering them, replacing them, or taking them off and leaving the chairs bare. It was a tussle between cost and haemorrhoids, basically.

'Brainwave,' I said. 'Linen shower caps. You just put them on and pull the ties tight. They're easier to make than actual covers or cases. I sent you a link to a YouTube video.'

'Oh yes,' said the customer, butting right in. 'My friend had those for her daughter's twenty-first birthday party. It was in an Irish pub and the actual upholstery was *nasty*.'

I said nothing. The trouble about being in a public-facing job in a small town like Cuento is that if you get into a slanging match or a fist fight, even in your private life, word gets round. So, despite the fact that this ghoul of a complete stranger had just tried to make my wedding sound old-hat and unhygienic, I couldn't tell her what I thought of her. She left after a silent moment anyway and I flipped the sign to 'closed' and snibbed the door.

'We've tasted all the cakes,' I said, 'but none of them were wedding cakes and no one seems able or willing to make a wedding cake, so my mum's going to bring one.'

'What?' said Sister Sunshine. 'Ciasto's wouldn't do a wedding cake? The Hamlet Bakery? The Soggy Bottom? None of them? I don't understand.'

'They gave me vanilla cake, something called "white cake" – I don't mean the icing – chocolate cake, red velvet cake. Ciasto's even had the nerve to offer carrot cake. That might have been a joke though. But not one of them offered a wedding cake.'

I was still fuming about our tasting day. Not only were the top three Cuento bakeries ignorant and incompetent but Taylor was disloyal enough to eat the whole of every sample and say he thought they were all delicious. Then he threw up out of the car window on the way home and blamed me, saying if I hadn't been so rude he wouldn't have been forced to choke them all down.

'I'll call them,' said Sister Sunshine, reaching for her phone. 'I really am astonished, Lexy.'

'Good, yes, you do that,' I said. 'Ask them for a price for stacking, icing and delivering my mum's cake.'

'What?' said Sister Sunshine. She was slow on the uptake today.

'Well, obviously, my mum can't bring a finished and decorated three-tier cake on the plane. So she's going to wrap the tiers and put them in her checked bag, well-padded. Then we can get it assembled when she arrives.'

'When is she coming?' said Sister Sunshine. 'And . . . checked bag? Lexy, have you seen the way baggage handlers throw luggage around. Your cake will be toast!'

'What?' I said. 'No, it'll be fine. That's the whole point. Wedding cake is fruitcake. My mum's making it this weekend and she'll be feeding it with brandy every week until she wraps it. It would take more than United ground crew to make a dent in it.'

'And that's the cake you want for your wedding,' said Sister Sunshine.

'Yes,' I said, patiently. 'Wedding cake.'

'That can withstand a long flight in a checked bag.'

'If the plane crashes, the black box and my wedding cake might be the only survivors,' I said.

'And you want me to ask one of my valued contacts in the professional cake-baking community to frost it for you.'

'Exactly,' I said.

'And what about the rest of the food?' she said. Her voice sounded a bit weak for some reason. 'Is your dad going to roast a hog and bring it over in his carry-on wrapped in aluminium foil?'

'The rest of the food seemed fine,' I said. 'Once we decided to go for the deluxe option. I know I said I was interested in the seventy-five dollar a head menu, but when it came to the bit, I went for a hundred and fifty.'

'Does Taylor know?' said Sister Sunshine, in the voice of a sickly kitten.

'Of course,' I said. 'He was right there. I thought he might put up a fight, but he just sort of caved.'

Sister Sunshine nodded. 'Let me know the new menu then,' she said. 'And I'll tell the stationers. Probably should be pretty soon.'

'I'll text you when I get home,' I said. Then I opened up her shop again and went on my way.

Todd and Kathi had each reappeared when I got back to the Ditch. Kathi was polishing the railings outside the Skweek and Todd was watching her, with a bottle of Raid in each hand in case the need arose.

'You're just in time,' Todd said. I must have looked blank. 'For the meeting with the Sex Volunteers.' He sighed. 'At the cemetery, remember?' He tutted. 'Lexy, you are one third of this business. Get a grip.'

'What?' I said. 'I'm fine with a trip to the cemetery, actually, because—'

'One condition,' said Kathi. 'You forget what is on the far side of the cemetery, you do not mention what is slated to take place on June twenty-first, you text no vendors and you do not call anyone from the car.'

'That's way more than one condition,' I said.

'Those are its sub-clauses,' Kathi said. 'Do you want to hear its main heading?'

'No, but—'

'Smart choice,' she said. She opened the door of Todd's Jeep. 'Get in the front.'

'I can go in the back,' I said.

'Where you will text florists and caterers and celebrants and jewellers and poor Taylor and your mother and fucking . . . I don't even *know* who else! And you'll hear nothing and be no good to us when we get there. Front seat, Lexy!'

'I wish I'd been there when you were planning *your* wedding,' I said. 'I would take great pleasure in reminding you how much organizing you did.'

'City Hall, pizza, bowling,' said Kathi. 'And we bought our rings at Sears.'

'Well, OK, bad example,' I said. 'I wish I'd been there when Todd was organizing *his* wedding.'

'We were interns trying to become residents,' Todd said. 'Yeah, it was fabulous but we took two days off from work, Lexy. Two days. Not two months.'

'Six weeks,' I said. 'Stop being so mean to me.'

'And there it is!' Kathi said, getting into the back seat and banging the door hard enough to make the Jeep rock on its chassis. 'Weaponized tears. The second last square on the bingo card.'

'What are you even talking about?' I said. 'What bingo card?'

'Anyway,' said Todd, glaring into the rearview mirror, 'we need to focus on this meeting. In one sense, we've gotten a result and good news for our clients. We worked out what was going on and we can assure them that it's finished. On the other hand, we have no real answers, which is bound to be an enormous disappointment to them.'

'So you didn't find out who Jane Doe was?' I said. 'Total dead end?'

'Bricked up and painted over,' said Kathi.

'But who paid for the headstone?' I said. 'That was a solid lead.'

'Ladies who lunch,' said Todd. 'Not their official title, but basically it was a bunch of do-gooders committed to no woman in Beteo County getting slid into a pauper's grave.'

'What a waste of money!' I said. 'They fundraise for dead people? They'd be better selling the corpses to those creeps up in Oregon and using the profits to help the living.'

'There she is!' said Kathi. 'I told you, Todd. The power of distraction.'

'What are you on about today?' I said. 'But I'm not wrong, am I?'

By then we were approaching the cemetery gate, and we all fell silent. Todd and Kathi were probably going over their report to the clients. I was drinking in what a pleasant drive it was, up towards the venue. The blossom on the street trees would be gone by next month, of course – it was drifting down now in the breeze – but the new leaves would still be small and fresh and there would be more shade. The houses on the left were few and well-spaced, set back behind ranks of oleander – *they* would be flowering next month! – and the cemetery wall on the right, if you didn't know what it hid, looked solid and comforting, with its big grey stones and the trees above. There was even a squirrel scampering along the top right now.

'Lex?' said Todd. I blinked. We were parked inside the cemetery gates and Todd was out of the car, holding my door open.

'Sorry!' I said. 'I was miles away. I was thinking about butterflies and doves and wondering—'

'Ahem,' said Kathi. 'One rule.'

'—wondering if the birds get confused when the monarch butterflies are migrating.'

'Sure you were,' Kathi said. 'You said "doves", not "birds".' She shook her head with a look of withering pity in her eyes.

'Because they migrate through the same territory at the same time,' I said. 'Ask Taylor – he'll back me up.'

'And the thing is he probably would,' said Kathi. 'Poor schmuck.'

'Here they come,' I said, nodding out of the windscreen to where the four Sex Volunteers were bearing down on us along the widest path, walking abreast of each other like just over half of the magnificent seven.

Bob Larch was still dressed for his actuarial past rather than his retired present, dapper and eager, like a little dog whose owner succumbed to an outfit while picking him up at the groomers. Juni Park was dressed in outdoorsy gear whose designer, if it wasn't Patagonia, could certainly be sued by Patagonia for infringement, the look only spoiled by the ubiquitous notebook and slim silver pen. Linda Magic looked as if she had started to dress to match Juni but then at the last minute decided to go to a rodeo. The hat was practical, I suppose, shady, loose on the crown, and you could carry your phone and wallet in the curled brim, but the boots were as bonkers as ever. I will never understand why women wear cowboy boots. It makes sense for short men– extra inches and a side of denial – but they make all women's legs look fat and turn their feet into little trotters. Mitch Verducci, completing the pack, was mooching along at the back looking so much like Devin in the old days before Della got a hold of him, that I felt quite misty for a second or two.

'So,' said Bob. 'Final report, eh? *Final* report?'

'Summative report,' said Kathi. 'We're signing off on the case. It wouldn't be ethical, under the circumstances, to keep charging you, but I have to warn you that there are questions outstanding.'

All four of the Sex Volunteers beamed at her. I wondered if her wording had been too convoluted for them to follow.

'Well, good then,' said Bob Larch, clapping his hands together and rubbing them as if he had caught an enormous bug and was trying to kill it. 'Where do you want to go? Walk and talk? Find a bench.'

'That seats seven?' said Kathi. She had never liked rubbing shoulders and her post-pandemic personal space was more of a zip code.

'There are two benches, facing, over by the dell,' said Mitch.

'Ideal,' said Todd and started walking, to show off that he had been so assiduous on this case that he knew where the dell was.

'I hardly think that's suitable,' Juni Park said to her young colleague through gritted teeth.

'What?' said Mitch.

'Sounds good to me,' Linda put in and scurried to catch up with Todd

We fell in behind them and followed, watching Linda draw abreast of Todd, overtake him, and then break into a trot. She had to be the most competitive woman ever born. When we got to the shady little dip where two memorial benches were set on either side of a small but elaborate gravestone in the shape of an angel, Linda Magic was puffing like a bull mastiff.

'Take a seat,' she said, shrugging out of her jacket and throwing it down on the shadier of the two benches. 'Sorry!' she said, snatching it up again. 'Take *any* seat.' She dithered a moment, not wanting to claim either bench but far too hot to put the jacket on again, then she hooked it over the angel gravestone and wiped her forehead using the side of her hand like a squeegee.

Todd read the plaque on the back of the nearest bench, said, 'Pleased to make your acquaintance, Edgar,' and sat, slinging one leg over the other and draping one elegant wrist over the armrest.

'Always weird,' Kathi said, plunking down at the other end. 'Please don't make me a bench when I go and have me spend eternity with strangers' butts on me.'

So I took the middle and the four Sex Volunteers squeezed in opposite, looking like the back seat of a bus.

'So you want the good news or the bad news?' Kathi said.

'Surprise us,' said Linda Magic.

'OK,' Kathi said, plucking her phone out of her back pocket and pulling up her notes. 'Well, like I said, this is a summative report, because the series of pranks or whatever you want to call them is over.'

All four SVs opened their eyes dead wide. It was disconcerting, almost unsettling.

'I'm sorry we couldn't produce anything that got the cops on board,' said Kathi. 'But at least we've worked out what the pattern is.'

The SVs frowned, pulling their brows down like security grilles at a bad-block bodega.

'They were running through the alphabet,' Kathi said.

The frowns deepened. Kathi couldn't see it because she was looking at her phone screen, but Todd and I shared a look.

'The alphabet?' said Juni Park and then Kathi *did* look up. A brain surgeon with his saw going would have looked up: Juni's tone was that icy.

'Pretty sick, huh?' said Kathi. 'Doing all that for shits and giggles.'

'That's not—' said Mitch.

'Oh!' Todd cut in. 'You're thinking there haven't been twenty-six incidents?'

'Exactly,' said Linda Magic. 'We're three short.'

'Two short,' I said. 'We're on twenty-four.'

'Are we?' said Juni Park. Then she looked up to one side and started mentally counting. Bob Larch looked down and started counting. Linda Magic's eyes were darting from side to side like a knitting machine, or probably more like an abacus. Kind of fascinating to see such an array of body language while they all did the same calculation. Mitch Verducci was the exception. He stared straight ahead. At me.

'You're Scotch, aren't you?'

'Yes,' I agreed. I've given up.

'Where in Scotland are you from? Edinburgh?'

'Dundee,' I said.

'Have you ever been to Edinburgh?'

'Oh many times,' I said. 'Scotland is tiny. It would fit into California several times over.'

'I'd love to go to Edinburgh,' he said. 'To the museum.'

'Um,' I said. The National Museum of Scotland was nice and everything – there's a dinosaur skeleton – but I'd never heard anyone plan a trip around it before.

'You know,' said Mitch. 'To see the tiny coffins.'

'What?' said Kathi. '*Children's* coffins?'

'No,' I said. 'Miniature coffins.' I remembered that much. 'They were found by a dog walker or—'

'Schoolboys,' said Mitch.

'Right, right,' I said. 'Buried in a—'

'Laid out in a cave, on top of Arthur's—'

'—Seat! Right,' I said, finally winning a point. 'You remember Arthur's Seat, right? The big hill in the middle of the city?'

'The whole place was hills,' Kathi said. 'What were these coffins?'

'Nobody knows,' said Mitch, in tones of wonder. Then he glanced at me. 'Right? Nobody knows?'

'Nobody knows,' I agreed. 'Something like thirteen—'

'Seventeen.'

'—little coffins with wooden dollies inside them and no one in a hundred—'

'Two hundred.'

'—years has been able to work out what they are.'

'Voodoo?' said Kathi.

'Nobody knows,' I said.

'Are they toys?' said Todd. 'Old toys can be way weird.'

'Nobody actually knows?' I said, wondering where he thought I might have got new information since Kathi asked me.

'Nobody knows,' said Mitch, in the kind of voice you usually hear saying things like 'with chocolate sauce' or 'rubbed all over your body'.

'Twenty-four!' said Bob Larch, quite a slow counter for someone whose whole career had been in financial services.

'I'm on twenty-two now running through them,' said Juni Park. 'I give up.'

'I got twenty-seven,' said Linda Magic. 'Let's trust Bob and the Trinity.' She beamed. 'So what's the good news?'

'Huh?' said Kathi. '*That* was the good news.'

Linda's eyes opened wide and her face started to change colour. She was really and truly the most insecure person I had ever met. First she gets into a running race to reach the benches ahead of the rest of us and now she was actually blushing over a little mistake that couldn't matter less.

'I'm sorry,' Linda said. 'I have brain fog from COVID. It's very upsetting.' I was a monster. 'I misspeak all the time and it's scary.' A real bitch. 'Like you're not in charge of your own mind?' Who had no business setting up as a counsellor. Linda gave a brave smile. 'Let's try that again. What's the bad news?'

'We have absolutely no idea why,' Kathi said. 'Some of the pranks were random: the pissing banshee, for instance. Some of them were mean, like the doughnuts and the noose and poor little Poppy Cliveson. Some of them would have been funny if it weren't for all the others, jokes about realtors being snakes, you know? But overall – not a scoob.'

'Not a what?' said Bob Larch.

Kathi glared at me, like it was my fault she had culturally appropriated Cockney rhyming slang and couldn't use it judiciously.

'Not a scoob,' I said. 'A Scooby-Doo. A clue.' No lightbulbs came on. 'We don't know.'

'OK, OK,' Bob Larch said, nodding sagely. 'Well, I think we can live with that.'

'I don't understand why you think it's finished at twenty . . . What was it?' said Linda Magic.

'Twenty-four,' Todd said. 'Because X and Z are pretty impossible initials for last names, but not quite so bad for first names. And they're covered: Xavier Reyes, the suicide and Zita Boulley, the schoolteacher who got the glass harmonica.'

'Ah,' said Bob. 'Right. Gotcha.'

'And is the glass harmonica one of the completely random ones?' said Mitch, making both Juni and Linda shoot him filthy looks for some reason.

'No, not necessarily,' I said. I was feeling like I hadn't contributed anything. 'Given that Zita possibly died of a seizure and given the theory – now outdated – that glass harmonicas possibly cause them, we've filed that under the "really nasty" column.'

'It's kind of a stretch,' said Linda. 'I never heard that. It's not like strobe lights or . . .'

'Menstruation,' I supplied, then felt as if I'd just farted at a funeral from the looks they gave me. We were sitting in a cemetery discussing pranks played on corpses but it appeared that there were limits.

'Maybe it was just opportunistic,' said Kathi. 'Maybe the glass harmonica was just . . . handy.'

All four of the Sex Volunteers stared at her with various expressions: dismay, mistrust, incomprehension and umbrage, like three brass monkeys and a bonus.

'How d'you mean?' said Bob Larch, eventually.

'Well, to scoop up that pesky Z,' said Kathi. 'Even Z *first* names don't present themselves all that often. Zack, Zoë, Zelda, Zander.'

'That's an X,' said Todd. 'But there aren't many Zebediahs these days.'

'Zuleika,' said Kathi.

'Zorro,' said Mitch.

'Zandra,' I put in. 'Zara'. They were completely legitimate names, but quite British maybe.

'Zemily, Zilliam, Zatherine and Zelizabeth,' said Juni, showing a playful streak we hadn't seen from her before.

'Thanks, Zuni,' said Linda. 'Zob? Zitchell? Any more.'

'Not from me, Zinda,' said Bob. 'How about you, Zodd, Zathi, Zexy?'

'I must say I'm relieved,' Kathi said. 'It's not the outcome you must have been hoping for when you engaged us, way back in January, but you're taking it very well.'

'No, it's not exactly what we were expecting,' Bob agreed. 'But I think I speak for all of us when I say you've set our minds at rest. Send us the final report and the final bill whenever you get round to it and thank you.'

He stood and shook our hands. Mitch did the same. Juni bowed her head sharply to each of us. Linda took her jacket back from the angel then stood and stared at us as if she wasn't going to shift until we had left. So we made our awkward goodbyes and went on our way. I checked over my shoulder once or twice, and even when the three of us must have been no more than bobbing torches, the four of them were still standing there like any of the other tombstones.

'I'm glad that's over,' Kathi said. 'Three of those dudes might call themselves local history buffs but I call them *all* creeps and weirdos.'

'Ghouls and geeks,' said Todd.

'No one goes to Scotland for the tiny coffins in the museum,' I said. 'What a whack job. What a quartet of whack jobs. Yeah, I'm glad it's over too. Now we all get the chance to concentrate on the wedding for five minutes in a row.'

'Finally!' said Todd.

'Exactly,' I agreed.

'Can't wait,' said Kathi.

'Me neither,' I said, beaming. I had the best best woman and bridesman in the world. They were so overcome with emotion and excitement right now, they couldn't even look at me.

PART TWO

TWELVE

Midsummer's Day again

If only I hadn't asked my attendants to loosen my dress, I would have had it to hold me up. As it was, I staggered and all of them – Todd in his Billy Porter tux, Kathi in her straight-up tux, Della in her bridesmaid's gown and Taylor in his kilt – surged forward to catch me, knocking heads and clashing limbs and leaving me to sink. Except that my mum and dad both slipped into the room right then and broke my fall. The three of us ended up in a heap on the floor, my head in my mum's lap and my dad holding my legs up. For some reason.

'Ow,' said Todd.

'What's happening?' said my mum. 'Lexy, are you drunk? Oh! Have you changed your mind? Because now's the time to stop it.'

'Has *he* changed his mind?' said my dad, craning over his shoulder to scowl at Taylor. 'Has he jilted you, chicken? Because if he has I'll put your feet down and biff him a good one.'

'Can you put my feet down anyway, Dad?' I said. 'It's killing my hamstrings. And nobody's jilted anyone. Has someone called nine one one?'

'You're ill?' said my mum. 'Injured? Where, darling? Tell Mummy what's wrong.'

I started to tell her but she wasn't listening. She had rounded on the rest of them, twisting my neck as she shifted. 'And you're all just standing there? What's wrong with you? Get an ambulance.'

'Sister Sunshine is dead,' said Taylor.

'Is it contagious?' said my mum. Give her her due – she didn't scramble to her feet to get away from me. 'Did Lexy catch . . . Wait. That's not true. I saw her wafting about like a rej— Well, I won't speak ill of the dead. But it's *not* true. She's alive and kicking. I just saw her. Oh! That means I can say what I want. Wafting about like a reject from the seventies.'

'*When* did you see her, Mum?' I said. I cranked my neck a couple of times to get the kinks out of it, then held my hands out so Todd and Della could haul me to my feet. Next the three of us hauled my mum up too.

'They're on their way,' said Kathi, who had evidently stepped aside and called the cops when no one was looking.

'Judith,' said Taylor. 'When *did* you last see Sister Sunshine? It's really important for you to remember.'

'Why?' said my mum.

Taylor was going to answer but Kathi put a hand up and stepped in between them. She knows how crucial it is to get witness statements unfiltered with emotion.

'To the best of your recall,' she said.

'I checked my watch,' my mum said. 'I saw we had twenty minutes till kick-off. I went to spend a penny and take one last look at my make-up, and that woman was just coming out of the cubicle next to me. She gave her hands a very cursory wash, Lexy. And her just about to handle your rings! I tried a look but she ignored me.'

'So that would be eleven forty,' said Kathi. 'At the bathrooms.' We all raised our wrists to check the time. I wonder how long it will take for the habit to die out, even among people who've been telling the time by their phones for years. We'll get there. Then people will clap their bums for a generation or two till the chips in our heads finally start to feel normal.

'Half an hour,' Todd said.

'So much time for someone to have left,' said Kathi. 'But let's go and hold the gates shut anyway.'

'What's going on?' said my dad. 'Has that strange woman twirled?'

'He means chomped,' said my mum.

'You might mean flaked, Keith,' said Taylor. 'And not exactly. She's been murdered.'

'Because Bertrand is there in the front row,' said my mum. 'Right where he promised he would be and he's going nowhere.'

'He might be *sitting* in the front row,' said Todd, waspishly, 'but he needs to get in line.'

'Did you hear me?' I said. 'Mum? Dad? Did you hear what I just told you about Sister Sunshine? Truly, this is not the time.'

There hadn't *been* a time. That was also true. Nevertheless, over the months of wedding preparations, as well as everything else I had to do to drive this happiest day of my life to perfection, I'd been forced to think up diplomatic answers to offers that were intrusive, inappropriate and unwelcome. One after the other, like late buses.

Surprisingly, given that it's Todd who has never met a boundary he didn't vault, it started with Della. 'Leagsaidh,' she said one day, slipping aboard my boat when I had a rare free hour with no client bookings. I knew it was serious because she said my name in Gaelic. 'I know you are not devout.'

Not devout? That was like saying that Sharon Osbourne was not reserved.

'And Taylor is not devout and Jewish too. But have you ever attended a wedding mass?'

'Uh, yeah. Yours.'

'Of course,' Della said. 'What do you think then?'

'I think it's January and I'm getting married in June and to get married in a Catholic church you need to be a baptized Christian, which OK, I am, but also a member of that specific church which is a shit ton of catechism classes. And you have to be in good standing with communion and confession and all that. Plus I'm pretty sure the other one has to be baptized too.'

'Which Taylor might be,' Della said. 'For all we know. And I said that to Father Jerry and he was kind of tickled. I think he would go for it.'

'Tickled?' I said. 'Tickled that an abandoned baby never knows if he's been baptized before his Jewish mother adopted him?'

'And as for the catechism classes and communion and confession,' said Della, 'you might need to postpone the wedding till the same time next—'

'What's this really about?' I said. 'Where the hell is this coming from? Because this isn't like you, Dells. This is nothing like you. This is . . .' I stopped dead, because it had suddenly occurred to me where this was coming from and I felt really stupid for not seeing it straight away.

'My mother wants you to convert me to Catholicism?'

'No,' said Della. 'Your mother wants you to get married in a church. She tried the others first but that went nowhere, so then she turned to me and I said I would give it a go.'

I was punching in my mum's number already – I've never put her on speed dial because I'm usually angry when I phone her and

I need the act of jabbing buttons so I don't swear at her when she answers.

'Mum?' I said.

'I'm just going to go,' said Della, slipping away.

To be fair to him, Todd was next up and pretty promptly too. 'Your mom's a maniac,' he said.

'Look who's talking!' I shot back.

Todd nodded, which was surprising. Then he said, 'My mom is indeed a whole lot, and even more on the side. But she got me thinking. Judith, I mean. Not Barb. Barb only ever gets me *drinking*.'

'Oh?' I said, glancing over at his profile. 'Thinking how?' We were on a road trip to the good Asian deli in the East Bay to get the eye-watering pickled chillies you couldn't procure in Cuento.

'I'm going to give you all the decisions and go along with whatever you say,' he told me. 'Seriously, absolutely whatever you want.'

'Can we start with what you're on about?'

'My ordination,' said Todd. 'Most of the best ones are in San Francisco, natch: the Holy Mother of All Churches, the Church of the Perpetual Groove Thang, Elvis's Chapel on the Road, Elvis's Chapel by the Bay, Elvis's Beach House Chapel . . .'

'You've got to be kidding.'

'But there are national organizations for that boring vanilla touch too. Universal Life Church, American Marriage Ministries . . . All online. Click of a button, Lexy.'

'Let's just buy our curry paste and pickles and never speak of this again,' I said. 'For your information though, if I was going to – and I'm not – it would be the Groove Thang, because how could you say no to that? Except, of course, that I completely am.'

I didn't see it coming from Kathi, mind you. She whistled at me as I crossed the forecourt one morning en route to Swiss Sisters, so I trotted up the stairs and entered the gleaming palace of clean clothes, where she was ready for the day.

'What's up?' I asked her.

'Nothing. It was just to say I'm all set to marry you if you want me to.'

It was so unexpected that I took a detour round by complete insanity 'You mean I dump Taylor and you divorce Noleen and you marry me?' Her face! 'No! Sorry, of course not. You mean, you officiate at the wedding when I marry Taylor, right? Of course, right. But, Kathi, why? Wait! Don't tell me: my mum, right? Just ignore her.'

'Oh, she's given up press-ganging *us*,' Kathi said. 'She's really on the case now.'

'Really on *what* case?' I said. I knew my mum was on the case of no jam jars, sacking, string or rope. She was on the case of linen, crystal, silk and roses. She was all over Taylor wearing Campbell clan tartan now that she'd given up trying to find an Aaronovitch version. But how could she be on the case of our celebrant?

'She's trying to find a Church of Scotland in San Francisco.'

'She won't succeed,' I said. 'It's the Church of *Scotland*. Clue in the name.' But I wished I felt more certain. San Francisco is the kind of place where you'll see everything if you hang around for long enough on the right corner. 'So, thank you but no. Please don't go to the expense and effort of getting yourself ordained, just for me.'

'Effort, right,' Kathi said. 'And anyway, I'm already all set up. Have been for years.'

'Why?' I said, not imagining there was much laundry/nuptials crossover.

'Noleen reckoned we could offer it as an add-on, back when the Ditch was a twinkle in her eye. She persuaded me.'

'Why didn't she get ordained, if it was her idea?'

Kathi gave me a stony look. 'Can you imagine Noleen officiating at a wedding?' she said. '"You're both nuts, but if you're determined, by the power yadda-yadda . . .".'

'She could do naming ceremonies too,' I said. '"Boy, I hope she's smart, because that is one ugly-ass baby. And what a dumb name."'

'Funerals,' said Kathi giggling. '"We all gotta go sometime, amirite?"'

And then I assumed I was done. Fifty guests would guzzle the good wine, eat the hundred-and-fifty-dollar menu with its whole sides of salmon and its beetroot rainbows, they would choke down wedding cake and like it, and they would do it all after Sister Sunshine married me, like I said. And Taylor, obviously.

But, when my parents arrived a week ago, laden with my mum's hatbox and my dad's kilt bag, and a whole suitcase full of Shredded Wheat, Marmite, Yorkshire Gold and McVities HobNobs (like they'd never heard of Amazon) – not to mention three tiers of cake, they had brought someone else along too.

'We saw his dog collar at the gate and he turned out to be sitting in the row in front of us,' my mum said. 'Of course, he might have been a Catholic, or a Baptist, or a Methodist, or a . . . What else is there? . . . but he had a backpack with the name of his parish on it and your dad Googled it, just quickly, before we had to turn everything off, and there it was! We had a twelve-hour flight to convince him.'

'You've kidnapped a minister?' I said. 'Bertrand, where are you supposed to be?'

'Ecumenical summit in Greenning,' he said. 'But Wednesdays are our days off and I'm sharing a room at the retreat centre, so a couple of nights here would be tickety-boo.'

'Are you allowed to marry people in foreign countries?' I said.

Bertrand's eyes flashed. 'I'll have to go online and fill in a form,' he said. 'But after that, why not?'

Why not? As I told Taylor afterwards, alone on the boat, why not was because he had clearly snagged that backpack from a charity shop and bought himself a dog collar off of Amazon, to try to get an upgrade on the flight over and was no more a Church of Scotland minister than I was. Why the hell would a church summit in Greenning have a Scottish minister at it? 'What does ecumenical mean, anyway?' I asked him. He told me, which to be fair did make it a bit more plausible, but still. I shut it down, no matter what my mum thought. And said. And would text me later to say again.

'Oh Bertrand.' I sighed, trying to make my face look rueful. 'That is so kind of you. And, Mum? You're one in a million. But the thing is, I've got a celebrant and she's not just a celebrant, either. She's also a wedding planner. She's project-managing the entire event.'

'That doesn't seem likely,' my dad put in, relying on his vast experience of arranging weddings in California perhaps. 'Are you sure she's not swindling you, Lexy? The realm of the wedding planner and the wedding celebrant are quite distinct.'

'So you'll understand that I don't want to hurt her feelings or put her nose out of joint, when she's still got my whole wedding to oversee.'

'Do you want to talk to Taylor about it at least?' my mum said.

'What?' I said. 'Why? What's it got to do with Taylor?'

'Wow,' my mum said. She was barely off the plane and already she had started making mysterious remarks for no reason, like the rest of them.

'Lexy?'

I opened my eyes. There she was in her RuPaul fascinator and her perfect make-up, peering at me as if I was a needle she was trying to thread. 'Bertrand? Hm? What do you say?'

'Mum,' I said. 'Forget the bloody wedding, for God's sake. Sister Sunshine has been murdered. There's more to think about than an over-priced party today.'

There was a moment of perfect silence as they all stood in a ring and gaped at me.

'It's a miracle!' said Della.

'It's an *overdue* miracle,' said Kathi, ripping off the completely over-the-top buttonhole I had guilted her into.

'I would have murdered someone months ago if I'd known that's what it was going to take,' said Todd.

'Welcome back, my darling,' said Taylor.

Which left my parents. And they were both glowering at me.

'Over-priced?' said my dad. 'We gave you a very generous budget, Lex, and you told us it wouldn't cover the bare minimum.'

'And it's not a "party",' said my mum. 'It's a sacred . . . sacrament.'

'Dad, I'm sorry,' I said. 'Mum . . . whatever . . . but someone has murdered the woman who was supposed to be marrying us ten minutes ago.'

'She said "us",' Taylor cried out. 'She's really and true back! Oh Lexy, I've missed you.'

'So now is not the time to remind me that it was *me* who insisted on her being here today, when you press-ganged that poor schmuck into missing a bit of sightseeing on his day off. OK?'

'By jings, that's a thought,' my dad said. 'Do you think Bertrand should maybe go home? If someone's picking off celebrants?'

'No one's picking . . .' I said. 'And people can't leave till the police . . . But maybe go and tell him to take his collar off, eh?'

It was nonsense but it got rid of both of them before I throttled one or the other.

'Should I take my dress off?' I said. 'What happens now?' We could all hear police sirens in the distance, getting closer.

'I got nothing to change into,' said Kathi. 'Della either. And if we're going to be sashaying around in this for the rest of however long, no way you get to duck out, sister. Look at Taylor, for God's sake.'

I looked at Taylor. He was wearing the full whack: lace-up shirt with flouncy sleeves; velvet waistcoat; dress Campbell kilt; sporran that looked like Jason Momoa's disembodied head; sgian dubh; tartan flashes; and dancing shoes with laces that climbed his socks like his shirt strings climbed his chest.

'You poor bastard,' I said. 'I'm really sorry.'

'I missed you so much,' said Taylor, his voice breaking.

'I'm sorry I put my foot down about your Star of David cufflinks,' I said.

'Never leave me again,' Taylor said.

Then the door to my dressing room banged open to reveal Noleen and Roger, with Devin just behind them holding both kids in his arms, Hiro asleep, Diego wide awake.

'Is it true?' Noleen said. 'Kathi texted me.'

'It's true,' I said. 'Can you believe it?'

'Nope,' said Noleen. She turned to Roger. 'You?'

'I want to believe it, but I don't want to get burned,' he said.

'Isn't it awfu— Wait, what are you talking about? Why would you want to believe something like that?'

'Oh yeah,' said Kathi. 'Well, there's that too. Sister Sunshine has been – Diego, honey? Put your fingers in your ears. – strangled with a string of inadequate floral fairy lights.'

'You don't say?' Noleen took the news in with a few solemn nods and then shook it off. 'But the headline is Lexy got her head out of her ass and stopped being a complete dick.'

'Uhhh, I took my fingers out again, Gramma Nolly.'

'Well, that's OK. It's a very special occasion, right, Della?'

'Can't deny it,' Della said. 'It was a wedding anyway but this is huge!' Devin had edged toward her and was now handing over the sleeping Hiro. The kids were getting too big to hold both at the same time, at least for someone who had never seen the inside of a gym and only really had muscles in his console fingers. Della hugged the warm little body close and started blinking as tears gathered in her eyes. 'That poor woman. She was annoying but no one deserves that. What happened?'

'No idea,' said Kathi. 'But here we go again.'

THIRTEEN

'What the hell are you wearing?' The commanding tones of Sergeant Molly Rankinson of the Cuento PD woke us all out of our daze. She even woke Hiro who can sleep through someone stumbling over a drumkit, as we all knew for a fact after Diego's last birthday. She could have been talking about any one of us, but I made a wager with myself and right enough it was Taylor her organ-stop eyes were trained on.

'The traditional dress of my should-be-by-now wife,' Taylor said. 'It's very . . . airy.'

Molly held up her hand. 'I don't wanna know. OK, so there's supposed to be a wedding, I realize that. But the venue is a crime scene and the deceased is the officiant and all the guests are witnesses at the very least.'

'Can you take names and let us cart the food back to the Ditch and at least have the party?' said Taylor.

'What? No! Are you insane?' Molly said. 'You can eat the food here. And I'd get going because the guests have already started.'

'Taylor,' said Todd. '"At least have the party"? Honey, I am ordained. Kathi is ordained. That blow-in of Judith's is ordained. You are getting hitched today, or my name isn't Theodor Mendez Kroger.'

'OK, Dr Kroger, since you've supplied your full name so very willingly,' Molly said. 'Let's start with you. Lexy, I'm taking over this . . . whatever this is . . . for the incident room, so you need to throw that big tail of yours over your shoulder and find another place to be.'

'It's called a train,' I said.

'Uh-huh. What's it for?'

That was a very good question to which there was no answer. 'Can I take my personal belongings?' I asked instead.

'You can't take anything that was brought into this room today,' said Molly. 'Unless it's prescription medications, EpiPens, or medical aids. Seriously, hit the buffet. It's going to be a long night.'

There was a mirror by the door of the dressing room, obviously supposed to let brides, bands and Bar Mitzvah boys check their outfits before they made their entrance, so I got to see the sorry little procession that trooped out. Me, with my face as white as my dress, Todd with even his diamonds looking dull, Kathi as undone as she could get by removing items and rolling or unbuttoning others. There's nothing you can do about the swing of a kilt and the smart clack of the segs in a pair of Highland dancing shoes so Taylor wasn't much changed, but Della, Devin and the Adorables wouldn't get a job advertising Disneyland today and Noleen, right at the back of the line, was the tin lid. Of course, Noleen's resting expression was the tin lid every day of life but she was extra dour-looking right now. I knew that for a fact, because the first person we met outside our little sanctuary – someone still bubbling and chirpy, who either hadn't heard the sirens or was on some kind of happy pills – asked her if she was one of my relations. That's right: Noleen was so fed up she had made herself look like a Scotswoman.

Out in the venue was a shadow version of what should have been happening. Where guests were supposed to be circling in airy little arcs and eddies, like soap bubbles, with glasses in their hands and smiles on their faces, they were circling in darting, furtive little jabs, with phones in their hands and worried looks. Instead of waiters – well, students in black shirts and trousers with trays of nibbles – there were uniformed coppers, also in black shirts and trousers but with clipboards. The caterers were grimly shoving all the prepared food out on long trestle tables at the back of the row seating. They had taken off the chef hats I'd paid for and now wore the bandanas that came free. I could hardly blame them.

Someone had turned off the fairy lights, out of respect maybe, and there's nothing more depressing than fairy lights when they're switched off. They're transformed into green electrical cables with prominent plugs and sockets and even more prominent safety labels. They make whatever they're wound around or draped across look the very antithesis of festive.

And someone from the venue staff had put their own playlist back on the sound system, instead of the ethereally Celtic mood music we'd had murmuring in the background while our guests gathered. I couldn't summon the energy to protest, even though the current track, while it maybe wasn't Radiohead, was certainly close.

Not to mention the fact that the table-staging – my dad was right: that *was* a stupid and unnecessary expression – was folded up and lying on its side against the closed open bar and, instead of my beautiful wedding cake, an even bigger, even whiter edifice had appeared. I watched as space-suited forensics and SOCOs trudged in and out of the crime scene tent and wondered why I couldn't feel anything.

'Lex?' Taylor said.

'Yeah,' I agreed, and turned away.

He and I had about ten minutes' worth of admin to take care of, paperwork and payments and bits and bobs of shutting everything down, and we had just managed to wade through it and head for the buffet table, when Molly and her sidekick accosted me.

'Ms Campbell? If you would accompany me to the interview room?'

'Is that different from the incident room?' I said. 'If not, can I please get changed? I'd settle for a dressing gown.' I tutted at her face. 'A bathrobe.'

'Are you cold?' said Molly. 'I can loan you a coat.'

She was giving me a measured look, out of a total poker face. I knew what she was up to. Witnesses had to be kept warm and dry in case they sued the police department but there was no law against looking ridiculous and she was clearly going to make me sit and stew in my wedding dress as long as was humanly possible. I had a good mind to strip to my basque, suspenders and white fishnets just to mess with her. The front bit of my wedding knickers was shaped like a love heart and they had no back at all. That would show her.

But actually I *was* a bit chilly, and the thought of sitting down in a thong was unsettling. OK, the seat covers were brand new but still. I swept past Molly and marched in the direction she was indicating.

The interview room was no more than a corner of the chill-out space. It was still bedecked with bubble-blowing machines for the kids although the balloon animal woman had long since popped her menagerie and gone. I sank down into an armchair and kicked off my satin slippers.

'They cost me two hundred dollars,' I said to Molly. 'And look at them.'

'Yeah, they're stupid,' Molly said.

I had meant they were grimy from the earthen floor of the hop garden but I didn't have the energy to argue.

'So, Ms Campbell,' Molly said. 'How long have you known Ms Fisher?'

'Who?' I said. Then it struck me that of course 'Sister Sunshine' couldn't have been her real name. 'Is her first name even Sunny?' I asked.

'Sonja,' Molly said. 'How long?'

'Six months,' I said. 'Half the earth's turn around the sun, she'd have said. Solstice to Solstice.'

'Would she,' Molly said. 'Still, people don't usually get murdered just for being annoying. How well would you say you knew her?'

'In one way, intimately. We've talked pretty much every day.'

'About a wedding?' I wasn't looking at her but I knew she was rolling her eyes.

'And she knew everything there was to know about *me*. Finances, family, my relationship with Taylor. She advised me on intimate waxing to accommodate the bridal underclackers I cannot wait to get out of.' I wriggled around until the string bit had stopped threatening to cleave me in two. 'But I didn't know much about *her*. Not even her real name. Sonja Fisher? How old was she?'

'Forty-one,' said Molly. 'When did you last see her?'

'I didn't see her at all today, I don't think. She was out there making it happen and I was in my dressing room with the hairdresser and make-up lady and my friends. Wait! Did I see her when I first arrived? Molly, I'm not trying to be difficult but I've been in a sort of a coma and I truly don't know.'

'How long were you "in hair and make-up",' Molly said, the quotes heavy enough to sink a dinghy.

'Is this for the investigation or just so you can judge me?' I said. 'Look, I'm not being deliberately arsey, but I am fried. I'll be in much better shape to answer all your questions tomorrow after a sleep.'

'You planning to huddle up with those chuckleheads you call partners and start getting in my way, as usual?' she said. 'Interfering in my active case, contaminating evidence, misleading potential witnesses, withholding information?'

'When did any of us ever do that?' I said, trying to make my eyes as big and innocent as I could get them, shoving down the memories of all the times Trinity had hung on to bits of news or found a way to get to interesting individuals, instead of leaving every last scrap of the work up to Cuento's Finest. I think I failed. I'm useless at poker. And at lying.

Molly raised the nearest eyebrow to me and kept scribbling in her little notebook.

'So, if I let you go home, you won't be calling a meeting of the gang and trying to muscle in? Because, Lexy, you have muscled in on cases that had diddly squat to do with you. Forgive me if it's hard to believe you'll leave this alone.'

'Molly, I assure you, nothing could be further from my mind. My wedding has just collapsed around my ears. I'm tired and stressed and upset. And my parents are here, so if I can shift myself to do *anything* it's going to be wine tasting in Napa, boat trips at Tahoe, the Golden Gate Bridge, Chinatown and the boardwalks of Old Sacramento. They've come a long way on a short visit and I want to show them a good time.'

'Right,' said Molly. 'About that. The visit might not be as short as they planned.'

'What are you talking about?'

'Your father didn't want Ms Fisher to officiate. Did you know that?'

'I wouldn't go that far,' I said. 'He's a celebrant himself in Scotland and early on they assumed I'd be going home for the wedding. But I wanted him to give me away and he was quite happy about it in the end. He paid for it. So what, anyway? What are you getting at?'

'Your mom's not "quite happy" about it,' Molly said. 'She fricking hates this place.'

'California?'

'The Garden,' Molly said. 'She thinks "Sister Sunshine" must have put the thumbscrews on you to get you to agree to a place that's so out of line with your taste.'

'Her taste,' I said. 'But again: so what?'

'Her taste, right,' Molly said. 'And she brought a pastor with her too, she tells me. All this way.'

'Um, she brought him "all this way" from Greenning,' I said. 'Not Scotland. And again, I fail to see . . .' My voice ran dry and my mouth dropped open.

'You look to me like you're starting to manage to see,' Molly said.

'You think my parents might have killed my wedding celebrant?' I said. 'That is the most ridiculous thing I have ever heard come out of your mouth in all the time I've known you. And talk about a wide field!'

'Yeah? They disapproved of her, they resented her, they thought she had an undue influence on you. And now you tell me they were paying for the wedding they reckoned she was hijacking?'

'Seriously, Molly, you need to get a grip. My dad? My mum? That's insane.'

'Who else had a motive?'

'If that's what you're calling a motive, who didn't?' I said. 'Todd wanted to officiate! Kathi was spitting feathers about – and I quote – having to do that dumb walk that makes you look like you shit your pants. Even Noleen was sick of fielding phone calls. Molly, weddings are irritating. Wedding *planners* are infuriating. Hippy-dippy wedding planners who talk about auras and omens are enough to send anyone off on a psychotic break. But come on!'

'Interesting,' Molly said. 'So Dr Kroger and the Mrs Muntzes had it in for Ms Fisher too?'

'No!'

'So you mentioned them in bad faith, trying to distract me from your mom and pops?'

'What? *No!* Is this a joke?'

'Yeah,' Molly said. She paused for a beat. 'Pretty dark humour, huh? OK then. Sorry about your wedding and you're good to go. Don't leave town and I can't stop you speaking to the press but I would appreciate it. Thank you.'

I was dumbstruck. Scratch that. I was thunderstruck. But also dumbstruck. I got to my feet without uttering another word and went to find the rest of them. Of course, I forgot what I was wearing and fell over the bloody train, proving Molly wrong about it being a pointless feature of any garment. There had to be twelve feet of it, all bunched up, and it cushioned my fall nicely.

Taylor was waiting for me on a tree stump near the stage where our ceilidh band should now have been playing.

'You want to go to the fancy hotel room?' he asked me.

I shook my head. I just wanted to go home, take off my underwear and burn it. I also wanted to take a picture of the weals all over my body where the boning and wires were digging in, as well as the chafing on my arse crack, and keep them in a folder marked 'never again'.

'Do you?' I said. 'Chocolate-dipped fruit and rose petals all over the bed?'

'We could spring some chocolate and fruit from our own buffet and take them home,' Taylor said. 'Petals too.'

'I'd rather order a pizza and have a bed full of crumbs,' I said.

'Well, we'd have to be pretty zippy anyway,' said Taylor, pointing across to the buffet table. 'Your mom's dividing up the leftovers and bullying everyone into taking the flowers with them.'

Right enough, my mum had laid her hands on a stack of Tupperware from somewhere and was dishing out food to all of our exhausted guests. There was a trail already starting to snake away from the dancefloor towards the car park, all of them clutching flowers and bottles of wine. I was sorry to see some of them leave without me ever getting to say hello to them – José and Maria from our lockdown, Todd's mother and her new squeeze who looked so much like James Brolin I half-expected an enraged Barbra Streisand to appear any minute and start a catfight. Arif and Meera, kids in tow and baby bump defying gravity, waved and signalled that they'd be in touch soon. I thought about trotting over to hug them but just then a 'psssst!' sounded at my elbow.

'Dad?' I said, turning to see him edging out from behind an enormous fig plant. 'What is it? Why are you skulking?'

'What's missing from this picture?' he said, nodding over to where my mum was overseeing portion control.

'What?' I said. For one wild moment all I could think was that Sister Sunshine was missing, and he sounded as if he might be confessing. Then I cursed Molly for putting crazy thoughts in my head.

'I've got the cake,' my dad hissed. 'They're welcome to the avocados and enchiladas, but your mum's cake is coming home with us. I'll fry you up a slice for breakfast, Lexy.'

'Fried wedding cake?' Taylor said.

'Try doing that with some egg-white fluff that passes for cake only if you're off your nut!' said my dad.

'Do you fry the frosting?' Taylor said.

'Oh, I've peeled off all that muck,' said my dad. 'Judith's cake is too good to be hidden under a ton of sugar and baubles. It needs no more than a slice of crumbly Wensleydale.'

'There isn't any crumbly Wensleydale within a thousand miles, Dad,' I said, and at long, long last I started to cry.

FOURTEEN

The only one of us who woke up the next morning in a sunshiny mood was Hiro. At three years old, and given the sample size of one, she didn't seem to realize that the previous day wasn't how the wedding was supposed to go. There had been dressing up, music, fancy food, all kinds of strange goings-on, and she had thrown fistfuls of petals about just like she'd been promised she would get to. That wedding was in the bag, as far as Miss Chihiro Muelenbelt was concerned.

For the rest of us, the next morning felt like a hangover of the soul. Also, we had drunk quite a bit after getting back to the Ditch, so it felt a bit like a hangover of the head and stomach too. And then it didn't help that my dad delivered his traditional quip – 'By, the nights are fair drawing in!' – like he did every twenty-second of June, to match his 'Nice to see a bit of light in the evenings again!' every twenty-second of December. It bugs the life out of my mum and her torn face started the pair of them bickering. It was displaced upset from the murder, clearly, but they're really good at it after all these years married and it was hard to listen to. So, instead of taking them out for breakfast which had been the plan, I ran away to hide in Todd's room. Taylor, needless to say, had used the unexpected gift of time as a chance to go down to the wetlands. I was glad because, with my mum there as a role model, I would probably have started displacement bickering too.

Todd was still in bed in his under-eye gels and tooth-whitening contraption, scrolling on his phone. Kathi was sitting on his dressing-stool, looking less happy to be back in her jeans and T-shirt than I had expected. Roger was long gone and thinking about him back in the paediatric HDU pissed me off even more, on account of how it made me feel guilty about my self-pity.

'Did you go for coffee?' Todd said, perking up as I came in. Then he saw my empty hands. 'Oh well.'

'Who's in the Skweek?' I asked Kathi. She only blinked at me. She hadn't opened up obviously, but she didn't want to feel guilty.

'I need an office,' she said, no qualms about guilt-tripping *me*. 'You said we'd talk about it again after the wedding.'

'Yeah, well, she said she'd start picking up coffee again too,' Todd murmured.

'I'll ramp up,' I said. 'Gimme a break.' Todd kept scrolling. 'What are you looking at anyway?'

'News,' Todd said. 'See if there's anything more about the murder.'

'And?'

'Prominent local businesswoman Sonja Fisher, aged forty-one, was murdered Wednesday at a private function in a popular Cuento venue. Fisher was strangled with a length of electrical wire by an unknown assailant. There were no witnesses to the crime and no obvious motive. The investigation, in its early stages, is ongoing. Latest details will be shared at a press conference this afternoon.'

'This is the *Voyager*?' I said. 'My God, I need to send Molly a basket of fruit every month for a year. And get The Garden to go halfsies. They really didn't use my name? Or say it was my wedding? Or specify what kind of wire? Or even where it happened?'

'And they said no witnesses,' Kathi put in. 'So they're not going to be assholes after all.'

'What do you mean?' I said, sensing that I had missed something.

'Good news,' said Kathi. 'Bad news for Molly, I guess, on account of how if everyone's innocent she's got to go on the hunt for an opportunistic rando, right?'

'What?' I said, trying again. Kathi shared a look with Todd, sucking her teeth and shaking her head.

'You tell her while I'm in the shower,' said Todd, throwing back his bedclothes. Kathi and I are old hands at not seeing Todd's bits when he gets out of bed. We've put in a lot of hours to get that way. As soon as his hand gripped the bias binding on the edge of his duvet cover, we both covered our eyes like invisible toddlers, and stayed that way until we heard the water running.

'While you were doing whatever you were doing yesterday after everything fell apart, Lexy,' Kathi said, 'I was gathering intel on the wedding guests turned witnesses. Asking them what they had told the unis about where they were and what they saw and whether they had alibis. And you know what?'

'They do?' I said. Her face crunched into a scowl. 'Aw come on! You said it was good news. You fed it to me.'

'Fair,' Kathi said. 'Yep, out of the forty guests who were there in addition to the wedding party itself, not one single one was alone around the time of the murder. The four of us were together, your mom and dad were talking to the ceilidh band. The other three Ds plus Meera and Arif and their kids were bugging the carp. Todd's mom was chatting up Father Bertrand. The woman's had a yen for a priest ever since that TV show with that guy . . .'

'*Ballykissangel*?'

'No, away way back. With that dude that played Jesus.'

'Mel Gibson?'

'No, but it might not have been him anyway. Doesn't matter. Taylor's buddies were all holding hands in a protective circle, obviously. Lexy, you have some boring parties in your future, you know. And the waiters were all getting final instructions from the boss. Even the two barmen alibied each other.'

'No one was in the bog?'

'That's the really beautiful part,' Kathi said. 'Did you know there were musical candles in all the bathrooms?'

'Yeah, of course. I paid for them.'

'What a dope!' said Kathi, cackling. 'OK well, Sister Sunshine reckoned eleven thirty was the time to light them and start them all playing. What *were* they playing?'

'I don't want to tell you,' I said. It was Michael Bublé, and it made me furious even thinking about the fact that not one of my so-called friends had stopped me.

'So two of the venue staff were taking care of that, meaning that they were together and the johns were free from the time Sister Sunshine gave the order to the time her body was discovered. Alibis all round. Police baffled.'

I nodded slowly. Todd's shower stopped running and both of us shot to our feet.

'We're going for coffee!' I shouted. Todd, despite the size and sumptuousness of his bath sheets, liked to walk around and air dry. I was halfway out the door, when I stopped as a thought struck me. 'So who killed her?'

'What?' said Kathi. She was out on the balcony already but she came back. 'What do you mean "so"? You thought one of your guests murdered someone?'

'No,' I said. 'But I suppose I assumed one of the caterers, or waiters, or the venue staff must have. Because if they didn't, who did?'

'It's hardly Fort Knox,' said Todd. He had emerged from his bathroom but he had a towel round his waist. Maybe he was learning some decorum. 'There's no boundary fence at all. The venue and performance space merge into the hop garden and the hop garden merges into walnut orchard on three sides. We know from past experience that the wall between The Garden and the cemetery is easy to get over. And OK there's a fence on to Turkey Farm Road, but with four gates. Vehicular in, vehicular out, pedestrian and delivery. None of them were locked. I checked.'

'You did?' I said.

'Of course I did. Have we met? So, yeah, someone came in from outside, got her alone in a quiet spot and crrk!'

'So . . . did you just happen to check that there were four unlocked gates?' I said. 'And, Kathi, did you just happen to share a few words with every guest and the entire staff, both permanent and contracted, covering where they were and when and what they told the cops?'

'What do *you* think?' said Todd. He was standing in front of his full-length mirror, working moisturizer into his face, neck and chest. He'd drop the towel any minute, but I couldn't drag myself away.

'Because I assured Molly that Trinity had no interest in this case,' I said. 'I pretty much promised her that we'd leave it alone.'

'Of course we're leaving it alone,' Kathi said. 'It's got nothing to do with any of us and there's no scope for Trinity to get involved in any way that could be helpful, or legal. Besides, we're too busy. Or, you know, we might potentially be too busy. If this thing we're waiting for pans out. Todd?'

'Nothing so far,' Todd said. He was standing on one leg like a stork, working body lotion into one of his perfect feet. It was putting a lot of strain on the towel and I looked away again quickly. 'Lexy, I checked the gates as possible escape routes in case of a swarm of bees or a cloud of gnats or a late migration of butterflies. You have no idea what a big ask it was for me to attend an outdoor event in the middle of a freaking farm.'

'And I was trying to work out who all had touched the food,' Kathi said. 'I didn't actually care where they were, so long as they hadn't been near the buffet table. I didn't want to faint from hunger and not be able to do that dumb prancy dancing you set your heart on, but I wanted to lock down some of the platters under Glad Wrap before they got contaminated.'

'Of course,' I said. 'Silly me. And, you know, I do appreciate it. I did. The dancing and the buffet and the great outdoors. Even though it didn't exactly go off seamlessly. So, cool. We're not investigating. And what might pan out? What are we waiting for?'

With perfect timing, Todd's phone pinged on his bedside table. He gestured to me to throw it over to him. Me, rather than Kathi with her good arm because Kathi had her fingers and arms and legs all crossed. If there was room in her trainers, she probably had her toes crossed too. I under-armed it over to Todd, who looked up and said a silent prayer before swiping to open the message.

'Yes!' he said. 'They got an answer!"

'Yes!' said Kathi. 'What's it say?'

'No!' said Todd.

'No?' said Kathi.

'P,' said Todd.

'P?' said Kathi.

'Pee?' I asked. 'Pea? What?'

'We contacted The Doe Pages,' Kathi said. 'They're a bunch of citizen detectives who match up missing persons with unclaimed bodies. Very cool dudes. And we got a hit.'

'We know who Jane Doe is?' I said. 'Our cemetery case is live again? That's fantastic.'

'Our cemetery case is more than "live again",' said Todd. 'Our cemetery case is ongoing, Lexy. We were wrong. Jane Doe isn't our F. The banshee taking a leak on her grave wasn't our last prank. Jane Doe, according to these online ninjas at The Doe Pages, was Nina Pradash.'

'So we have no idea why the banshee was where it was,' said Kathi. 'And we're short one F?'

'Oh God,' I said.

'Yeah and we have two Ps,' Kathi said. 'I don't get it either, Lexy.'

'That's not what I meant,' I said. I was thinking furiously. Did it make sense? I was horribly sure that it did. I should tell the other two. If I was lucky, they might show me how wrong I was. I've never wanted more to be utterly and completely wrong.

'OK, We have two Ds,' Kathi said. 'Nit-picker. Sorry, Todd.' Todd didn't care for talk of nits in general conversation and particularly hates this expression that references people touching them.

'That's still not what I meant.'

'Oh my God, Lexy!' said Todd. 'All *right*. D'Ambrosi doesn't go under D and we have two As. Let me call you an Uber to the goddamn point!'

'If you would let me *tell* you what I meant!' I said. 'The alphabet is complete. The series of "pranks" is over. But we can't investigate it.'

'We're short an F,' said Todd. 'How is the alphabet complete when we're short an F?'

'We might have a first name F,' Kathi said, scrolling on her phone. 'But it made more sense that X and Z were the special cases. There shouldn't have been a problem finding a last name with an ordinary initial like F. Let's see . . . Kermit, Puja, Joey, Hamza, Debbi, Les, Pauletta, Zita, Max, Albert and Mary, Phillip, Poppy, Larry, John— Aha! Frances Ernst. Professor Ernst with the dolls had a first name beginning with F. So we're *not* waiting for last name F before we can say it's done.'

'No,' I said. 'We're not. We've had our last name F and it's no mystery why it was left until last and it certainly wasn't a prank.'

'What. Are. You. Talking. About?' Todd said, clapping his hands together near my face. With every clap the rolled bit of his towel overlap loosened a little. And all the body lotion on his palms made the claps into wet smacks that rang in my ears.

'Lexy, you had a real tough day yesterday,' Kathi said. 'And you'd been functionally insane for six weeks before that. You're tired and you're upset about Sister Sunshine. Why don't you leave this to Todd and me.'

'Her name's not Sister Sunshine,' I said.

'Well, no,' said Todd. 'That would have been too neat if someone who'd actually been baptized Sister Sunshine turned into a Solstice-bothering wack-a-doo like she was. No disrespect intended.'

'That family who blew through in spring with the kids called Candy and Bobo?' said Kathi. She had done a rush job on the children's ski jackets when one of them had projected barely swallowed grape juice all over the back seat. 'I wanted to ask when they decided they didn't want their daughters to be president one day.'

'Sister Sunshine's real name was pretty *ordinary*,' I said.

'Sonja?' said Todd.

'That's not the *ordinary* bit,' I said.

'What's her last name then?' said Kathi. 'I did hear it but I forgot it.'

'Because it's so *ordinary*,' I said.
'Fisher,' said Todd. 'Oh shit.'
'Fisher,' I agreed.
'Fisher?' said Kathi and her tone told me the penny had finally dropped. 'Is there any chance that's Phisher with a P-H?'
'No,' I said. 'It's Fisher with an ordinary F.'
Todd's towel dropped off. He might have caved his stomach in to take a huge breath and reduced the circumference of his waist so much that there was nothing for the rolled bit to hold on to. But it was hard to avoid thinking that the towel was as flabbergasted as the rest of us and had swooned.
'Throw me some boxers from that top drawer, Kathi,' he said. 'We need to go get some coffee and talk this through.'

They didn't take much convincing. We took our coffees to the UCC arboretum, which had finally calmed down again after its moment in the sun in 2020 when every class, consultation, date and break-up took place in its shady acres. Now it was back to a few senior walking clubs and the squirrels again.
'OK, first of all, this gets rid of the pile up of Ds, Ps or As,' I said. 'The banshee wasn't at Jane Doe's grave at all. He was up that tree because it gave him a view over the wall to The Garden. He was on stake-out, waiting for Sister— for Sonja.'
'But she has nothing to do with the cemetery,' said Kathi.
So, actually, they took a bit of convincing. 'Secondly,' I said, 'when the banshee came streaking in our direction, I thought at first he was on a beeline for me. Then he swerved and I think he started heading for Sonja instead.'
'Oh my God,' Lexy,' said Todd.' You think he thought you *were* Sonja? And then he saw her in the nick of time?'
'Maybe,' I said. 'If he had the wrong glasses on.' Sister Sonja Sunshine had been willowy with long flowing blonde hair. I was roughly the shape of a barrel with bushy hair the colour of bracken. 'Anyway, the third point is that she ran away. Remember? She vamoosed. She knew.'
'She knew what?' said Kathi. 'Did you tell her about the cemetery pranks?'
'They didn't come up,' I said. 'We had so much to talk about. I mean, given the parameters – where fairy lights and candle-scent matter – we had so much to talk about. I really am sorry.'

'Yeah,' said Kathi. 'Please don't retake your vows for your tenth anniversary.'
'Anyway, I'm not sure what I think she knew, but she knew something, right? Had to.'
'It's not too outlandish to cut and run when a stranger is sprinting towards you screaming holy murder. What did she say when you asked her about it the next time you saw her?'
'Um,' I said.
'No way,' said Kathi.
'We were deep in discussions of whether to hire chairs or buy seat pads,' I said.
'So you didn't touch on the fact that . . . Wait. How soon was it?'
'The next day,' I muttered.
'And you didn't touch on the fact that the night before you had been accosted by a howling maniac who came at you over a cemetery wall?'
'We hadn't quite given up on recovering the existing seat pads, or maybe just going with hard wooden chairs,' I said. 'I'm not defending myself here. I'm just telling you.'
'Defensively,' said Kathi. 'But you're right about one thing. She definitely knew more than she let on.'
'Thank you,' I said. 'For the second bit. Up yours for the first. But what makes you think so?'
'Because it's one thing that you didn't ask her because your head was so far up your ass you could have shouted it from behind your back teeth – no offence – but why didn't *she* bring it up with you? She didn't ask what happened after she left? Or apologize for leaving? Or share any theories about what the hell was going on?'
'Or even reassure me that the venue wasn't a known haunt of violent maniacs,' I said. 'You're right. That *is* weird. It didn't strike me at the time but that is totally cuckoo!'
'We need to go to Molly with this,' Todd said. 'She's going to absolutely love it!'

Cuento PD went through dispatchers like Todd goes through skincare regimens (lucky for me because I use up his half-bottles when he moves on to the next big thing) and I didn't recognize the young man who sat behind the desk today.

'Is Sergeant Rankinson in?' said Todd. 'We have information about the Fisher murder.'

'All of you?' he said. 'How come?'

It was either a good point or a question so dumb I couldn't frame an answer. So either he was made for this place or he'd be off to greener pastures very soon. In the meantime, he rang through the back and Molly was with us before you could say, 'I missed my honeymoon for this face and this welcome'.

We trailed through to an interview room, all three of us trying to hang back so we wouldn't be first. If I had been wearing trainers I would have stopped to tie both my laces, one foot after the other, so's not to be in the vanguard. Because, we could guess how Molly was going to react to the news that the cemetery pranks she had so resolutely refused to investigate had been nothing but the run-up to this murder she was now neck-deep in.

It didn't make much difference in the end. We sat in a row on the opposite side of the table from Molly and it was clear that she'd pick on whoever she wanted to pick on. Which, it turned out, was each of us one after the other.

'Come on then,' she said to Todd. 'You first while I'm fresh.'

'We saw the person who killed Sister-Sun-Fish-Sonja-Fister,' said Todd. No one else alive could reduce him to gibbering jelly like Molly.

'You all gave witness statements that you were together in that room during the window of opportunity,' Molly said. She swung round and fixed a glare on Kathi. 'What changed?'

'Not yesterday,' Kathi said. 'Earlier. One night in April. We witnessed a failed attempt.'

'All of you?'

'But not together,' I said. 'I was with the victim and these two were staking out the perpetrator.'

Molly gave us all a long hard look and then said, 'I'm going to need a cup of coffee.' She took a deep breath. 'Or maybe a quart of gin.'

FIFTEEN

'That was completely unnecessary,' said Todd. We had finally escaped from Molly's clutches after almost two hours of intense grilling.

'And really ungrateful,' Kathi said. She had offered Molly all her notes and charts and been given a brush off like a shower of dandruff on a tuxedo.

I had been going to offer my stash – well, the scrap of bombazine mainly – but I'd changed my mind now.

'We're just as bad,' I said. 'We should have gone straight from the cops to the Sex Volunteers.'

'And yet here we are,' said Todd. Where we were was sitting in a row at the bar of Barvissimo in downtown Cuento, each with our stiffener of choice: a June Bug for Kathi and a Mudslide for Todd. They had ordered these drinks one time in the middle of a flaming row, the topic of which was long forgotten. Kathi had found her insect-themed cocktail unexpectedly delicious and Todd had never tasted anything better than the Kahlua and extreme dairy he had chosen purely to upset Kathi with its dirty name. I was having a cup of tea, since the head waitress here was Welsh and had drummed the recipe into the entire staff. 'If you can make a Bloody Mary, you can make a bloody cuppa!' she would say, and so Barvissimo had become my favourite drinking spot in town.

'But, you're right of course,' Kathi said. 'We need to tell them asap.' Todd opened his mouth but managed not to speak. Kathi sighed. 'Just say it.'

'I'm over it,' said Todd.

'Waiting is worse!' Kathi barked. 'Say it so we can move on.'

'Jesus,' I said. '*I'll* say it. Rocky.'

'Thank you,' said Kathi. 'Yeah, c'mon. Drink up and let's go.'

Todd drained the ice-cream dregs from his glass and then ran a finger around the inside to scoop up the last of the cream and toffee sauce. 'We could order the same again and call them instead.'

But I was with Kathi. We needed to tell the Sex Volunteers that their annoyance had become a class one felony and we needed to do it in person. Apart from anything else that would make it easier to gauge if any of them was harbouring thoughts of suing us for not preventing it, not even foreseeing the possibility of it, in the course of six long months.

'Juni and Bob strike me as the litigious wing,' I said, as we drove off. 'Linda's too perky and Mitch is too . . .'

'Isn't he just?' said Kathi. Todd did not disagree.

We were headed to Juni Park's place first, since she was on the same side of the railroad tracks as the Ditch. Technically, that is. But the self-storage and budget-motel end of the south side of town shared no other features with the rolling acres of La Aplastado, where sprawling bungalows were dotted around sparsely in between greens and fairways as the single coil of streets wound its way lazily towards the country club at the centre. Juni Park's house was sand-coloured and neat, with tall, shining windows and glossy dark-green shrubs nestled up to its walls like the dust bunnies on my boat nestled up to the skirting boards. There was a triple garage disguised as more house and a glimpse of an inkblot-shaped pool and mini-me hot tub in the rear, locked behind elegant black railings. The house was empty, the mellow chimes of Juni's doorbell echoing inside and not so much as a pet dog stirring.

We moved on, trundling round on the big road to the only slightly less expensive streets over on the west side of town, where the lesser of Cuento's two country clubs was to be found. This was where Bob Larch's careful money management had landed him a two-storey house with double garage and a rectangular in-ground pool. His shrubs were dusty and his hot tub sat proud on a bit of decking but it was still the sort of neighbourhood where we felt we should knock and then beat a retreat if no one answered. And no one answered.

So we looped back towards Linda's patch, a funky neighbourhood where the street names – Calormen, Archenland, Cair Paravel and Calaver, just to take a few of the more bonkers examples – had led to its nickname: Narnia. Narnia had community gardens, bike paths, a pond full of deafening frogs and aggressive ducks who destroyed the tender crops in the community garden, and – so I had heard – a homeowner's association that made the Stasi look like Buddhists. Linda's house was painted purple with orange trim and had stalactites of macrame hanging-planters on the porch which were so thickly clustered I was sure she must come and go through the back door. Narnia wasn't the kind of place where neighbours would challenge you for checking the rear of a house, or not unless you were carrying a single-use plastic bag anyway, so we trooped round there, skirting Linda's above-ground pool. It had been colonized by a duck overflow and, as a consequence, had grown a green scum topping thicker than Todd's June Bug, as well as a mud surround and an impressive aroma. We banged on the door and peered in the kitchen window past the row of essential herbs – mint, parsley, basil and cannabis – growing in pots there. There was no answer.

'Right,' Todd. 'On to the Badlands.'

'Why, where does Mitch live?' I asked.

'First and A,' said Todd.

That was so far downtown you kind of forgot about it, tucked in there around the roots of the university, where for every real house there was another that had been turned into a student centre, a second-hand bookshop, or an infeasibly specific little lab where one kind of test was done on one kind of sample for one kind of research in one department, but by five hundred students at a time. I hadn't been to 1st and A since I had been married to Bran and didn't know how to navigate an American town or why the larger houses had enormous Greek letters on their walls or what 'catty-corner' meant.

'Maybe we'll find *all* of them there,' said Kathi, edging past the pool with both eyes on the ducks in case they flapped their wings suddenly and drenched her in green water.

'I can't see Juni Park attending a meeting surrounded by Mitch's bongs and beer cans,' said Todd. He was picking his way over the ground with his eyes on his feet in case of worms.

So it was me who saw, when we arrived at the front of the house again, the unexpected and unwelcome sight of Molly, standing on the other side of the street staring back at us.

'Guys,' I said.

'Well, this is going to be interesting,' Molly called over. 'Entertain me. What are you doing here, right after an interview during which you all promised me you weren't going to interfere?'

'We're not,' I said. 'We were here on a social visit. But there's no one in. Why? What are *you* doing here?'

There was no chance in hell Molly was going to tell us, but we worked it out for ourselves anyway. Because not only was the house across the street from Linda's surrounded by sunflowers, but it had enormous painted metal sunbursts stuck into the patches of grass on either side of the drive and – this was the clincher – a big X of bright yellow crime scene tape over the front door.

'Is that Sister Sunshine's house?' I said.

'Whose house is *that*?' said Molly, instead of answering.

'Linda Magic,' said Kathi.

'Fricking Narnia,' said Molly. 'Who the hell is Linda Magic and why are you looking for her?'

'One of the S— Four people who employed us to solve the pranks in the cemetery,' said Todd. 'Who tried to get the *Voyager* to take an interest and failed. Who tried to get *you* to investigate, which is – you know – your job, and failed.'

'What were you going to say?' said Molly. 'S . . .?'

'I changed my mind about saying it,' said Todd. 'The big clue was when I didn't say it.'

'Say it,' said Molly.

'Sex Volunteers,' said Todd.

Molly held up a hand to stop him saying any more and shook her head. 'Well, at least they got their wish. We just did a press conference with the *Voyager* where the April attempt you reported came up and I can assure you they are on it. But when was this that these "Sex Volunteers" tried to get the PD involved?'

'Seriously?' said Kathi. 'You're going to deny that the Sex Volunteers tried and then we tried and then they tried again and then we tried again not even an hour ago?'

'I was tuning you out except where it was relevant.'

'It was all relevant,' I said. 'And you ignored it for months and now someone's dead.'

'Aaaaaand we're done,' said Molly. 'Except for this. What did you say to Ms Magic? And what did she say to you? Because if you've contaminated a witness in advance—'

'She's not in,' I said.

'Lucky for you,' Molly said. 'Now git gawn.'

It still fascinates me when people here say things like 'git gawn' and 'critter' and 'gosh-darned' for real, but I've managed to stop smirking.

We bundled into the Jeep and, doing the fifteen miles an hour both decreed by the Narnia residents' association and necessitated by the free-range goats, chickens and homeschooled kids, we made an exit.

'Let's not go to Mitch's nasty lair after all,' Kathi said. Todd's hint about Mitch's household hygiene had hit home.

'You know what I'd like to do?' I said. 'Go back to Jane Doe's grave. Now we know her name – Nina Pradash – I want to pay my respects. We could pick up some flowers on the way.'

'You wouldn't mind being so near The Garden?' Kathi said.

'Enh,' I said.

So we chose the least supermarket-looking bunch of daisies and roses in the Narnia supermarket and trailed back over town to Turkey Farm Road and the big banshee tree overhanging Nina Pradash's and Vellanda Argyle's graves.

Where we caught up with all four of our missing Sex Volunteers.

'What brings you here?' said Todd, getting the question in before they asked us, with greater authority.

Linda Magic said, 'We're planning a new—'

Just as Bob said, 'We were reviewing an old—'

While Juni Park went for: 'We've lost our—'

And Mitch managed: 'We found a—'

Then Linda took over and said, 'Our process is hard to explain.' She was flipping back and forth through a notebook as if she was about to start reading stuff out.

'Actually,' said Kathi, 'we need to tell you something. And it's not good. How aware are you of what letters of the alphabet have been covered and what letters are still to go?'

'You said they were all done!' said Mitch, nervously zipping and unzipping his hoodie until the teeth whirred.

'We thought they were,' Kathi said. 'We assumed Jane Doe here was an F. But she's not. And then there was this murder.'

'*What?*' said Bob Larch. 'Oh! You mean the murder at the venue? I saw it in the *Voyager*. But . . . are you investigating it? And so you haven't been thinking about our problem? Because that's OK.'

'Well, no,' said Todd. 'It's not that. It's that Sister Sunshine's real name was Fisher and we think she's the far-from-grand grand finale. The F you were waiting for.'

'But-but-but . . .' said Juni, waving her slim silver pen as if it was a wand and she could use it to make all of us disappear. 'But she was killed somewhere else!'

'Over that wall,' said Todd, pointing. 'And that's where she was targeted the night there was someone in the tree too.'

'But-but-but . . .' said Bob, patting all his pockets one after the other, as if he was searching for a notebook or pen of his own. Or as if he wished he had a zip to whirr. 'Murder?' he asked us imploringly. '*Murder?*'

'Wow,' said Mitch. It was such an inadequate response to the situation that all three of his friends turned on him.

'Wow?' said Linda. '*Wow?*'

'Anyway, so we just wanted to give you a heads-up,' said Kathi. 'The cops are going to go public and they're going to want to talk to you, but you shouldn't take any of their shit. OK? Because another thing is that they're going to deny that you tried to get them to listen to you. They've more or less said so.'

'Go public with what?' said Mitch Verducci. 'A connection between an escalating series of mystifying occurrences and a murder?'

'And also, Mitch,' said Bob Larch, pointedly. 'The police are going to want to talk to us. Which some might say was the more salient point.'

'Yeah, but don't worry,' I said. 'You tried multiple times, right? Don't let them guilt trip you over that now. Or shift the blame or anything like that. OK?'

'We tried to get the police to listen to our worries,' said Juni Park. It wasn't a question. It wasn't really an echo either. What was it?

'You did, right?' I said. 'Didn't you?'

Juni looked at Linda and Linda looked at Bob. Bob looked at Mitch. 'Of course we did,' said Mitch. 'What's up with everyone today?'

'So now it's blown up into something much more serious,' Kathi said. 'Don't let them slither out of responsibility.'

'No way,' said Mitch. 'Feet to the fire. Truth to power. All that jazz.'

'Mitch,' said Juni. 'Stop talking. We need to discuss these developments before we go on the record. It concerns us all.'

I was lost and I wasn't alone. Kathi looked at Todd and he looked at me. I looked at my watch. 'Guys? I've got to go. I've got a client coming in. Can I take the Jeep and you get an Uber when you're done here?'

'I think we're *all* done here,' said Linda Magic. Then she dug deep and managed a little laugh. 'Sorry! That came out way too ominous-sounding. I'm just upset.'

'Of course you are,' said Todd. 'As well as everything else, she was your neighbour.'

'She was?' said Mitch. 'That's . . .' His voice died as the three others wheeled round to glare at him. 'News,' he said. 'That's news. I'm allowed to say that, aren't I?'

'Across the street and down a little,' said Linda, ignoring him. 'But yeah.'

'So you know all kinds of stuff about her that won't be in the general consciousness?' Mitch said, making Bob and Juni both start clamouring nonsense. They might as well have been la-la-la-ing.

'*What?*' he said. 'I just meant you could probably help the cops work out who killed her. What else?'

'What a strange individual that Mitchell Verducci is,' said Todd as we made our way home. 'Even the other three Sex Volunteers obviously think so.'

'And it's so surprising,' said Kathi. 'Guy that organizes cemetery tours with a bunch of other weirdos twice his age? You'd think he'd be extra-normal.' Todd ignored her. 'So, Lexy,' she went on. 'How come you have a client when you were supposed to be on your mini-honeymoon?'

'Someone called in a crisis,' I said. 'I didn't have the heart to refuse her. Them, actually. It's couples counselling but for some reason they picked me.'

'Don't tell them what happened to your wedding,' said Kathi. 'They'll fire you.'

But she couldn't have been more wrong. The couple that presented themselves at the door of my consultation room twenty minutes later knew exactly what had gone down at The Garden the day before. That was the main reason they picked me.

'I'm Collins and this is Cody,' the woman said. 'Thank you for seeing us, Lexy.'

Cody nodded but added nothing, seemingly used to his partner taking the lead. I would put them at about ten or twelve years in, with more than one kid but not more than three. Women like Collins tended to get ruthlessly efficient when the second baby came along, taking on the role of communications officer without a backward glance, rather than wasting time while their husbands marshalled their thoughts. With a fourth child though, the family CEO dynamic started to fray, and they turned the corner to being human and flawed again.

'Of course,' I said. 'So, let's start with some background. How long have you been married?'

'We're not married,' Collins said. So much for my hard-won expertise. 'We were supposed to be getting married in three months' time. Autumn had it all in hand and now we don't know what to do.'

'Autumn?' I said.

'Autumn Gold,' said Collins. 'Our wedding planner and celebrant.'

'Ah,' I said. 'And has something gone wrong?'

Collins gave me a look that silently screamed 'Duh'. Cody was watching her, whether for cues or out of adoration it was very hard to say.

'"Has something gone wrong?",' said Collins. 'Well, yeah, I'd say something went wrong when she was murdered yesterday.'

'I'm sorry, what?' I said. 'Did you say she was murdered yesterday?'

'Oh my God, you don't know?' said Collins. 'I didn't mean to break such devastating news! I thought you would know! I thought you were her client too.'

'I'm confused,' I said. '*My* wedding planner and celebrant was murdered yesterday. I'm sure yours is fine. You just got a garbled message. Somehow.'

Collins was staring at me. 'That's right,' she said. 'Sonja Fisher. I'm confused about why you're confused.'

'Now I'm really confused,' I said. 'My wedding celebrant was called Sister Sunshine, real name Sonja—'

'Fisher, right,' said Collins. 'We knew her as Autumn Gold.'

'Business plan,' said Cody suddenly, making me jump. 'Sonja was a brilliant businesswoman, in an overcrowded market. Four websites, four names, four complete stock switches. She was Gentle Blossom in spring, Sister Sunshine in summer, Autumn Gold in fall, and then Crystalline Ice in wintertime.'

'That's . . . nuts,' I said. 'Or it would be nuts, if it was true. I've seen her house. It's wall-to-wall sun.'

'All summer,' said Collins. 'Then it's leaves and gourds all fall. Icicles and shit through the holidays, and then pinker than Barbie.'

'That's not the genius part though,' said Cody. 'Any fool could do that.'

'Not relevant, babe,' said Collins. She turned to me. 'Can you help us? Do you have your receipts? Did she deal with your caterers and florists and dress designer and videographer? Because she had everything – all our paperwork and all the contacts and we can't begin to pick up where she left off. We tried the police but they were entirely unsympathetic.'

'Hang on,' I said. 'Do you want to talk to me as a fellow client of your wedding planner? Not as a therapist? Because that's not appropriate *at all*. I'm going to need to insist on clear professional boundaries.'

'Yeah, right,' Collins said. I stole a glance at Cody. He would be happier in the long run with someone a bit more shambolic. Living up to Collins would finish him off before he was fifty.

'What do you mean "yeah, right",' I said.

'You didn't mind Sister Sunshine blurring boundaries when it was helping you but now you're all ethics and scruples instead of helping me?' I noticed she said 'me' instead of 'us' even though she was talking about her wedding to Cody and I opened my mouth to point that out. Then I remembered some of the things I'd said in the lead-up to midsummer and I closed it again.

'Blurring boundaries?' I said.

'You're making out you know nothing about it?' said Collins. 'No one is that innocent.'

'I'm not claiming to be innocent,' I said. 'Just uninformed about this particular matter. Cody, can you help?'

Cody was only too pleased. 'The reason it's such a brilliant business plan and no one else does it,' he said, 'is that it's probably illegal. Or at least . . . Nah, it's illegal.'

'It being . . .?' I said. 'Because if Sister Sunshine was mixed up in a crime then that might be the motive for her murder and might even lead straight to the culprit. You should tell the police.'

'But it's the *perfect* crime,' said Cody. 'It's a victimless crime. She booked wedding venues, you see? She took venue dates off the open market by booking them herself and then she sold them on to her clients as part of her package. No one else does that.'

'Ohhhhhhh,' I said. My mum had been adamant that I shouldn't have been able to book my wedding venue less than six months out, but it all made sense now. 'But where's the crime?' I said. 'That sounds fine to me.'

'Extortion,' Cody said. 'Unfair business practice.'

'Extortion of what?' I said. This made no sense to me whatsoever. 'Unfair to whom? The venues? The rest of the wedding-industrial complex?'

Cody beamed. He really was enchanted by this business wheeze.

He was headed for a life as a crashing work bore, regaling his wife and family, possibly even his friends, with the minutiae of his office arrangements. Either that or he would dream up doomed infallible plan after doomed infallible plan and drag Collins through multiple bankruptcies. 'No, it was her clients she defrauded,' he said. 'She wouldn't have stayed in business if she hadn't treated the rest of the vendors with kid gloves. But weddings? You're not looking for repeat business.'

'But what was it she *did*?'

'I just told you,' Cody said.

'Pretend I'm really stupid,' I suggested, 'and I need to have it spelled out to me.'

'OK,' said Cody. 'Take us. Coll and me. She told us she might "manage to get a date" because she had just heard of a cancellation but we had to move quickly because it would soon be snapped up.'

'Oh my God!' I said, all thoughts of boundaries gone. 'That's almost word for word what she said to me!'

'And that kind of high-pressure selling technique might be fraud all on its own, but combined with false representation . . .'

'False representation of what?' I said.

'Because she had the date in her back pocket and it was going nowhere. Plus a cancellation is usually cheaper, right? But this was the full retail price from the venue and her mark-up too.'

'But it worked?' I said.

'On a bride?' said Cody, which was a good point. 'And once the bride pounces, Autumn Gold has a wedge. She got you a miracle date so of course you trust her to do everything. And you don't even notice the slow drip of enhancements and additions and upgrades and extras . . .'

He had just described my life from January to June. 'But how is it a victimless crime?' I asked.

'Duh,' said Collins, out loud this time. 'Because the bride gets her dream wedding.'

And the mother and father of the bride get a bill the size of Alaska and the groom gets months of wishing he had never met the bitch and florists and caterers and wedding dress designers all over the world get yachts.

'Well, I'm sorry to say, Collins and Cody,' I told them, 'that all the orders and invoices and delivery notes and receipts pertaining to my aborted wedding are still wherever Sister Sunshine kept them and it could be months before the police are finished with her paperwork and financials. So I can't help you, as a fellow client, but here we are with forty minutes left and I might be able to help you otherwise.'

'With what?' said Collins.

'Pre-wedding counselling,' I said. 'I think it's a pretty good idea, although alien to me as a buttoned-up Brit, obviously. In fact, I'm surprised Sister Sunshine never offered it as part of the deal.'

'Pre-wedding counselling?' Collins appeared to be struggling with the concept. 'Like how to not stress out about the seating plan? How to not guilt yourself about billing the bridesmaids for your bachelorette?'

'Not exactly,' I said. 'Maybe pre-*marriage* counselling is a better way to describe it. You could talk about what made you both sure you wanted to marry. What your expectations are. Have you discussed children? Money? Long-term plans? Dealbreakers? A wedding is just a party, but building a marriage is work.'

'Yeah, yeah, we did all that,' Collins said. 'He's hot and I'm hot. I want a housekeeper and two vacations a year – one beach, one ski. Two kids. There's plenty money. Long-term I'd like a weekend place in Tahoe. He's not allowed to get fat.'

I let the silence ring out for a few beats before I spoke again. I suppose it was admirable in a way: at least she wasn't hiding how shallow and horrible she was.

'Cody?' I said, trying to put my message into my eyes, although how do you say 'run' with any facial features except your mouth really?

'Yes, ma'am,' said Cody.

'Anything to add?'

'I don't want a fatty either.'

I was wrong. They were made for each other. 'And how about if one of you becomes seriously ill?' I said. 'What about multi-generational living with elderly parents in years to come? Does either of you have a religious faith to pass on?'

'What a downer!' said Collins. 'Did you thrash all that out with *your* honey?'

'Yes, Lexy,' said my mum, suddenly appearing in the doorway. 'Did you? Because you're being a bit of a wet blanket to these two lovely young people right at the start of their adventure.'

'Judith!' I said. It would be intolerable for Collins and Cody to find out she was my mum. 'I'm in session.'

'You're not parliament,' she said. 'I'm Lexy's mother,' she added, shaking Collins and Cody's hands, 'and I've been happily married for forty years. I can let you in on the secret of how it's done and I won't charge you a penny.'

I couldn't wait to hear what kind of mad crap she was going to come out with, but she surprised me. I think she surprised herself. She certainly blew the boots off Collins and Cody. 'Each of you be an open book, but each of you don't read too closely. No matter what, don't tell your gal pals or your buddy boys what an idiot he is or a what a drag she can be. And pick a sex night. It doesn't have to be only that night but make sure it's always that night.' She thought for a moment then shook her head. 'Nope, that's everything. You're welcome.'

SIXTEEN

'I can't stop thinking about my parents' sex night,' I said to Taylor, when we were tucked up in bed after a pleasant evening of tacos on the forecourt. My mum and dad had floated around in the pool until they were prunier than a pair of sundried walnuts, and I had taken photos of them draped over their flamingo inflatables with their drinks floating in mini-flamingo inflatables by their sides. I'd keep the pictures up my sleeve for blackmail purposes in the future.

'Ew,' said Taylor.

'I know, right? They've been here eight days so they must have—'

'Not them,' said Taylor. 'That's your "ew". No one thinks about their mom and pop having sex, Lexy.'

'Your mum was a single parent,' I said. 'Talk about getting off on a technicality.'

Then we felt the boat dip as someone stepped aboard at the porch end. 'If that's my mum, at least I'll know their night isn't Thursday,' I said. 'That's what's wrong: I think I'll be able to narrow it down by a process of elimination and then I won't be able to stop thinking about it.'

'Double ew,' Taylor said, as the bedroom door was swept wide open.

'Todd!' I said. 'Come in. No, please don't knock or anything.'

'What?' said Todd. 'I *didn't* knock. Lexy, you didn't drink any wine tonight, did you? But that's a conversation for another time. Point is, can you drive us to the cemetery? We had a call on the bat phone.'

'What conversation is this?' said Taylor.

'Um, are you sure, Todd?' I said. 'Now that things have stepped up seventeen notches to homicide, maybe you should leave it to Molly and her crew.'

'No way,' said Todd. 'The thing that's going down tonight is definitely prankish.'

'Taylor?' I said. 'Are you going to forbid me to go? I'd have to obey if you did.'

'Your wedding experienced a rapid unscheduled disassembly, in case you forgot,' Todd said.

'And you weren't going to "obey" anyway,' said Taylor. 'Although it would have been pretty funny.'

'Is she coming?' Kathi's voice sounded from the back of the motel, where she must have been standing in a bath shouting out of a high bathroom window. She was obviously not fit to drive.

'Jesus,' I said, batting back the covers and getting out of bed.

I had on a camisole and frilly shorts, still somewhat in honeymoon mode, and was glad of the chance to show them off. But of course Todd wasn't satisfied. 'Way to give up as soon as the ring's not even on the finger, Lexy,' he said, wagging his finger at my attire.

I dropped a sundress on over my shoulders and shoved my feet into my flip-flops. 'What have they told you?'

'Balloons,' said Todd. 'Some students were walking through the cemetery on a dare and saw a buttload of balloons tied to a grave. One of them had been on a local history tour of the place and still had Linda Magic's number in his phone.'

'You have my spousal permission to tangle with balloons,' Taylor said, turning over on his side to face away from us. 'Even water balloons. But maybe make sure the grave junkies told the cops too?'

Todd looked sober enough to me as he held back the oleander and toyon bushes to let me pass round the side of the motel and it occurred to me that maybe he had simply wanted the three of us together but felt he had to persuade me on factual grounds.

'I'm right back to normal now, by the way,' I said to him. 'You don't need to tiptoe round me anymore.'

'You *were* a howling maniac, to be fair,' said Todd, taking my advice and running a marathon with it.

'I wasn't,' I said. 'I was a fairly standard bride. It's just I'm usually so great – so low-maintenance and so reasonable – that it stuck out.'

'OK,' said Todd. I couldn't see him but I knew he was laughing. 'Did Taylor tell you that? Do you strike Taylor as low maintenance?'

'Taylor says what he thinks,' I said, trying to sound lofty. 'He just said "grave junkies", straight out. I think if he had something to discuss with me, he'd spit it out.' I realized I was following my mum's marital advice, loyal to Taylor when talking to Todd.

'There's straight-talking and there's straight-talking,' Todd said. 'I thought "grave junkies" was a little unfair.'

'What'd I miss?' said Kathi. She was out front, leaning up against the side of the Jeep and definitely over the limit. I felt a pang of guilt, pretty sure she was still decompressing from the angst of having a named part in my wedding. I'd make it up to her somehow.

'Todd reckons people who volunteer to hang around graveyards and turn them into a tourist attraction shouldn't be accused of being into graves,' I said.

'The Freaky Four?' Kathi said. 'It depends which one you're talking about. Hey, Judith.'

My mum and dad's room door had opened and my mum put her head out. She was shining with night cream and dressed in a long T-shirt-style nightie with Minnie Mouse on the front. Surely it couldn't be Thursday then.

'Are you going out sleuthing?' she said. 'Can I tag along? Your dad's asleep, Lexy.'

'Wore him out, huh, Judith?' Kathi said, with a leer. Then her face fell suddenly. 'I might be drunk.'

My mum added a pair of sensible slip-on sandals to her outfit and picked up her handbag from just inside the door. Then she closed it quietly and came over to join us. 'I saw students out for breakfast in their jammies this morning,' she said. 'And I thought: why not? While it's warm enough, why the hell not?'

'Because we're a professional outfit and we have a reputation to uphold?" I said.

Kathi blew a raspberry. 'Hop aboard, Judith, and come see the magic happen.'

It wasn't hard to find the grave in question. A balloon rose into the night sky as we pulled up by the cemetery gates and another one followed while we were making our way towards the spot in question. We arrived just in time to see a third eddy gently upwards, its string waving goodbye.

'Wow,' said Kathi.

'I'm surprised the headstone isn't floating away across the town,' said my mum. 'Like that old man's house.'

There might not have been enough balloons tied to the gravestone in front of us to dislodge it from its base in the grass, but there were more than I'd ever seen in any one place except a balloon shop. They jostled and squeaked against one another in a profusion of colour, making the chunk of grey granite look as if it had had a rainbow perm.

'How are they even attached?' said Todd. 'Oh right.'

There was a kind of rope hairnet over the top of the headstone with the balloon strings knotted on to its mesh. That made sense, I supposed. Whoever did this must have assembled it somewhere else or they'd definitely have been here – them and their helium pump – too long to have gone undetected.

'"Amelia Florez",' I read from the inscription. '"*Esposa amada, mama, abuela, tia. Con dios ahora*".'

'Florez,' said Kathi. 'With an F.'

'Yeah but it can't be,' Todd said. 'I think this is a fluke. Florez is a Mexican name. I bet it's her anniversary and the family did this in her honour. We're not as repressed as you guys.'

'Sicilians?' said Kathi. 'Oh you mean, Lexy and Judith?'

'I'm not repressed,' said my mum. 'I think it's pretty. Lexy, you have my permission to do this for me when I'm gone.'

'I thought you wanted cremated,' I said.

'Even better,' said my mum. 'All these balloons would definitely carry an urn up, up and away. Do you need a tissue, sweetheart? Do graves get to you?' This was to Kathi who was sniffing repeatedly. I smothered a laugh at the idea that Kathi would touch her face with someone else's tissue. Mind you, it wasn't like her to sniff either.

'You OK?' I said.

'I'm hungry,' Kathi said. 'And I'm sure I can smell snacks.'

I lifted my face and sniffed the air. I could smell something too. 'What is that?'

'It's so familiar,' said Todd. 'But, out of context, I can't seem to put my finger on it.'

'It's coming from over there,' said Kathi, literally following her nose away from the gate towards the newer sections of the cemetery, closer to the shared wall with The Garden.

'Keep your eyes peeled though,' I said. 'And stay away from big trees.'

'Yeah but what *is* that though?' said Todd. 'It's not taffy apples. And it's not fried onions. It's *so* familiar.'

'Not to me,' said my mum. 'It smells nice though. If we'd had anything but tacos for dinner I could get quite peckish off of that smell.'

'The tacos didn't agree with you, Judith?' said Kathi. It sounded like sympathy to the uninitiated. I knew she was sounding out the likelihood of my mum farting, or worse, in the Jeep on the way home.

'Oh, delicious!' my mum said. 'But so filling. You think a wee round flat thing and a dab of this and a dot of that wouldn't be much, but by the time you've got the rice and beans and cheese and cream and guacamole, it would choke a pig. Mind your feet, there!'

Kathi was drifting off the path and in danger of tangling with a wreath. She dropped her head until she had sorted herself out, then lifted it again with a deeper sniff than ever. 'It smells kind of burnt,' she said. 'But good burnt. Not bad burnt.'

'And buttery,' said Todd.

'I can see something,' I said, pointing. 'Look over there.'

A couple of rows beyond us and a couple of graves along, there was a patch of white in the darkness, a pretty blinding kind of a white with the moon shining down on it. It was a mound of something, rounded and solid.

'Is it an igloo?' said my mum. 'Can you still say "igloo"?'

'A butter igloo?' said Kathi.

'Is it popped balloons?' I said.

'It's certainly popped,' said Todd, as he strode to the edge of the grave. 'It's popcorn.'

'Popcorn!' said Kathi. 'Of course!'

'That is a lot of popcorn,' I said. 'Is there even a headstone under there?'

'One way to find out,' said Kathi, starting to snap on a pair of the latex gloves she always had about her person. 'Place your bets, folks.'

'Should you touch it though?' I said. 'Shouldn't we just call the police? Now that they're finally willing to tie the two cases together.'

Kathi had both gloves on now. 'Take a pic so we can replace them just right,' she said and then she plunged both hands into the apex of the popcorn igloo. 'How do you even pop this much popcorn?' she said.

'They would have had to start a year ago if they did it how we do it,' my mum said. 'In a pan on the hob with a knob of marg.'

'But even back in the present day,' I said, 'with a popcorn machine, it's not nothing. Maybe they bought it.'

'Already popped? That's going to stick in the memory of the popcorn vendor,' Todd said. 'Best customer of the year.'

'Found it!' said Kathi. She was scraping at the mound with both hands, like a mole. 'Shine your flashlight on this, Todd, will you?'

Todd shuffled forward, nudging his feet into the foothills of the popcorn mound without stepping on any and flattening it, and then directed his torch over Kathi's shoulder.

'Well, well, well,' she said. 'Jonathan Ford. Ford with an F. How do you like them Fuji apples?'

'We better put it back,' I said. 'I don't mind helping and getting buttery hands. They can't fingerprint popcorn, can they?'

In the end, we all pitched in to reheap the popcorn over the top of the grave, checking and rechecking against the picture until it looked the way it had before.

'And now we call the cops,' I said.

'Or we call Linda Magic and tell *her* to call the cops,' said Kathi. 'Tell her she should have called the cops straight out of the gate. We don't even have to admit we were here.' She had sobered up, apparently.

'Well, we better skedaddle asap rocky,' Todd said. 'In case anyone sees us. If the *Voyager* went public with news of the pranks after the presser, there might be some true-crime tourists moseying on over here.'

'Wouldn't they wait till morning?' said my mum, with a yawn. 'I'd wait till morning if it was me.'

'If they're in the crossover part of the Venn diagram of true-crime junkies and graveyard fans?' said Kathi. 'No way. Yep, Lexy, you're right. We need to haul buns.'

I was almost sure they were dialling up the American for my mum. Mosey? Haul buns? If one of them said 'lickety-split', 'raincheck' or 'booger' I'd know for sure. 'OK,' I said. 'What's the quickest route back to the gate and the Jeep?'

Todd lifted an arm, looking like Crazy Horse Mountain, and led us in an admittedly straight line, diagonally across the rows of graves, in completely the opposite direction from where my sense of direction, the skill Taylor calls my 'nonsense of direction', would have led me. And thank God he did, otherwise we would have missed it.

'What's that noise?' my mum said, when we were about halfway there, in sight of the wall that ran along Turkey Farm Road.

We all stopped walking and listened. There was a faint burbling, chuckling sound and an even fainter splishing and splashing.

'Water feature?' I said. Nothing about American graveyards would surprise me. When the weather is good enough to turn everything solar, it's amazing what pops up. Like Christmas trees covered in fairy lights miles out in the country in the middle of a field. An integral solar water feature in a gravestone would be nothing.

'No way,' said Todd. 'It would never get a permit. What *is* that?' He swerved from his path and, with an ear cocked, he started tracking the sound.

'It's getting louder,' I said.

'Because we're getting nearer,' said Kathi.

My mum drew level with Todd and said, 'Awwwwwww. Shoosh, everybody, and watch where you're shining your torches. We don't want to frighten them.'

I crept forward to see what she was looking at and almost let out an 'Awwwwww' of my own. There was a child's round, inflatable paddling pool set up on a grave in front of us and half-filled with water, on the surface of which a handful of tiny ducklings were bobbing around, peeping and chirping and beating their stubby little wings to cause miniscule tidal waves that then freaked them out and made them cheep even more.

And of course the grave this was all happening on belonged to a Gerhardt Friedrichsen. Friedrichsen . . . with an F.

'We can't leave them here,' my mum said. 'They might get eaten up by a bear before the police arrive. Or a boa constrictor or a crocodile.'

'I'll give you a skunk, a possum or even a raccoon,' said Kathi. 'But we're a long way from bear country, Judith, and about three thousand miles from the nearest crocodile.'

'Good!' said my mum. 'And no boa constrictors either?'

'A little closer,' Todd said. 'Five hundred miles due south. But, if these cuties have been OK so far, they'll probably be OK till Animal Control comes for them. We really seriously need to go.'

And we were in the nick of time. As we pulled away from our parking space by the gates another car – another Jeep, in fact – was pulling in behind us. This one was a Jeep the like of which was very familiar here in Cuento. It was what Noleen called a sorority Jeep, a pastel-hued going-away-to-college present from doting parents. And it was stuffed to the roll-bars with girls.

I put Todd's Jeep back in neutral and waved to them in the mirror. Then I stepped down and walked back.

'I told you we shouldn't have waited for Jayden to get out of the shower!' one of them said. 'We're not first.'

'First what?' I said.

'We're not doing anything wrong, ma'am,' the girl in the passenger seat said. She was golden and near-naked with long shiny hair and little string bracelets up both arms and round her legs too, like she had too many friends for her wrists and had had to use her ankles.

'*Ma'am?*' I said.

'Sir?'

'Wow,' I said. 'First what?'

'We heard the press conference and we're murderinos so here we are, ma'am, sir, ma'am . . . ma'am?' I couldn't think what she was on about until I realized that Todd, my mum and Kathi had all come to join me and were being addressed.

'You're murderinos?' said my mum. Surely she didn't know what that meant. I hadn't a clue.

'Uber murderinos,' said another golden, near-naked, shiny-haired girl leaning forward from the back seat. 'Did you see anything?'

'Ultra murderinos,' said a third. This one was completely different in that she had a UCC hoodie on so she was only half-naked. 'Is it true that the Wedding Whacker laid a trail of clues through the cemetery for, like, months?'

'Wedding Whacker?' I said. 'The person who murdered Sonja Fisher? Don't you think that's a little disrespectful?'

'The Eclipser?' said the driver. 'Because he snuffed out Sunshine?'

'*Did* you see anything?' said Hoodie.

'Is there anyone else in there?' said Friendship Bracelets. 'We thought if we came now, at night, we'd get our stuff live way before those be-yotches get their be-yotch butts down from Sac. Even though it's like way scary.'

'I have no idea what any of you are talking about,' said my mum. 'But you sound like you know how to enjoy yourselves, I'll give you that.'

'Yeah, you have fun, ladies,' said Todd. 'Knock yourselves out.'

'You don't want to come with and protect us, do you?' said the last of the gang, speaking up for the first time in a girlish voice and with a batting of her lashes. This was Jayden, fresh from her shower, with her wet hair gleaming gold and her gaydar lost down the plughole.

'You knock yourselves out,' said Todd, again.

When we were back in the Jeep, I asked him if he wasn't worried that they would destroy evidence.

'Murderinos? Never,' he said. 'But they will guard those ducklings with their lives. I wouldn't like to be the boa constrictor on a road trip that thinks it's snacking on duck tonight.'

'I know you're laughing at me,' my mum said. 'But I don't care. It sounds so glamorous. Say some more.'

'After I phone this in,' Kathi said, already punching numbers. 'Hello? Oh hi. This is Kathi Muntz, PI. Can I speak to Sergeant Rankinson, please? Oh, she's done for the night already? Hm? Oh, she's out chasing a lead. Well, could I leave a message for her, please? Yeah, can you tell her that I've had a call from my client Linda Magic warning of more activity in the Cuento Cemetery? In light of what happened yesterday, though, my associates and I didn't think it would be appropriate for us to go along there. But someone from the PD might want to check it out?' She paused. 'Huh? Oh, home. Just hanging.' She paused again, listening. 'Is that so? Well, OK. I'll look out for—' She stopped. 'Oh really? I see. Well, you got my report. I better go now. You have a safe shift now, you hear me? OK. Thanks. Bye. Shit. Fuck. Kill me. Hit the gas, Lex.'

'Problem?' I said.

'Molly left the precinct to come and find us at the Ditch about a half hour ago,' Kathi said. 'She's probably there right now waiting for us. So where the hell have we been?'

'A casino?' said my mum. She was still sure the mythical America she'd seen in the movies was just around the next corner.

'Mother, you're in your nightie,' I said. 'Late night gelato?'

'Judith, could you pretend you wanted to drive down a freeway under the stars?' said Kathi. 'Just for shits and giggles.'

'What do you mean "pretend"?' said my mum.

'What about traffic cams though?' said Todd. 'We *could* say we took Judith to see Bran's beige barn.'

It wasn't a bad idea. In fact, now he had said it there was no chance I'd get away without showing both my parents where I had spent my short marriage.

'Or,' said my mum, 'Walmart. And I was in my nightie so someone would take my photo and post it online.'

Genius. There was a Walmart in Muelleverde and we could take the camera-free back roads there and back. Or claim we had anyway.

SEVENTEEN

We met her in the car park.

'Leaving?' I said. 'I hope you haven't been bugging my dad.'

'Or my wife,' said Kathi.

'Or my husband,' said Todd.

'I came to see you guys,' Molly told us, 'to double-check that you were making extra sure to butt out. Where ya been?'

'Where ya goin?' said Kathi.

'Cemetery,' Molly said. '*Where* did you say you'd been?'

The temptation to keep this snappy dialogue going with an echo was strong as it was nuts, like how you always want to fling yourself off any cliff edge you get close to, or touch a plate some waiter just told you was hot enough to burn.

'Walmart,' my mum said. 'But it didn't work. No one took my picture from behind, giggling at me for being out in my nightie. I'll have to step it up a bit. Lex? I might need to borrow something.'

'Do you have tattoos you could show off, Judith?' said Todd. But my mum just smiled and waved and headed for her room. I'd have been happier with a more definite denial, personally.

'So you got the message then,' Kathi said. 'If you're going to the cemetery.'

'Yeah, I got the message that you'd got the message that something was going down in the old boneyard again tonight,' Molly said. 'Dispatch told me along with telling me that you told them you were at home. You know, when actually you were at Walmart.'

'Messages get garbled,' said Todd.

'Which is why we keep a sound file of all of them,' said Molly. 'If I lend you a knife, would you consider cutting the crap?'

'Or you could go to the cemetery,' I suggested. 'In case anyone who heard the press conference or read the *Voyager* doesn't want to go to Walmart, and tramples all over the crime scene. I'm saying crime scene, guessing you're no longer thinking of it as a "prank scene".'

'Don't push it,' Molly said. She considered saying more but in the end simply shook her head and made her way to her car.

'Nightcap?' said Todd. 'We can go to mine because Roger's on nights all week.'

'I'm bushed,' Kathi said.

'Yeah, me too. I'm done,' I said. 'Let's go out for breakfast in the morning. I want my mum and dad to experience the Red Raccoon while they're here anyway.'

Not only did they experience it, but I got a photo of their faces when the waitress banged down their plates. They'd gone for the tall stack, even after I'd tried to explain that pancakes here were different from pancakes there. What with the Canadian ham, country potatoes and three fried eggs, I wasn't making plans to cook them any lunch.

'That's a gammon steak,' said my dad. 'And what are those balls?'

'Whipped butter,' I told him. 'The wee jug is maple syrup.'

'Todd,' my mum said, 'I want to apologize from the bottom of my heart for the pancakes I made you eat last Christmas.'

'You're good,' said Todd, over his spinach egg-white scramble and fruit cup.

'Eggs and syrup,' said my dad. 'What a world!'

'Aaaaaaaanyway,' said Kathi. Her hangover had meant that she only ordered coffee and a piece of dry toast.

'Ford, Friedrichsen and Florez,' Todd said. 'What do we think?'

'Balloons, popcorn, kiddy pool full of ducklings,' Kathi added. 'I haven't had time to research the departed in question but unless they're all carnies, I don't feel too hopeful about one answer fitting all.'

'It's the first time there have been multiples on one night,' I put in. 'And the first time there have been multiples of the same initial too. Except D, if it's Doe, or P if it's Pradash. Or A if D'Ambrosi—'

'Right, right, right,' said Todd, which was fair enough. It did threaten bamboozlement every time we started in on it. 'So maybe Jonathan Ford . . . had a squeaky voice? Or . . . insisted that all his wives had breast enhancements.'

Kathi snorted. 'And Amelia Florez . . . what's funny about popcorn?'

'Maybe she was a dental hygienist,' said Todd.

'Or a really bad decorator,' I offered, proud to show off my grasp of American cultural life. 'If they had "knocked-down" the headstone too, I'd be sure of it.'

'Isn't it something, Judith?' said my dad. 'They're speaking English but they might as well break into Klingon.'

'And the kiddy pool full of ducklings?' said Todd.

'Marx Brothers?' said Kathi. 'Kind of a stretch, though.'

My dad made a peculiar noise in his nose and the back of his throat. I put down my fork and stood to prepare the Heimlich, but he waved me off. 'That's "Gaun yersels" in Klingon,' he said.

'Or,' said Todd, 'and hear me out because I think I'm on to something here: it *is* completely random, except for the fact of the three Fs.' I wound my hand to get him to keep talking, which the waitress mistook as a request for refills because I've got nothing much in the way of a cultural grasp to show off about.

'Warm that up for you, hon?' she asked my mum, hovering with two jugs of coffee.

'In the microwave?' my mum said. 'No offence, but this is really terrible coffee and boiling it isn't going to help.'

'Is it?' said the waitress, flipping open both the normal and decaf jugs and peering inside.

'No,' I told her. 'It's fine. Mum, it's diner coffee. That's what it tastes like.'

'Finally I understand Starbucks,' my mum muttered, as the waitress slunk off again. 'But go on, Todd. Don't let Lexy derail you.'

'OK,' Todd said. He pushed aside the bit of his titchy breakfast he couldn't manage and dabbed his lips. 'We think Sister Sunshine's murder was the culmination of a series of pranks.'

My mum and dad both nodded, through bulging mouthfuls of pancake.

'Paradigm shift,' said Kathi. 'No recognizable crescendo.'

'Damn,' said my mum. 'I understood a bit there, but it's gone back to normal. Keith, put some syrup in the coffee. It helps.'

'None at all,' said Todd. 'And for that reason among others we have to conclude we are not dealing with a sane mind here.'

'Right up your street, Lex,' said my dad. He never did learn the difference between what I did and psychiatry. I smiled at him anyway because he had the maple-syrup jug upside down over his coffee cup to let the last of it drop out in a thin stream. Neither of them knew you could just ask for more.

'But look what happened,' Todd said. 'The first *Voyager* article about the murder didn't mention the cemetery at all. Didn't mention much of anything. And so what's the murderous maniac's next move?'

'Ohhhhhhhhh!' said Kathi.

'What?' said my dad. 'You're right about the coffee, Judith.'

'Ohhhhhhhh!' said my mum. Then she grinned. 'I'm lying. Not a clue. Lexy?'

'Oh, I never know what they're on about when they start this game,' I said but, even as I was speaking, I suddenly thought that this time maybe I did. 'Unless . . .' I went on. 'Do you think the murderous maniac was . . . I don't know how to put it . . . hammering it home?'

'Exactly!' said Todd. 'Three big bonkers Fs all on the same night. They might as well have hired a plane to write "Duh!" in the sky.'

'And if only they'd waited one *more* night,' I said, 'Molly was about to go public with it anyway. In fact, they might even have still been in the cemetery releasing ducklings or wiping the butter off their hands when the presser went down.'

'Remarkable,' said my dad. 'Not a word. Not a single word. "Releasing ducklings"? "Presser went down"? Klingon, I'm telling you.'

'Didn't you fill him in when you got back?' I asked my mum.

'We had other things to be—' my mum managed to get out, before I bolted for the loos to avoid hearing the end of the sentence and having to know officially that it *was* Thursday after all.

My parents decided to go on a downtown walk after breakfast. They foresaw a great deal of excitement: my dad looking at tools in Deuce Hardware and my mum looking in the windows of all the nail bars. She couldn't wrap her brain round the number of nail bars and wanted to see for herself if each and every one could truly have customers in a town this size. That left Trinity itself to wander home, trying to work out what – if anything – to do next.

'We've turned it over to the cops,' said Kathi. 'I think we're done.'

'That double D still bothers me,' said Todd. 'Or double P. Or double A.' *He* was allowed to run through the options, apparently.

'We could make a report to the Sex Volunteers,' I said. 'A final report?'

'We made a final report,' said Kathi. 'And then another one.' We were waiting at the end of the block just before the road goes under the tracks to the wrong side of town. It's an annoying place to have a traffic light with a pedestrian crossing, since it means skulking outside the police station where, surprisingly often, we might be seen by Molly when we don't want to be.

'We need to make a final, final report,' I said. 'We all know things come in threes.'

'Except when they come in twenty-fours,' said Kathi. 'Hey! Speak of the devil!'

I was sure she meant Molly, not that I've got a guilty conscience or anything, so I looked down towards the cop shop but all was quiet there. Todd and Kathi were both looking up the street in the other direction.

'Did they see us?' Todd said.

'Who?'

'That car,' said Kathi, pointing. 'That was our clients. They *must* have seen us. They drove right past.'

'And we're so notable,' said Todd. He meant he was, but Kathi and I appreciated his kind gesture.

'They must have been in the police station,' I said. 'Maybe Molly hauled them in. Even so, why would they drive past without even a wave or a toot?'

The light changed and we crossed the road, away from the receding bumper and the puzzle, right into Molly's path. She was outside the front door of the cop shop, as if she'd been waiting for us.

'Yo!' she said in case we were going to pretend not to see her.

'It still bugs me that you say "Oy!" back to front,' I muttered. Then I lifted my voice. 'Yo, what?'

'Where you been?' she said, as we trooped over. 'Walmart again?'

She definitely didn't believe us about that, but she couldn't prove anything. Or so I assumed until she started speaking. 'That was a real good guess you made last night, you know.'

I waited with a polite smile on my face. Todd waited with a smile so polite it was infuriating. Kathi was stony-faced and Kathi's stony face is worthy of Easter Island.

'You remember?' Molly said. 'When you warned dispatch that someone might head on over to the cemetery and tamper with the evidence?'

'Not quite,' Kathi said. 'We passed on a message from our clients that someone might do that. And you've already had the opportunity to check that out with them.'

Molly frowned. 'What? Never mind. Way to miss the point, Muntz. The possibility of evidence-tampering was actually the takeaway there.'

'And did someone?' said Todd. 'Has someone? Did you catch them?'

'I'm working on catching some of them right now,' Molly said. 'Which would give me a grand total of ten separate collars.'

Kathi whistled. 'Ten, huh?'

I was confused. There were four sorority moppets in the pink Jeep. If Molly was hinting about trying to trick us into an admission – and she was; she's not exactly subtle – wouldn't there be eight? Or, if she wasn't aware of my mum's presence – which she was, though, then seven. Ten made no sense to me.

'You doing a little mental arithmetic there, Lexy?' she said.

'Me? No,' I said. 'Trying not to fart. We've been out for breakfast.'

Kathi moved away from me a step or two and Molly screwed her face up. I can still deploy the California distaste for crudeness to my advantage at times. I'd have been screwed if I'd moved to New York.

'Last night,' Molly said, 'we found a couple trying to spice up their marriage with a little roll in the popcorn.' She looked at us as if her eyes were lasers. We all managed to do a passable Tucker Carlson impersonation. Popcorn? *Huh?* 'And a pair of schoolkids huffing helium, thinking we wouldn't miss a few of the balloons.' Balloons? *Huh?* 'And a carload of murderinos rocked up too. Two of them took charge of the wildlife, like good citizens.' We didn't skip the Wildlife? *Huh?* faces completely, but my heart wasn't in it and Todd and Kathi looked uncomfortable too. 'The other two chicks were partying at the bounce house,' Molly said, 'but I'm still counting them all in together.'

'Bounce house?' I said.

'Bouncy castle in British,' said Todd, which was an excellent save and God knows what he would have done otherwise.

'So . . . you didn't know about the bounce house,' said Molly, as if Todd's save had never happened. 'But you did know about the rest of the crap.'

'Whose graves were they at?' said Kathi. 'There's no alphabet left. Are they starting again, but faster?'

'There was no pattern,' Molly said, even though she must have noticed the three Fs. And if the bouncy castle was on the grave of an F too, two-year-old Hiro would have seen the connection. Bloody *Trump* would have seen the connection.

I was dying to admit we had been there and ask her about the fourth grave, but Kathi was the PI here and it was her call.

'Ah, but they didn't do them in order last time either,' Kathi said. 'Truman was first, Cliveson came second. So, you see, Sergeant Rankinson, whichever four initials got the . . . what did you say? . . . balloons and birds and whatnot . . . it probably *is* the start of another set of twenty-four.'

'Twenty-six,' said Molly. 'Whatnot was a nice touch, Mrs Muntz. But I'm afraid your theory is a no-go. Last night the graves that got the extras were three Fs and a D. Well, possibly a D. Jane Doe.'

I gasped. I couldn't help it, even though Kathi sent me a withering look. And then I did much worse than gasp. 'Someone put up a bouncy castle on Jane Doe's grave?' I said.

'That's one of four options,' said Molly. 'What a lucky guess.'

'Shit,' I said.

'If that's shorthand for "Wow, I'm shit at this", I can only agree.' Molly gave me a hard stare, then opened the police station door behind her without even looking for the handle, spun on her crepe sole and walked away.

'Lexy!' said Todd, when the door had swung shut again.

'I know!' I said. 'I'm sorry!' But now we know we're right, don't we? It was a big sky-writing "Duh", like you said. Three more Fs and another go at the grave where the first attack happened. Hey, maybe the second attack started there too.'

'What?' said Kathi. 'We know it did. The banshee was up the tree above the bounce house grave. But *did* the dragon-mask attack start there too?'

'What?' I said. 'Oh right. No, I meant the second attack and the third attack. Or, you know, I meant the first and second attacks on Sister Sunshine. Not the night I got cat-scratched. What I'm saying is maybe the killer came over the wall on my wedding day to strangle Sister Sunshine and once again they had been hiding in that tree.'

'And it's not just that it's the best, most climbable, handiest tree for the purpose, right?' Kathi said. 'We're not missing something obvious, are we?'

'It isn't,' said Todd. 'We're not.'

'Jane Doe. Nina Pradash, Vellanda . . .' I said. 'No. There's no other way to make it fit, except the tree. We're not missing . . .'

'. . . anything,' Todd finished off for me. 'I just said that.'

'We're not missing . . .' I said.

'Someone blown out your pilot light there, Lexy?' said Kathi.

'Nah, it's nothing,' I said. 'Let's go home.'

I made it as far as the street before I stopped again. I looked back at the police station, the car park, the driveway, the door. Then I looked up towards the downtown and down towards the Ditch.

'What?' said Kathi.

'Right,' I said. 'What?'

'What?' said Todd. 'Actually, you know what? Never mind! Tell me later once you've recovered from your slow-mo.'

'Right,' I said, nodding. It was beginning to come clear. 'What? Never mind?'

'Switch her off and switch her on again, Todd,' Kathi said.

'I'm quoting Molly,' I said. 'Molly just said, "What?" and then she said, "Never mind".'

'She did?' said Kathi.

'You had just told her that we were passing on a message from the Sex Volunteers. And she said "What? Never mind". And then carried on to tell you you had missed the point.'

'Yeah, she was pissed because I corrected her,' Kathi said.

'But I don't think that's what it was,' I said. 'Can you remember the other thing you said?'

'Uh no,' said Kathi. 'Why, what'd I say?'

'You said she had already checked out for herself that what you were telling her was true.'

'Duh,' said Kathi. 'Right. Because the Sex Volunteers were just here. We saw them driving away. Maybe she needs new batteries, Todd.'

'But the thing is,' I said, 'that's not the only time that's happened. I can't remember when, but sometime in the last six months, I said to Molly that the Sex Volunteers had reported disturbances to her – or something; I can't remember the details – and she was exactly the same then. Like "They did? Huh?".'

'You know, Kathi, she might be right,' Todd said. 'Molly wouldn't take any blame for ignoring the Sex Volunteers' complaints.'

'Pig-headed denial,' Kathi said. 'Right on brand.'

'Perhaps,' I said. 'Only . . .'

I looked at the door of the police station again, and around the car park, and over at the pedestrian crossing, and towards the downtown and then finally down under the railway lines towards the ditch, the tomato fields and the back roads towards Mulleverde.

'We didn't actually just see the Sex Volunteers leaving the police station car park,' I said.

'That's right,' said Todd in a slow, careful voice, as if he was trying to get a chimp to put a knife down. 'We saw them drive past us while we waited to cross.'

'But I was *looking* at the police station,' I said. 'And then the car drove past in front of my eyes. You see?'

'Nope,' said Kathi.

'They weren't parked in here,' I said. 'Molly just confirmed it. They hadn't been to see her. And, like I said, it's not the first time it's happened. I saw them, walking in single file like The Beatles.' Todd squeaked. 'Not beetles. *The* Beatles. Abbey Road. And I thought they'd been to the cop shop because where else would they have been? But Molly denied it that time too.'

'They might have been to see us at the Ditch,' Kathi said. 'Let's go ask.'

'Not last time,' I said. 'But yeah, possibly today. Let's go and ask anyway.'

But the Sex Volunteers hadn't been to the Skweek to look for Kathi – 'Not that I should be working out of a laundromat anyway,' she said – and they hadn't asked in the office where to find any of the Trinity staff – 'Not that I'm employed to answer questions for you anyway,' Noleen said – and they hadn't been to the boat to find me, otherwise Diego and Hiro would have seen them because they were playing pirates onboard and Della was sitting on the porch watching them – 'Not that the slough is deep enough to drown in in June but anyway'. And they hadn't texted Todd or been seen by the family of tourists who were floating around the deep end of the motel pool or by Devin who was 'working from home' at the shallow end.

'Maybe they had business in Mulleverde and they heard there was traffic on the freeway,' Kathi said.

I ran up the stairs to the top walkway and stood on tiptoe to get a glimpse of I80. 'It's moving OK,' I shouted down. 'And what business could they have in Muelleverde? There's two pancake shacks and a Friends of the Library bookshop. Where the hell were they? Twice.'

I trotted down the stairs again and stood in the forecourt waiting for inspiration to strike as the sun beat down mercilessly on our heads. I glanced over at the tourists, hoping they had enough sunblock on, and was reassured to see an oily slick on the surface of the water all around them. Noleen would have to tip the pool cleaner extra but at least Kathi wouldn't be shaking sheets of skin off the bed linens before she washed them.

'Come on then,' Todd said. 'Spit-balling rules: no idea too dumb to float.'

'Maybe they enjoy countryside walks,' said Kathi.

'Although some ideas get really close,' said Todd. 'That's not countryside, Kathi. That's agricultural land. No, if Lexy's right and the Sex Volunteers weren't at the PD, and weren't here at the Ditch, then they might have been . . . at the self-storage facility? Where else could they have . . . Yep, must be.'

Of course. I smacked myself on the forehead with the heel of my hand. I walked past it every day I went to downtown or Swiss Sisters without a car and I was so used to looking at it I didn't see it anymore. I had never been inside – naturally, being Scottish – even though the size of my boat meant I had a more legitimate need for the place than almost anyone else in Cuento, unless there was an actual old woman literally living in a shoe with three sets of triplets.

Thankfully for whoever owned the business, indeed for whoever owned any of the eleven, yes eleven, self-storage facilities in Cuento, not many people had the same definition of 'need' as me. Despite the fact that most of the houses in town had such enormous garages that the houses looked like afterthoughts, and despite the fact that no one actually parked their cars in there, *and* that numerous houses also had basements, plus the fact that it wasn't legal to sell a house in California unless it had fitted wardrobes in the bedrooms, the good citizens of Beteo County 'needed' self-storage for the surfboards, snowboards, toboggans, skis, pedallos, wetsuits, golf carts, fishing rods, tents, hang-gliders, cross-trainers, rowing machines, exercise bikes, road bikes, trail bikes, mountain bikes, tricycles, tandems and unicycles they would never admit they weren't going to use again. Didgeridoos they had shipped home from Australia after the trip of a lifetime. Guitars they had lugged round Asia on gap years. Steel drums and bongos and congas and djembes that they swore to learn to play once they'd got them home. Oh, the self-storage needs of the people of Beteo County! They 'needed' self-storage for the antique furniture, carpets, paintings and chests full of china they wished their grannies had sold. They 'needed' self-storage for clothes they might slim back into, become able to carry off or land a job for, children's artwork they'd end up paying therapy bills about if they ditched it – and speaking of children – for cradles and strollers and cots and scooters and seesaws and trikes, Wendy houses, dolls houses, Barbie houses, Lego and teddies and bouncy chairs, baby clothes and toddler clothes and girls' clothes and boys' clothes, and the frocks of every princess of every Disney movie ever made, packed in tissue like the wedding dresses and prom dresses and outgrown tuxes and ugly sweaters, and – speaking of Christmas – for the fake trees and lights and inflatable reindeer and Easter, Independence Day, Halloween and Thanksgiving decorations they were still paying off on their credit cards, years after deciding it was too much faff to put them up and take them down again. And the motorbikes, boats and classic cars they were definitely going to finish fixing one day.

But, in spite knowing all of that, I still couldn't see why volunteers who organized cemetery walks would need more than a laptop, a printer and maybe a reference book or two.

'Let's just ask them,' Todd said. 'Let's go right now and ask them. Why are you being weird, Lexy?'

I blinked. How much of that had I said out loud.

'Go where though?' said Kathi. 'All around their houses again? Why not just call?'

'Look,' I said, 'if they're all together, can't we make a stab at guessing where it is they're headed? Let's at least try the cemetery first. And let's walk. In case there is actually somewhere else down here they might have been coming and going from that we wouldn't notice if we zip straight past in a car.'

'What? Why? What's with you?' Kathi said.

I didn't know. But here's something I do know: Todd asked why I was being weird and Kathi asked what was with me. So, later, when it turned out that I wasn't being weird at all and what was with me was a subconscious, gut-level but entirely correct, premonition of extreme dodginess, they should both have grovelled their apologies. Fat chance. When it turned out that my guts were golden and also it turned out – coincidentally, I admit – that my suggestion of walking led to us cracking the case, Todd and Kathi were struck by total amnesia.

EIGHTEEN

What made it even more infuriating was that they were quite happy to credit my dad, who was simply a fourth warm body in the mix.

We met my parents at the entrance to the forecourt, my dad carrying a pool scoop and a citrus picker and beaming from ear to ear. I had no idea if he was going to donate them to the motel as leaving gifts or check them as excess baggage but he looked happy. My mum had a sack of groceries that she was holding in her arms like a baby.

'They asked me "paper or plastic?", Lexy,' she said. 'It's just like being in a movie.'

'Where are you off to?' my dad said, standing both his new tools upright and holding them like Alpine poles.

'Cemetery,' said Todd.

'Excellent,' said my dad. 'It was pretty exciting when Judith chummed along. My turn this morning!' He pecked my mum on the cheek, loaded her up with his shopping as well as her own and fell into step with us. 'Thanks for telling me to bring a hat by the way, Lex,' he said as we hit the road. 'It's as hot as you told me it would be and I'd be hard-pressed to find anything except a baseball cap in the shops here.'

'You don't want a baseball cap, Keith?' said Kathi, who had a permanent dent round her forehead, and ears that bent outwards.

'No offence,' said my dad and, perhaps thinking of equity, turned to Todd and said, 'I don't want a nose stud either.'

'I'll rethink my Christmas gift plans,' said Todd drily.

We were now passing the self-storage facility's front gate and I suppose we had slowed. How could we not, when we were newly convinced that this was the frequent – well, twice over – destination of our clients for reasons we couldn't fathom? So I suppose we were almost stationary when the guy came out of the warehouse door, in his grey and orange livery to match the signage.

'Great!' he shouted. 'You came back! Furby had to go but he told me to look out for you.'

'Keep quiet and let me do the talking,' Kathi said, without moving her lips. 'Aw, we missed Furby?' she said.

'Yeah, but it's cool, it's cool,' said the kid, jogging towards us. 'And, you know, if you're cool, then maybe we don't write up a whole bunch of paperwork? No harm, no foul?'

'Fine by me,' Kathi said.

'Ms . . . Park?' said the kid. He was a moonlighting student as were so many of the service-industry frontliners in Cuento, and not the only one who tended to make you wonder how the hell he had got into a degree programme.

'Ms Magic,' said Kathi.

The kid grinned at me. 'You're Ms Park then,' he said. 'And Mr Verducci?' My dad opened his mouth, enticed by such glamour, but Todd cleared his throat. 'Me obviously,' he said. 'And this is Mr Larch.' My dad thought about that and decided it would have to do.

'Well, like I said,' the kid went on, 'no harm done.' He held out his hand in a fist, palm down. Kathi held out hers like a cup, palm up, and we all watched him drop a shiny key into it.

'I could have kicked myself when I realized I'd left it,' Kathi said. 'Did I literally walk away and there it was hanging out of the door?'

'Well, on the ground nearby,' the kid said, 'but no one else had been in that section so we knew it was you. Strictly speaking, we're supposed to take the key and add a master padlock and write up the incident and . . . man, you know!'

'I do,' Kathi said. 'Rules and regs, amirite? Rules and regs up the wazoo.'

'Cool,' the kid said. 'But . . . you know what? Maybe I should ask for some ID. You know, just . . .'

Kathi put her head on one side and gave him a kind look. 'How many foursomes, two men and two women, do you deal with on the average shift?' she said, extracting a twenty from her wallet and pressing it into the kid's hand. ''Preciate you saving us the admin, son.'

'Sure,' the kid said. 'Yeah, sure. Like, if you're happy, why would I go making work, right?'

'Right,' Kathi said.

'Right,' said the kid.

'Or I tell you what,' Kathi went on, 'if you're antsy about security, you can come with us right now and double-check that this key really does open that lock and we're who you know we are. How about that?'

'That'll work,' he said. Kathi gestured to him to go ahead and, unbelievably, he did. 'It's along here.' He turned and led us back in through the warehouse doors, up a set of open stairs and along a corridor, cold and grey and endless-looking from being so featureless. 'This is it,' he said, stopping at one of the metal doors with discreet numbers on little brass ovals. Then he gave a leering wink. '*If* you're who you say you are, anyway.'

Kathi inserted the key, turned it and pulled the door ajar.

'Good enough for me,' the kid said. 'You all have a great day, you hear.'

We watched him disappear along the passageway and go bounding back down the metal staircase with his whistles echoing.

'That is terrifying,' said Todd. 'I hope to God he's not pre-med.'

'That's who's going to be running the world?' said my dad. 'Thank God I'll be dead.'

'He's bound to realize what just happened and come back,' I said.

'I'm touched by your optimism,' said Kathi, 'but just in case you're right, we better hurry.' She pulled the door all the way open and we filed inside.

The smell was the first thing that hit. It wasn't as fresh as it had been the night before but it was still burnt and buttery and, if we had had any doubt, the three-foot-long plastic bag full of countless other scrumpled-up plastic bags all with a few unpopped kernels in their corners would have swept them away.

'Oh. My. God.'

'People really say that, son?' said my dad.

'This is a helium cannister,' Kathi said.

'And this is a heavy-duty air pump,' I added. 'Still, it must have taken a while to blow up a whole bouncy castle.'

And it wasn't just from the night before. It was all there: doll boxes, bacon wrappers, the storage case for a glass harmonica, a few nets of hay, almost finished, as if some goats and donkeys had feasted on most of it, a sturdy box with a carrying handle and airholes, which had 'LIVE POULTRY' stamped on the side in red letters, and of course the whiteboard with the map of the cemetery in permanent marker, and with names on numerous graves, and with lots and lots of crosses. Cliveson was crossed off. So was Nabhan, and Lavelle, and Quinn, and our old friends, D'Ambrosi, Kellog and Yount.

'Oh. My. *God!*' Kathi was standing in front of the board.

'What?' I said.

'Jane Doe,' she said. 'Nina Pradash. They got her down as X.'

'X!' I said. 'We never even thought of X! Wow. Of course! X!'

'I'm always getting on at your mother for asking what's happening when we're watching Bourne films,' said my dad, 'but I'm seeing the other side of it now. What's everybody on about?'

'Our clients killed my celebrant, Dad,' I said. 'Our clients did all the pranks themselves. And this was where they prepared them.'

'The call was coming from inside the house!' said my dad.

'Exactly, Keith,' said Todd. 'We were wrong about Xavier Reyes, being X *and* R. Jane Doe was X.'

'Damn,' said my dad. 'I thought I had it there but you've lost me again.'

'So . . . we must be wrong about Zita Boulley too?' said Kathi.

'Oh. My. God.' My dad was pointing at the whiteboard.

'What?' I said. 'Dad! What?'

'Nothing,' he told me. 'I thought it was my turn to say it, that's all.'

But Kathi was looking at the board for real. 'Z,' she said. She glanced at my dad. 'Zed, Keith. Look, everyone. There *is* a Z. Zeigler. But no cross against it.'

'Where . . . Where is that?' said Todd. He bent closer to the map. 'And what are those things marked with the little boxes? They're not graves.'

'Oh. My. God!' I said.

'Fill your boots, Lex,' said my dad.

'No, I'm not kidding,' I said. 'Those little oblongs are benches, Todd. That's the grave the Sex Volunteers took us to have that chat that time. Remember? Mitch suggested it and the others looked like they wanted to kill him and then . . . Oh!'

'Yes!' said Todd. 'Linda Magic broke into a sprint to get there before us and she hung her jacket over the memorial so we didn't see the name.'

'And that's the only one left,' Kathi said. 'Jane Doe was X. The murder was F—'

'But,' said Todd, 'what about—'

'The ducks and balloons and popcorn and shit were extra Fs,' Kathi said, 'because the *Voyager* didn't break the story—'

'But they've only marked Friedrichsen,' I said, pointing.

'Maybe they only meant to *do* Friedrichsen,' said Kathi. 'Before the murder. But then, afterwards, they hammered it home with Ford and Florez—'

'But why would they do any Fs, before the murder?' I said.

'Look, never mind that now,' Todd said, sounding strained. 'Point is, there's only Z to go and they were just here, collecting what they need for it? Right?'

'But it's going to be a damp squib after a murder,' Kathi said. 'I hope.'

'Yeah, it's sure to be,' Todd said, but he sounded less sure than I had ever heard him.

'So,' I said. 'Nine one one? And try to explain all of this? Again! Or . . . Trinity to the rescue?'

'If I've got a vote,' said my dad, 'I think you shouldn't count on being able to explain this to anyone. I'm at sea and I'm looking right at the whiteboard.'

'Dad, can we drop you off at the police station? And you bring Molly back here and show her?' I said. 'And tell her we've gone . . . to . . .'

'Another case?' Kathi suggested, then she wrinkled her nose up and shook her head.

'Shopping?' said Todd. 'No that's too me and not enough you two.'

'Tell her we've gone to patrol the cemetery,' I said. 'If she wanted it off-limits she should have put some of her yellow ribbon round the perimeter. Tell her whatever you want, Dad. Let's go.'

'Do you think she'll put me in the drunk tank?' said my dad. 'Or even a room with a two-way mirror? Is there a desk sergeant? Will they all have holsters you can see when they're in their shirt-sleeves?'

He didn't really want answers. He was just living his best life: a walk-on part in a cop show. 'Don't accept anything from the vending machine,' I told him. 'And tell them we found the key on the pavement.'

'Sidewalk, Lexy,' my dad said.

'Stop off and tell the kid to keep his mouth shut and say nothing,' added Kathi. 'He's as dumb as a box of rocks but he doesn't deserve to be fired for it.'

'Gotcha,' said my dad, trying the word out for the first time as far as I knew. 'You go. I got this. And hey, be careful out there.'

'I love you, you numpty,' I said, dropping a kiss on his cheek before skedaddling.

We drove to a side street off Turkey Farm Road, parked the Jeep and went the rest of the way on foot, watching carefully for any or all of the Sex Volunteers, who actually no longer deserved an affectionate nickname.

It was baking hot, the shade trees dusty and dry-smelling already even this early in the summer, and the sunny gaps between them making my scalp pulse.

'We need a cover story,' said Todd, as we passed through the gates.

'If they're even here,' I said. 'Won't they wait till nightfall?'

'So we identify a good surveillance spot,' said Kathi, 'and decide on shifts. I can take the first six hours if one of you goes to the Skweek when Della leaves to pick up the kids.'

'Shouldn't we have . . . I dunno . . . binoculars or night-vision thingies?' I said.

Kathi patted the side pocket of her utility vest. 'I got protein bars too,' she said. 'And a hip flask.'

'Yeah?' said Todd.

'Of water,' said Kathi.

Turned out we were all wrong anyway. The Sex Volunteers weren't setting up their last hurrah, or leaving again having done so, or planning to arrive under cover of darkness. And that's not all they weren't either.

'They're here!' Kathi hissed as we edged towards the two benches, sneaking from gravestone to gravestone like the cartoon Pink Panther. She went for her binocular pocket but stopped at the first rasp of Velcro.

'What do we do now?' breathed Todd. 'Lexy, you have a better view. What are they doing?'

'Bob Larch is biting his nails and Linda Magic is . . . crying,' I said. 'Juni Park is fiddling with that bloody pen. I can see Mitch, but I don't know what he's doing. He's got his head down.'

'I wish we had gone for the cops,' said Todd. 'Or told Keith to bring them here, at least.'

'Oh, sod this for a game of soldiers,' Kathi said. It was one of her favourite British sayings but I was never sure if she knew what it meant. In this instance, if she was using it correctly, it would be accompanied by her—

I yelped, as Kathi proved she knew exactly what she was saying by standing up and striding towards the two benches and the angel statue. Todd and I hustled after her. My pulse was rattling and my heart felt as if it was lodged just behind my back teeth, but Bob was still biting his nails and Linda was wiping her eyes. Mitch was fiddling with his phone and Juni was wringing her hands as best she could without dropping her silver pen. No guns. I calmed down a bit and waited for someone to say something.

'I believe this is yours,' Kathi said, holding up the little shiny key. 'We've just spent a pretty interesting half hour in your unit. And the police are on their way.'

'How did you get the key to a private storage unit?' said Juni Park.

'Someone dropped it,' I said.

'Bob?' said Linda. '*You* had the key. You dropped it?'

'On the ground, outside our unit,' Bob said. 'It's over, Lindy. I wanted it to be over.'

'It's only just beginning,' said Mitch, speaking for the first time. 'It's going to be huge.'

'How did you know it was ours?' said Juni.

'We got lucky,' said Todd, which had the advantage of being true.

'So, obviously, we'll go to the police,' said Mitch. 'If you insist.'

'If . . .?' I said.

'And it might be better that way,' he went on.

'Mitch, for God's sake,' said Bob. It came out like a wail.

'If we insist?' I said. 'Might be better? I can't even work out which one of you . . . Not a single one of you is making any sense!'

'Why are you still so upset?' said Linda Magic. 'Is it your wedding?'

'I'm "still" upset too,' Kathi said. 'Quirk of mine.'

'I'm also "still" upset,' said Todd. 'And I've been married for eight hundred and fifty gay years. What the hell is wrong with you people?'

'Oh no!' said Juni Park. She glared the other three. 'Look at their faces! I told you it wouldn't work.'

'Was it you?' I said. 'Which one of you did it?'

'We all worked together,' said Bob Larch. 'Using our different strengths.' His words made me feel sick.

'They're not talking about Operation Berendt,' said Juni.

'We never settled on that name,' said Linda. 'Operation Masquerade is still my favourite.'

'Tiny Coffins,' said Mitch. 'Works on more than one level.'
'Eyes Wide Open,' said Bob. 'I never agreed that was too much of a clue.'
'It doesn't matter!' Juni said. Yelled, really. 'They're not talking about our initiative.'
'There's not much in it,' I said, 'but, Juni, *you* are making a tiny wee bit more sense than the rest. No, of course, we're not talking about whatever you're all talking about. We just want to know which one of you killed Sister Sunshine.'
'No, no, no, no, no, no,' said Mitch. 'I gave that up. They made me.'
'*What?*' I said.
'None of us killed Sister Sunshine,' said Juni. 'Someone killing Sister Sunshine ruined everything.'
'What garbage is this?' Kathi said. 'What heaping stinking garbage are you trying to make us swallow right now?' I knew she was really angry, because the imagery she was using was enough to make her gag in other moods. 'You're trying to tell us that after you had mopped up twenty-three letters of the alphabet with stuff that could just about be called pranks, even if some of them were real nasty pranks . . .' She ran out of breath, but luckily Todd was there to take over.
'And then one of those last three letters matched the name on the grave where a banshee climbed a tree to stake out a murder victim, and then the second last letter matched the name of the victim and then here you all are at the last letter of all . . .' He lifted his arms and shook his head.
'That there's some *mistake*?' I finished off for him. It was short but it was punchy.
'That tree overhangs more than one grave,' said Juni Park. 'That would have been extremely sloppy.'
'And plus the bounce house was our X,' Mitch said.
'And that poor woman had five different names,' said Linda Magic. 'Blossom, Sunshine, Gold, Ice and Fisher. I don't know what the chances are that one of her five would match up to a certain particular one of our twenty-six, but it's like that thing of how many people you need in a group to be fifty-fifty of a shared birthday, isn't it?'
'What?' I said. 'Three hundred and sixty-five and a wee bit for the leap years, of course. So Sonja *Fisher* is a humungous coincidence. You must think we're stupid.'

'A little bit,' said Bob Larch. 'It's twenty-three.'
'Right, until the murder,' said Todd. 'What's your point?'
'No, it's twenty-three *people*,' said Bob. 'Before you get evens on a shared birthday. And we haven't done anything for Z. This is simply where the benches are.'

'So you're really claiming you didn't kill Sister Sunshine and then do a big triple drumroll of Fs to make sure people got the message?'

'What?' said Linda Magic. 'Of course we didn't. We did the Fs to make it plain that we *hadn't* done an F yet. That we *didn't* kill Sister Sunshine. And we put that bounce house up at X when we did to make it plain that the . . . why did you say "banshee"? . . . was nothing to do with us either.'

'Huh,' I said.

'There was a majority opinion that it was the right thing to do,' said Mitchell Verducci. 'Three against one.' No prizes for guessing who the one was.

'Look, budge up a bit, will you?' I said. 'Let's all sit and talk this out.'

Todd did a big fake 'counsellor' sneeze but he also started directing people to the right bench: him, Mitch, Juni and Bob on one; Kathi, Linda and me with our elephantine arses on the other. He can't resist making the point of what fantastic shape he's in, even at moments such as this.

'OK,' Kathi said. 'Start with this. What was the point of the pranks?'

'To put us on the map,' said Juni. 'We're never going to be as steeped in history as Savannah.'

'Ahhhhhh!' said Todd. '*Midnight in The Garden of Good and Evil*.'

'Huh?' I said.

'It's a book by a man called John . . . Ahhhhhhh! Hence Operation Berendt? . . . about the historic graveyards of the city of Savannah. It really shot the place into the tourism stratosphere.'

'But *Masquerade* has a proper puzzle,' said Linda. 'Like ours.'

'*Masquerade* the Jimmy Stewart movie?' said Kathi.

'Cary Grant,' I said. 'But surely you meant the children's book with the real live treasure hunt in it? We had a copy in the house and I remember my dad telling me about before the jewel was found. All the proto-Pokémon-Go madness gripping the nation.'

'But it was a children's book!' said Mitchell. 'And the riddle is solved. The treasure's been found. The tiny coffins of Edinburgh, on the other hand, are still as mysterious as ever. And more relevant.'

'But we solved your riddle even before you finished it,' said Kathi. 'An alphabet of pranks.'

'Is only the first level,' said Bob Larch. 'You fell right into our trap. Bwah-hah-hah-hahhhh.'

'Oh we did, did we?' said Todd, sounding more pissed off about being bested than he had when he thought he was talking to four murderers.

'We hoped that the less mentally agile of the fans would think exactly what you thought,' said Mitch. 'But even at that we thought you'd file Jane Doe under X.'

'Yes,' said Linda. 'That was disappointing.'

'What are you talking about?' said Kathi.

'Another reason to go with Operation Eyes Wide Open,' said Bob. 'Or Eyes Wide Shut. Or Operation Angels or something like that. We needed to give people an extra push, to make sure they ended up here.'

'Ohhhhhhhh!' I said. 'Here with the weeping "Blink" angel?'

'What are you dribbling on about?' said Kathi.

'It's an episode of *Dr Who*,' said Mitch in a voice that was equal parts scorn and shock. As if she had asked who wrote *Hamlet*.

'But all three of us agreed that once the serious contenders had gotten past the alphabet and not been distracted by the specifics,' said Juni – neither Todd, Kathi nor I said 'none taken' out loud but we were all thinking it in spades, I'm sure – 'and once the cream of the crop had solved the Nina Pradash red herring, eventually they would realize that what they were left with was Z. The Zeigler family are the only ones with that initial in the whole of this graveyard. We were so proud of it. We worked so hard.'

'And?' said Kathi. 'Then what?'

'And then some crass and clumsy idiot came galloping through the middle of years' worth of work and murdered Sonja Fisher.'

'That's not what I meant,' said Kathi.

Linda Magic beamed. 'I know. You meant "What's the next part of the quest?". We got you!'

'But to return to Sister Sunshine being murdered,' I said.

'A thing we would *never* have done,' said Mitch. 'You must be able to see that, you three. We wouldn't have killed someone! If we'd been caught, the riddle would be ruined. There would be no puzzle left. Just some grubby little crime scene.'

'But wait though,' I said. 'Mitchell, wasn't it you who wanted to claim the Sister Sunshine murder? Like . . . fold it in?'

'Exactly,' said Mitchell. 'Gift horse and mouth, right? Only I couldn't get the rest of them on board. It would have been so perfect. So unsolvable, so impossible to tie it to the rest. Because it *wasn't* tied to the rest. See? It would look random, because it *was* random. People would be beating a path to our cemetery forever, trying to make sense of it.'

'And we'd know all that,' said Bob Larch, leaning forward so he could address Mitchell at the far end of the bench, 'only if our families told us about it on their monthly visits. Because you're not allowed social media while you're serving a life sentence for murder.' He stopped glaring at Mitch and turned beseeching eyes on Kathi and me. Todd was too close for him to focus on. 'It's all gotten completely out of hand,' he said. 'Please help us.'

But it was too late. They hadn't put the mee-maws on so we hadn't heard the squad cars, but we all heard the tramp of police-issue footwear on the raked gravel paths and the creak and squawk of their shoulder radios too. Molly was at the head of an impressive cohort of plain clothes and back-up uniforms, including Soft Cop and Mills of God, and she started speaking as soon as she had us all in view.

'Bob Larch, Mitchell Verducci, Linda Magic, Juni Park, you are under arrest for the murder of Sonja Fisher. You have the right to remain silent.' Her minions were hard at work with the handcuffs and suddenly Todd was all alone on his bench. 'Anything you say can and will be used against you in a court of law.' Linda was plucked out of her seat between Kathi and me. 'You have a right to an attorney. If you cannot afford one, one will be appointed for you. And if I had more officers here,' she went on without so much as a pause for breath, 'then the three of *you* would head for jail right along with them. I have had it! So, fair warning, do not push me.'

NINETEEN

We were all sitting on the porch of the boat when Taylor came back from the wetlands.

'Good day?' he said, kissing my head and dropping on to the floor beside me to take off his boots and dangle his feet in the slough. He's got to wear long trousers, thick socks and sturdy boots year-round in case of snakes, black widows and water leeches so, in June, July and August, it is not great to be around when he peels them off. He unzips the bottom of his trousers before the drive home, naturally – Taylor owned no clothes without an element of transformation until he bought his kilt – and he used to take his boots off and leave them in the back-passenger footwell with the socks stuffed inside, letting his feet sizzle away in flip-flops with the car AC set to Siberia and angled downwards, but I vetoed that after this one time when he forgot to take his boots, with their sock stuffing, *out* of the back-passenger footwell and left the car parked in the sun for a week while we were on holiday. I truly thought something had died in there. Something bigger than a rodent too. So we've come to an arrangement: he takes his boots and socks off out here on the porch, throws his socks in the slough and puts his boots – full of really cheap, perfumed cat litter – on the narrowest bit of the side deck not near any of our windows. Of course, I never meant him to do it when we had company but now wasn't the time to bring it up.

'Your feet smell,' said Diego.

'*Papi*,' said Della. '*No seas malo.*'

'*Lo siento, Mama*,' said Diego.

'*Tio* Taylor,' said Hiro, quite quietly for her. 'Your feet are nice and stinky. Yay you.'

She smiled with pride and gave her big brother a withering look, enjoying the chance to show him how kindness was done.

Taylor, incapable of taking offence at something so blameless as smelling like a burst sewer, ruffled each of their little heads en route to the side of the boat to plunge his offending extremities in the greenish, lukewarm slough and probably kill a few fish.

Kathi stared at the children's heads for a minute or two, probably wishing she could snatch them both up and plop them in the bath right now to scrub Taylor's hand and transferred-sock filth off of their curls. I saw her fight it, with deep breaths and a deliberate turn of her head to face the other way. I was so proud of her. Unfortunately she saw me being proud of her and flipped me the bird.

'No!' said Hiro, back to full volume. '*Abuela* Kathi! Bad finger!'

'Ahhhhhhh,' said Taylor as his feet hit the water. 'Oooooh, that's better.'

'Hard day?' my mum said. 'Ours has been thrilling.'

'Too thrilling for little ears,' I said. 'I'll tell you later.'

'We're leaving anyway,' Della said. 'Bath time, *niños*!'

Grumbling and bargaining, Diego in particular making an environment-based case for less washing, they made their way back to the motel, passing Noleen and a jug of Margaritas.

When we were all served, we filled Taylor in. He's a rewarding person to regale with stuff, unstinting on wows and whistles, always ready with a follow-up, and not above a set-up question to hand over glory. He did one of them right now.

'So your clients are a bunch of murderers?' he said. 'You can turn this into a true-crime bestseller. Or a podcast anyway.'

'Of course, our clients aren't murderers!' I said, quite polite since we were still technically in the honeymoon period, and also my parents were there.

'Bullshit!' said Kathi, for whom neither of those two things was a factor.

'Stick to ornithology, birdbrain,' said Todd, since Kathi had bagsied the other tactic and going clever with the putdown was all that was left for him. 'We believe our clients. Anyone who saw their faces when the handcuffs were slapped on knows they're innocent. As far as murder goes. Unfortunately, Molly wasn't facing that way. She was giving *us* the stink-eye.'

'So what do you do now?' Taylor said. 'Keep out of it and wait for the cops to catch up?' The look he gave me wasn't exactly stink-eye but it sure as hell wasn't rose-petal-eye either.

'No,' I said. 'What we do now is work away behind Molly's back doing what she should be doing, proving that our clients are innocent, ideally by finding the real murderer.'

'That sounds dangerous,' said Taylor with half a glance towards my parents.

'Probably,' I said.

Taylor waited for my mum and dad to weigh in on his side, clamouring and wittering, trying to ban me from taking chances with my precious, only-child self, proving that he knew my parents well enough to be getting fond of them but he didn't know them like I did.

'That's my good girl,' said my dad. 'And all the gods go with you!'

'Judith?' said Taylor.

'Lexy, if you're sticking it to the man, can I come?'

I could hardly say no. They had flown thousands of miles and spent thousands of pounds for a wedding that didn't happen. If my mum decided she'd rather work a Trinity case than see Monterey or Mount Shasta or even Bodega Bay where they filmed *The Birds*, then I could hardly sit there and refuse her outright.

Instead I played for time, hoping something would come to me in the morning.

Luckily, my dad had zero interest in finding Sister Sunshine's killer and they're joined at the hip after all these years. And, besides, the early stages of an investigation are a lot of library work and arguing. And, most crucial of all, Roger let them have his convertible, after which they were a goner. My mum tied a scarf around her head like Grace Kelly and my dad worked out he could drive an automatic with his arm round her and they took off for the Pacific Coast Highway, telling me not to worry if they stayed out all night, because the glamour of it all would only be complete if there was an 'iconic roadside motel' involved.

'What's the Ditch?' said Noleen, as we waved them off. 'Chopped liver?'

'I hope Roger's got top-flight insurance,' I said, as my dad hit the wrong side of the road, remembered, over-corrected and kicked up a plume of dust from the gutter.

'Right then,' Kathi said. 'Into the office. Oh, wait!'

'Jesus,' I said. 'Porch of the boat. Let's go.'

'She was single,' said Todd, once we were ensconced, 'and childless. Her parents are dead. She was an only child. She ran her own solo business. Her friends have had only nuts-but-kind things to say about her and her client testimonials are wall-to-wall five stars.'

'But it can't have been a random killing,' Kathi said. 'Because it was a crazy place to do it and it was the second attempt. So someone somewhere in Sister Sunshine's life had a motive to murder her.'

'How do you know what her friends have been saying?' I asked.

'Memorial Facebook page,' said Todd. He took his phone out of his pocket, hit some buttons and tossed it over to me. I hate him throwing his phone around on deck. He'd never take the blame if it ended up in the slough.

On the screen was a picture of Sister Sunshine inside a floral frame with a flickering candle filter over her face so that she looked as if she was endlessly dripping out and sniffing back in a long yellow snotter. I dragged my eyes away and scrolled down.

Todd was right. These were real friends, not Facebook lice, as attested to by the fact that the messages were accompanied by photographs of hugging, smiling groups featuring Sister Sunshine. There they were at Burning Man, at Earth Day, at an olive harvest, in a sunflower field, in an almond orchard, making snow angels, in holiday bars with leis round their necks, on dusty hillsides with keffiyehs up over their mouths. And every single one of them had plaudits and paeans for Sonja Fisher. 'A shining light', 'a force for good', 'following her own wandering star', 'best foot massage in the northern hemisphere' . . . And then there were the eulogies from her clients over the years: 'Everyone said we couldn't get married on skis but Crystal made it happen'; 'Gennie made our promise ceremony everything we dreamed of. I only wish she was a doula too'; 'Sister S is the spirit of Summer and made our day dazzle', 'With a combined age of 97, we knew a June wedding wasn't for us this time, and Autumn brought joy to our Golden Day'.

'Professional contacts?' I said.

'Keep reading,' said Kathi. 'Or no, don't, pass it back, because my God, you read slowly and you breathe loud too. But the florists she works with offered free flowers for her funeral and three different caterers are bargaining to donate the repast.'

'The what?'

'Funeral food,' said Todd.

'Purvey,' I said. 'Gotcha. So who else is there? A MAGAt? Someone making a political point? Because she was quite . . . alternative . . . wasn't she?'

'In Flagsville, Kentucky, she might have been,' Todd said. 'In Bibletown, Missouri. But in Cuento? If some unhinged right-winger started taking out hippies in northern California, there'd be no one left.' It was a fair point.

'Nah, this is personal,' Kathi said. She was still scrolling down the memorial page on Todd's phone. 'This is someone with beef and no one on this page even has any smoked tofu, which makes sense because who's going to have beef with a wedding planner?'

I opened my mouth to speak. Not that I had anything to say but sometimes, when there's a vague thought wafting around the back of my mind like a dust bunny and I start talking, it balls up and falls out. They mock me but it's worth it for a good cause. Anyway, on this occasion, Todd cut me off before I got going.

'If her job is even relevant,' he said. 'We don't know anything about her past, her relationships, even her other neighbours apart from Linda. My God, Linda!'

'I know,' I said, completely distracted from my dust bunny. 'I can't stand thinking about the four of them sitting in jail. I mean, they're beyond weird but, like you said, if "weird" got you locked up in northern California, there'd be no one to drive the buses.'

'So we talk to her neighbours?' Kathi said. 'Or I talk to her neighbours, flashing my PI license at them?'

'Meantime though,' said Todd, 'and don't shout me down before you hear me out, Lexy.' That's never a great opening, but I managed to keep my mouth shut until I had heard more. 'Remember that time you were trying to be a good witness and you sucked at it?'

'No.'

'And remember how we got past the problem?'

'No.'

'And it cracked the case.'

'Wait . . . No.'

'Exactly,' he said. 'You're doing my arguing for me here! You don't even remember it, so it obviously wasn't a big deal, so there's no problem doing it again, despite all your bitching.'

'Hang on,' I said. 'Are you talking about hypnotizing me? Because I was pretty clear last time that that was a one-shot deal. I can't believe you would want to put me through it again.'

'Put you through what?' said Todd. 'You knew nothing about it. As far as you were concerned, you zoned out for a little while, like you do when you get a head massage. It was hardly traumatic.'

'Yeah, but I wasn't trying to remember the details of my wedding celebrant strangled with a string of fairy lights, was I?'

'What?' said Todd. 'Oh my God! What do you take me for? I didn't mean regress you to your wedding day. I meant take you back to the night of the Jane-Doe-tree-peeing-banshee incident. If you could recall any more from then, we might really be motoring.'

'Huh,' I said. 'But I haven't forgotten anything from that night. Unearthly scream, pounding footsteps, punched in the face, you two turned up.'

'What?' Kathi had raised her head from Sister Sunshine's memorial Facebook page at last. 'You didn't get punched in the face the night of the Nina Pradash overhanging branches.'

'I hate to be argumentative,' I said, 'but I still had open wounds and bruising when I went to meet Sister Sunshine for the first time days later. I'm still surprised she didn't ditch me right there and then in case I tarnished her brand.'

'Oh, is that right?' said Todd. 'You were in The Garden with Sister Sunshine and someone who was staking her out punched you in the face and the cuts and bruises hadn't healed by the time you went to meet Sister Sunshine for the first time so she could take you to show you the venue, where you were when someone was staking her out.'

'Stop!' I said. 'You're making me dizzy. OK, two different nights. I made a mistake. Shoot me.'

'I'd rather hypnotize you,' said Todd. 'To see if there's any tiny improvement we could make to your not-at-all ropey recall.'

'I was in the midst of an unusual psychological period,' I said.

'Telling me,' muttered Kathi, without looking up.

And there was the dust bunny again. 'Beef,' I said. 'Cut face from a punch.'

'Kathi,' said Todd. 'We need to take Lexy to the emergency room. She's having a neurological event.'

'Shut up, the both of you,' Kathi said. 'I've found something. I've found someone who didn't love Sister Sunshine.'

'Posting on her memorial page?' said Todd. 'Tacky. Read it out.'

'"Sonja Fisher was a good businesswoman, with the ruthlessness to make it in a tough market. I hope she died happy with her choices."'

'Wow,' I said. 'That's horrible.'

'But interesting, right?' said Kathi. 'It was posted by someone called "She's The One" – quite the ego there, huh? – and this She's The One, if I check quickly, has . . . yeah, it's a new account, opened five days ago, no friends.'

'Sounds like as many friends as she deserves,' said Todd.

'At least Sister Sunshine didn't see it,' said Kathi.

'Unless . . .' I put in. 'I wonder if there are comments on her business websites. Kathi, look up "Sunniest, summeriest, lightest, brightest Solstice, flowers and frills weddings in California".'

'Is that her website address?' said Todd. 'I can't agree about her being a good businesswoman. That is a branding disaster.'

'No,' I said. 'That's more or less what I Googled to find her that first night when Linda Magic was trying to sign me up to get hitched in a crypt.'

'"Sister Sunshine",' said Kathi, reading off her phone. '"The Sunniest Celebrant in the State."'

'Comments?' said Todd.

'Site's locked,' said Kathi. 'Must be nice to be the cops, huh? They've shut this baby right on down.'

'Although, to be fair,' I said, 'it wasn't Linda who wanted me to get married actually in a mausoleum surrounded by corpses and cobwebs.' I would have been hard-pressed to say whether Todd or Kathi hated the sentence more. 'That was Taylor. I'd forgotten.'

'Hypnosis could help you remember all kinds of things,' said Todd, but I was already calling. Taylor's ringtone for me was a seasonally adjusted birdcall, set very low, so it wouldn't be a problem if his phone rang when he was in a hide, but he still sounded freaked when he answered.

'Lex? Everything OK?'

'Remember when you said we should get married in a crypt?' I started with. Then I gave him a good long time to catch up. I'm already a great wife, in my opinion.

'Wasn't that in January?' he said.

'Yeah. So?'

'So, couldn't this wait till I was home?'

'No. What was that about?'

After a huge pause – or maybe a pause that long should be called a silence – he said, 'You won't like it, so I'm not going to tell you.'

'I'm putting you on speaker,' I told him.

'This is quite young to be turning into your mother,' he replied. Damn him; he really did make me laugh even when he was annoying me.

'Say that first bit again,' I said, holding the phone up to Todd and Kathi.

'The part where I said, "I'm not going to answer your question about the crypt because you won't like it"?'

Todd and Kathi burst out in great big gratifying hoots and yelps of laughter.

'Oh Taylor, Taylor, Taylor,' Todd said. 'I can laminate a little card for your wallet. Top five staying-married tips.'

'Or I could get Noleen to explain it to you,' said Kathi. She looked at Todd. '"You won't like the answer so you're not going to get it"!' Then they both cracked up again.

'I'll see you tonight,' I said.

'Does this need flowers?' Taylor asked me and the note of dejection in his voice set me off cackling too.

'Don't you dare,' I said, when I had got a hold of myself again. 'The wedding flowers are still opening, some of them. They're getting bigger before my very eyes!'

So he was laughing too as he rang off and it was only as my smile faded into a warm glow of fondness I realized he hadn't answered me. 'What are you doing?' I asked Kathi, to distract myself.

'Looking up "She's The One". Do you think someone would more likely call themselves after a terrible movie or a terrible song? What do we think?'

'I've never seen the movie but the song's OK,' I said.

'Ewwwwwwww!' said Todd. 'No way, Lexy. That song is *nasty*! Her unfillable private place? Her cream that he'd like to polish his boots with?'

'What?' I said. 'This must be a remix.'

'Wait, Todd,' said Kathi, still hunched over her phone. 'There are two *different* songs, I think. Bruce Springsteen with his dirty boots – and I agree, ew – and then a Robbie Williams one which' – she scrolled up a bit – 'has no lyrics at all. My God, it's like baby's first word book. I was young, I am old, that is up, this is down. And yet it says here it's one of the top ten first dance songs at British weddings. Oh my God, this is tragic. Ed Sheeran, Michael Bublé . . . Who the hell's Chris Rea?' She looked up when the silence got awkward. 'What?' she said.

'Did we ever hear what Lexy and Taylor were planning to shuffle round the floor to?' said Todd. 'Because from the look on your face right now, Lexy, I'm guessing it's something *pretty funny*.'

'That's not what's wrong,' I said. 'And it was Toploader's "Dancing in the Moonlight".'

'Who?' said Kathi. She and Noleen had a serious concert habit and she didn't care for not having heard of musicians that other people knew.

'Or maybe something by The Magic Numbers,' I said, but I'd over-egged it.

'Yeah, no way you were still deciding, day of,' said Todd.

'Stop distracting me,' I said.

'Brides be crazy!' said Todd.

The sun had been up for hours in real life but, in my mind, that right there was the moment of light dawning, of birds chirping a symphony and of sweet peace stealing over the land.

'You OK?' said Kathi. 'You look weird.'

'Todd,' I said, 'you're a genius. Well, more of an accidental idiot savant, but thank you anyway.'

'Go on,' said Todd.

'*Who'd* have beef with a wedding celebrant?' I said. '*What* caused the state I was in from January to June this year? And *why* choose a username that's one of the top wedding songs and say of a dead woman that she was a ruthless business dealer who might regret her choices?'

'Are you confessing?' said Todd. He didn't sound quite as jokey as I'd like.

'Not me,' I said. 'Not *actually* me. But not far off. Listen, you know how Sister Sunshine's schtick – man, that's hard to say – Sonja Fisher's schtick – Jesus, that's worse – was telling couples she had just got a cancellation and they had to move fast before it was snapped up again?'

'Is that legal?'

'Never mind, she won't be doing it in the future. But here's what I'm thinking. What if my wedding really *was* a cancellation? I mean, what if Sister Sunshine gave me the date because someone else she was hustling didn't sign up in time and so I ended up with someone else's wedding day. And that other bride – whoever she was – couldn't get over it and so she . . . did what she did.'

'Lexy!' Kathi said. She put down Todd's phone and stood up and came over and put her arms round me, squeezing me till my bra creaked, kissing me on my forehead with such a fierce kiss that there was an audible pop when the suction gave way.

'What's all this in aid of?' I said. Kathi's physical-affection setting is close to Scotland level (sober Scotland level, that is; drunk is another stinky, sloppy, germy question altogether) and she was usually such respite for me.

'The ring,' said Todd. He was saying it into my hair, because of course he'd piled on; there was no hug ever hugged that Todd wasn't willing to turn into a group hug. 'Kathi, I think you're right.'

I extricated myself from both of them, leaving them with their arms around each other but both facing me. 'Ring?' I said, but I was tracing a line down my face so obviously the thought was bubbling its way up from somewhere.

'The night of the dragon-mask attack,' Todd said. 'The ER nurse said you would probably get an infection from the depth of the cut because people's fingernails are gross.' Kathi let go of him and stepped away. 'And you said you thought it was a ring, not a fingernail, and she said the cut would definitely get infected in that case because people clean their fingernails a lot more often than they clean their rings.' Kathi looked down at her wedding ring, a ring she removed on a weekly basis to scrub both it and the band of skin underneath it. She swallowed hard.

'So here's what I'm thinking,' Todd said. 'What if it was a new ring, like a brand-new ring, like the just-slipped-onto-the-finger engagement ring of a bride-to-be? That would mesh with what you're saying.'

'Oh God, Lexy,' Kathi said, surging forward and throwing her arms round me again.

'OK,' I said, shifting Kathi off to the side a bit like a bag of shopping. 'I get that. But the second night, the night of the banshee—'

'When it was coming straight for you and then it shrieked and swerved and went for Sister Sunshine instead . . .?' said Todd. He covered his mouth.

'Maybe it didn't,' said Kathi. She was still clutching me.

'It did,' I said. 'I was standing right there. You were miles away and I saw it clearly.'

'No, Kathi's right,' said Todd. 'Yes, the banshee swerved, but it wasn't going for Sister Sunshine. It was going for that ridiculous Hobby Lobby explosion of a mood board she'd set up for you.'

'I thought it was pretty,' I said. Then, realizing I might be somewhat missing the point, I added, 'But of course it was going for

Sister Sunshine. We know it was, because on my wedding day – presumably not all dressed in black with leather gloves on, although who knows – it *did* go for Sister Sunshine. It *killed* Sister Sunshine.'

'Lexy!' Kathi put both her arms round my neck and squeezed. It wasn't so much a hug as a wrestling move. When I spied Todd bearing down again too, I worked my jaw free and said, 'Public toilet, cockroach, bowling shoes, ant heap,' so that they both fell back out of arm's reach. 'Sorry,' I said. 'But calm down. What's wrong with you?'

They shared a glance then Todd nodded at Kathi telling her to go ahead.

'OK,' she said. 'Think back to your wedding day, Lexy. You slept in a shared room with your mother the night before, right?'

'Don't remind me,' I said. '*Do* remind me never to share a room with my mother after Mexican food, though.'

'And we drove you to the venue,' Todd added. 'Then hair and make-up and then you wanted a meeting with your attendants and Della brought the baby and we were all there, or you know, taking it in shifts because we needed breaks for sanity and self-care and basically, until you went walkabout and saw the . . . fairy lights . . . you hadn't been alone all day.'

'And I'm grateful,' I said. 'I could do without the casting up and guilt-tripping because I'm not sure how much more sorry you expect me to get. I'm sorry, right? Never again, but what's your point?'

'Simply this,' Kathi said. 'The murderer must have known that the window of opportunity for getting to the intended victim when she was unprotected was the run-up to the ceremony because, once the ceremony started and then afterwards at the reception, there was zero chance that the bride would be alone for a moment.'

'Celebrant,' I said, honestly thinking she had just suffered a slip of the tongue.

Kathi shook her head. 'But guess what? It didn't work. Because of the extreme entitlement and total disregard for the needs of others, you had at least one minion dancing to your tune every single second of the goddam day.'

'This is completely gratuitous,' I said. 'If I write "sorry" on my bum and moon you every night for a month through your bedroom window, would that be any good?'

'So the murderer, full of rage and determined to mete out punishment, did what the banshee didn't do.'

'Huh?'

'Swerved to Sister Sunshine,' Todd said.

Kathi put her knuckle in her mouth and bit down to keep from crying, or maybe to keep from hugging someone who had just said, 'bowling shoes'. I hope it was the shoes thing because it didn't work for the crying; tears were pouring down her face and dripping off her chin to make dark splashes on her polo shirt.

'Oh,' I said.

'Oh?' said Todd.

'Yes, oh. You're telling me I was the target and the banshee only murdered Sister Sunshine because it couldn't get to me?'

'Yes,' said Todd. 'That's what we're telling you. Could you maybe channel January-to-June Lexy, and have a little reaction, please?'

'Yep,' I said, as my eyes rolled up in my head and the pair of them faded to grey.

TWENTY

First things first – and even though I hated myself for caring more about my own skin than I had about Sister Sunshine's – I needed to get the scrap of black fabric I had snatched from the banshee, plus the photographs of the cut on my face from the night of the killer crocuses, to Molly, without delay.

'Killer crocuses?' she said, stopping writing and looking up at me over the top of her reading glasses. She hadn't worn reading glasses when I first met her and, thinking about her getting older, I found myself hoping she had someone in her life and wasn't married to her job.

'You've been given all this information twice before already,' Kathi said. 'The grave of Joey D'Ambrosi was defaced by the planting of crocus bulbs that spelled out an accusation of incest.'

'No,' I said. 'Joey D'Ambrosi had seaglass saying he killed his wife. The bulbs was Mr and Mrs Truman, with the accusation of . . . inappropriate behaviour.'

'As opposed to incest?' Molly said.

'Actually,' said Todd, 'the seaglass was how an accusation of murder was levelled at Mr and Mrs McKerran.'

'Ahem,' said Mills of God. We all started. Molly actually jumped. It was like a fire extinguisher suddenly piping up. 'It was tumbled glass, not authentic seaglass, and it spelled out the slander of incest with respect to William and Betsy Truman. The accusation that Mrs McKerran killed Mr McKerran was laid out in crocus bulbs and Joey D'Ambrosi's accusation of . . . inappropriate proclivities . . . was expressed in the medium of polished pebbles.'

'Wow,' said Molly. 'And yet you have a cheat sheet of call numbers taped to your dash. You know, Lexy, a date would have worked too.'

'Right,' I said. 'Well, that photo of my face was taken on whatever it says on the time stamp on whatever day it also says, in January, and I'm pretty sure it was Sister Sunshine's killer's engagement ring that raked my face. Like that piece of bombazine, which I managed to rip from a garment one night in April, has left a hole in one of Sister Sunshine's killer's outfits.'

Mills of God held open an evidence bag and I dropped the little scrap in.

'Taffeta,' he said. 'What kind of outfit *was* it?'

'Well,' said Todd, 'at the time we thought it was a costume – bat, vampire, banshee, something along those lines – but it might have been a black wedding dress. Or it might have been a guy. On account of how women can't pee out of trees.'

'Speak for yourself,' said Molly, which came out ruder than I think she meant it to and also quite nonsensical. 'So there was either a woman or a man in a tree wearing either a Halloween costume or a wedding dress. Anything else?'

'No other *physical* evidence,' I said. 'And I hope you know – I mean, please write it down – that we hotfooted it along here to turn it over as soon as we realized it was germane. I mean, just because it was January and April and now it's June, that doesn't mean we've been holding it back.' This wasn't strictly true and I hoped she wouldn't focus on it.

'Realized how?' said Molly. Damn.

'Right,' Kathi said. 'OK, Sergeant Rankinson, this is by way of a theory and we all know how much you love Trinity's theories but, if you would just hear us out, because I think we're on to something.' She took a deep breath and began.

Molly didn't hear us out. She stopped writing when we were halfway through and put the cap back on her pen with an unwarranted firmness a minute or so later. Long before we had all said everything on our minds, she folded her arms and sat back.

'A bride?' she said. 'A cancellation murder? I've heard it all now.'

Mills of God cleared his throat again. 'My daughter . . .' he began but a look from Molly quelled him.

'If only you'd seen Lexy in the run-up to midsummer,' Kathi said, 'you'd have no trouble believing it. But you must have seen brides-to-be in your personal life.'

Molly snorted. 'No.'

'You've never been a bridesmaid for a sibling or school friend or old college buddy?' Kathi said.

Another snort. 'No.'

'How'd you manage that?' said Kathi, sounding awed and a bit wistful. They really were quite a pair of pigs to me still, days on end after I'd snapped out of it.

'Listen,' Todd said. He was holding his phone up to her. At first

I didn't recognize the squawking and bleating that came out of it, then I got my ear in and realized it was my voice, high and fast, as if I was going to explode any minute. '. . . and it clearly says on the labelling that these are *sets* of glasses. Sets! For champagne, red wine, white wine and water. And if they were all the same height that would be normal and if they were all different heights that would be quirky but purposeful, but the water glass is the same height as the red wine glass, but the white wine glass is taller and the champagne glass is taller than the white wine glass, so my wedding meal table is going to look like the bric-a-brac stall at the last gasp of a really cheap yard sale and I might as well have red fucking solo cups.'

'I don't sound like that,' I said.

'I started taping you on speed and a half,' Todd said, 'because I was running out of storage space on my cloud.'

'It's a really good thing you have an alibi for the time of the murder,' Molly said. 'Was Ms Fisher responsible for the horror of your stemware?'

'My daughter . . .' said Mills of God. I was less sure he was trying to support me, coming round to the idea that he had leftover trauma he needed to get off his chest. Molly killed him with a glare in any case.

'So you could try asking around all the florists and that for a name,' I said.

'We are already looking at Ms Fisher's business contacts, *and* her clients,' Molly said. 'But thank you for your information. I'm sure I don't need to tell you again that it's an offence to interfere with an active police investigation.' She stood, gave us all a hard look and left.

'How did it turn out with your daughter?' I asked Mills, once she had gone.

'She calmed herself down on the big day with cannabis edibles and threw up on the pastor.' I only hoped they didn't have a videographer. But I bet they did.

Back out in the sunshine, I'm sure I wasn't the only one who felt like they'd just been in the headteacher's office, getting ticked off for putting gum on the seats of the school bus. We were giddy, the three of us.

'I like thinking that Mills has got a wife and family,' I said.

'Mills?' said Kathi. 'Mr Memory!'

'Molly would be a better detective if she wasn't so stubborn,' Todd said. 'And it's not going to help in the long run if we solve the case out from under her. She'll only become more cussed and dead set on her own way. So maybe we should do what we're told.'

'Yeah?' Kathi said.

'Lemme think about it,' said Todd. 'OK, I thought about it.' He stuck his tongue between his lips to blow a raspberry then saw Kathi's face at the thought of all that spittle and tucked his hand under the arm of his sleeveless T-shirt instead. He waxes everything so he's got lovely slick skin to make armpit farts with. This one was a belter. 'I still think it might have been a black wedding dress,' he said. 'Completely unrelated to that though, I say let's go visit Spence the wedding-dress designer to see how he's getting on after the trauma of the fire. And if the subject of Dita Von Teese and/or the question of non-traditional hues should happen to come up, then Sergeant Rankinson can bite me.'

'And we're all going?' I said. 'I'm pretty tired and even if I did have some energy I should really use it up on my parents.'

'Honey,' said Todd, 'if you think you're getting to go back to the boat and curl up in a ball just because there's a target on your back, you are sadly mistaken.'

'Or, like I said, because my parents are here.'

'No way,' said Kathi. 'But not because it would be flaking out and dumping us with all the work, Lexy. You're coming with us because you can't be left on your own because we all believe that someone has tried to kill you once already and, for all we know, is going to try again. And you can't rely on your parents to protect you because you can't tell your parents, you maniac, because it would break them. Jesus.'

So I was wrapped up in a glow of love as warm and snug as a cashmere blanket as we all got into the Jeep and cranked up the A/C against the sweltering heat – as it was the sort of day to make anyone wish she was wrapped up in a glow of love as cool and fresh as an icy spritzer – and headed for the causeway.

Spence's new bridal store was indeed in a much ritzier bit of Sacramento, with pom-pom bay trees in stone pots at either side of the entrance and the kind of hush that only comes with new, above code, building specs. As the door whispered shut behind us the sound of the midtown traffic disappeared without trace and we found ourselves ankle-deep in dove-grey carpet, breathing in subtle floral perfume and staring up into the onyx eyes of a security guard who stood like the God of All Gyms and Emperor of Tight T-shirts, with his enormous arms just about folded over his enormous pecs and his enormous thighs pressed together, although this meant that his enormous feet were still about a yard apart. Spence was taking no chances with his new gaff, it seemed, and had employed 'A Presence'.

'Perry!' said Todd.

'Todrick!' said The Presence, who did not suit the name 'Perry' at all.

'You know each other?' I said.

'If you go to the same gym then Todd's doing it wrong,' Kathi said.

'Dr K was there when I had a shoulder injury fixed with an epidural anaesthetic,' Perry said. 'We musta talked for two hours, huh Doc? Pro tip: take the knock-out. It's really boring lying there awake while someone puts you back together. Or it would have been if this dude wasn't the biggest gossip in the whole of Sac County.'

'Happy to help,' said Todd. 'Sorry we had to strap you down.' He turned to the two of us. 'We can't let patients turn their heads and view the procedure in case they panic and bolt. Perry was hard to persuade.'

Perry shook his head and made a waving it all away gesture. 'Hey, I usually pay extra for straps and buckles,' he said, then he laughed a rich baritone laugh that started deep under his feet down in the old, abandoned mines from the '49 Goldrush.

'Peregrine!' came a voice we recognized. 'What have I told you about brides and bondage stories?' An artfully pooled curtain behind the reception desk was swept aside and Spence stood framed in the archway.

'Hey!' he said. 'Look who it is! My favourite customers! You retaking your vows already? My dress was that good?'

'He says that to everyone,' Perry muttered.

'That's marriage for you,' Spence said, kicking one foot up to the side. 'We get to rehear the same stories over and over until one of us cuts out the other one's tongue.'

Truly, I thought to myself as we left Perry to be 'A Presence' some more and followed his husband into the belly of the boutique, every pot's got a lid.

'So what can I do for you for reals?' Spence said, when we had arranged ourselves on the little Louis XVI armchairs in his viewing area and got ourselves served with champagne.

'Well, it's a long shot,' I said. 'But did you hear what happened at my wedding?'

'No!' said Spence. 'Please tell me it wasn't someone standing up and saying, "Yes, I do object!" because I've always wanted to be there for one of those.'

'Um, no,' I said. 'We didn't get that far.'

'Jilted?' said Spence. 'And you want to know if I can take the dress back? Well, sure I can but not for full refund because of the alterations. Or you could give it to me to dye red and you keep it as a ballgown.'

'Right,' I said. 'That would be a godsend because all my ballgowns are getting shabby from overuse. But funny that you should mention wedding dresses of many colours.'

'Wait! *Are* you retaking your vows?'

'Spence? Hon?' came Perry's booming voice from the foyer. 'Why don't you shut up and let *them* tell *you*?'

Spence sighed dramatically. 'He insisted on helping out – he gets very bored after the end of term. He's a kindergarten classroom assistant.'

None of us reacted out loud, but surely I wasn't the only one who pictured tiny little bold kids climbing him like a tree and tiny little shy kids peeing their pants in terror at the sight of him.

'But in this instance he might have a point,' Spence went on. 'Tell me.'

'Lexy's celebrant was murdered at the venue before the vow-taking,' Kathi said. 'I see from your face that you knew her. Sister Sunshine? In summer, anyway. Well, we think we saw the murderer a few months before the attack, and again a few weeks before the attack, and on one of those occasions we managed to get a scrap of fabric from the miscreant's clothing. Which we think might be a wedding dress. Except that it's black. Refill?'

Spence had drained his glass in three gulps while listening and nodded, holding it out for a top-up.

'Man, if only we hadn't handed that fabric over to the police!' I said.

Kathi raised one eyebrow and dug into her pocket, drawing out a familiar looking swatch.

'What?' said Todd. 'You gave Molly a decoy?'

'I cut it in half and kept a piece,' Kathi said. 'They'll only shoot me if they find out.' She leaned forward and gave the scrap to Spence, who held it up to the light, sniffed it, felt it with his finger and thumb and then downed the other glass.

'I don't think this is a wedding dress,' he said.

'Yeah, we knew we were clutching at straws,' said Todd. 'Ah well.'

'No,' said Spence. 'If I'm right, it's a crinoline tuxedo.'

'A what?' said Kathi.

'Billy Porter,' said Todd and I in unison. I turned to Spence. 'Right?'

'Right,' he said. 'I haven't sold many of them since menswear escaped the closet but I haven't sold *none*. Usually white, I have to say, what with the whole wedding thing, you know. The crossover between a guy who wants a crino-tux—'

'Stop trying to make that happen!' shouted Perry. 'Crino-tux sounds like a procedure!'

'—and a guy who wants to be married in black is very small.'

'But don't most guys get married in black here?' I said. 'Because of the lack of kilts?'

Spence nodded thoughtfully and tapped his teeth. 'I'd like to talk to you about kilts sometime,' he said. 'But when two guys are marrying and one of them goes for a' – he lowered his voice – 'crino-tux, it's usually white.'

'What about when both of them . . .?' said Kathi.

'Never happened yet,' said Spence. 'I've only had one guy who wanted to marry a woman in one too.'

'You mean he wanted to wear one to marry a woman in, or he wanted to marry a woman who was wearing one?' said Todd.

'I'm confused,' Kathi said.

'You should put them in the window if you want them to start moving,' Perry said, appearing in the doorway. 'You just need to think up a better name for them that doesn't sound like it might need follow-up care. You would also need to believe me about—'

Spence held up a hand. 'No,' he said. 'I gave in about where the silverware goes in the dishwasher and I gave in about who the real hero of *Toy Story 3* is, but I am not going to risk another fire just to prove that you're wrong.'

'Why not call it the "Porter"?' said Todd. 'There's a neckline called Bardot and a bag called Birkin, after all.'

'Tuxoline, Crinedo, Edoline,' said Kathi. Wordle has warped her.

'Vegetable shortening, hair restorer, intimate ointment,' said Todd.

'Why not call them floor-length black tie?' I said. I turned to Perry. 'Believe you about what?' Sometimes I can't switch off being a relationship counsellor just because no one's paying me.

'I don't think the fire was a hate crime,' said Perry. 'Don't get me wrong. It was a crime and it was hateful, but it wasn't homophobia. It wasn't gay-bashing.'

'But didn't you say the message accused you of pandering to "abominations"?' said Kathi.

'That "undermined marriage"?' added Todd.

'Yup and yup,' said Perry. 'But in all our long life of slurs and hate, we have never once been attacked so . . . generally. No Bible verses, no nasty names, no salivating descriptions of the sex they *so* clearly wish they were having. I think this one was something else.'

'Like what?' said Kathi.

'I don't know, but something.'

'Oh shit,' I said. 'I think I do.' Kathi and Todd turned enquiring looks my way. 'I think it was more personal than a hate crime and I think the timing wasn't a coincidence.'

'Oh shit,' said Kathi.

'Oh shit, you've thought of something that's going to help us find out who torched my store?' said Spence.

'Oh shit,' said Todd. 'Yes, Spence, but the arson's going to be a side dish. So's the punch in the face with a brand-new ring on, and the charging about the cemetery over-dressed to the nines. The main course is murder.'

'Huh?' said Spence.

'The abomination was my wedding,' I said. 'It undermined marriage because I hopped into someone's date on a cancellation. And neither the bride nor the groom were very happy.'

'I *knew* it was a guy that night!' said Kathi. 'I *said* it was a guy!'

'Excuse me,' said Todd. 'You said it was a banshee.'

'Excuse *me*,' said Kathi. 'The Sex Volunteers said it was a banshee. I simply relayed the message.'

'You guys sure do have fun,' said Perry. Then he saw my face and sobered. 'Sorry.'

'Don't worry about it,' I assured him. I almost meant it too. 'Kathi? Todd? Excuse *me*, actually. It doesn't matter if the bride hid in the cemetery in February and raked my face with her new ring. And it doesn't really matter if the groom was up a tree peeing in his Porter in April. It matters which one of them put a firebomb through Spence's back window in March and it matters which one of them murdered Sister Sunshine.'

'If he peed in his crino-tux he doesn't deserve to own one,' said Spence.

'We'll tell him,' I said. 'If we find him. Spence, this one and only guy who wanted to wear the garment in question to marry a woman? What colour was it?

'It was black,' said Spence. 'I thought I told you.'

'And I'm assuming you still have his name?' I said, ignoring the claim that his word salad had been plain-speaking. 'And her name? The bellicose bride and the gross groom?'

'Lex,' said Todd. 'You don't think you maybe turned over two pages at once there? I mean, sure, it would be neat if Spence here sold the exact . . . garment . . . to the very guy, but it's a long shot. What we need to do is ask all the wedding designers in the city and maybe the state, narrow it down.'

'Way to make me feel special,' Spence said.

'OK,' I said. 'OK, we need to narrow it down to wedding designers who sold more of the very unusual garments in the most unusual colour – black – for the most unusual kind of wedding they get bought for – hetero – *and* had their boutique burnt down the same day I was there?'

Todd, to give him his due, blushed. 'So, *do* you have the names and contacts, Spence?' he said.

'Somewhere,' Spence said. 'In my records. For sure. But what with the fire and the fact that that account was closed, I would have to wait until I'm home with my archives. I can probably get it to you by later this evening.'

'Appreciate it,' said Kathi. 'Email this address.' She handed over a business card. 'Unless you'd rather tell the cops yourself. Miss out the middle man.'

'So . . . you explain the reasoning to the cops and take all their scorn and scepticism and I come along fill in the last missing piece?' said Spence.

'Yeah,' said Perry. 'Like when I make cream puffs to take to a pot-luck, and fill then and frost them and you carry them from the car.'

'Like when I trim the Christmas tree and I'm still stuck up the ladder when you switch the lights on,' said Spence. It was June. It's not every grudge-bearer can even remember their Christmas grudges in June, much less produce one without a run-up.

'Like when my wife waits until I've cleaned the entire house from top to bottom and then asks people I don't even know round for canasta,' said Kathi. That was a grudge from a long time back, I reckoned. They didn't live in their house anymore, because Kathi liked to keep it clean, and they only ever had us round. And what even was canasta?

'Like when my husband waits until I've packed my own suitcase for a trip and then decides he's only taking a carry-on,' said Todd. That wasn't remotely relevant but it was probably all he could dredge up. Roger is a saint.

'Anything from Love's Young Dream?' said Spence, looking at me.

'My partner wanted to get married in a crypt because the people buried there were Jewish,' I said.

'That's not the same thing at all,' said Todd, suddenly on relevance patrol.

'No, I know,' I said. 'It's just it popped back into my head because we were talking about early trips to the cemetery like that night we chased you two and you hid there.'

'A lo-ho-hot of fun you have,' said Perry.

'And I wouldn't even consider it,' I said. 'But I'm thinking now if I had said yes then Sister Sunshine would still be alive.'

'Taylor might be dead though,' Kathi said. Todd nudged her. Maybe he thought he did it subtly but they weren't sitting all that near each other and he had to scooch down in his chair to reach her with one toe. He had had quite a lot of the champagne and it looked like I was driving home. Again.

'What?' I said.

'Nothing!' said Kathi. She gave her empty glass a hard stare. 'Is this extra strong, Spence? To open wallets?'

'What do you know about Taylor suggesting a wedding in a crypt?' I said.

'Nothing,' said Todd, wide-eyed.

I turned to Spence. 'Hope to see you again sometime,' I said.

'Thanks for all your help. I've got to go. I need to tell another wild tale to a sarky mare of a cop and I need to speak to my beloved too.'

'Ohhhhh, you're in trouble!' said Perry pointing to Todd and Kathi with a wagging finger. 'Lexy, you're a strict one, aren't you? I'd really like to get to know you all better and maybe hang out sometime. Cemetery chases, tree-peeing banshees and sex volunteers? I'm in!'

TWENTY-ONE

'Any idea where my parents are?' I asked Noleen when we got back to the motel. She was in the pool, floating flat on her back in her usual swimming attire of an oversized basketball jersey and a pair of long shorts *so* oversized they made the top look body-con. When she floated on her back, of course, the slinky material clung to every inch of her and left nothing at all to the imagination except for skin tone, but I would never tell her and we were always careful to weed out any photographs.

'Gone on a bike ride,' Noleen said.

'It's a hundred degrees!'

'But there are no hills. They're making the most of it. Oh, and they asked me to tell you that they're taking all of us out for dinner tomorrow night before they fly home but they've left it up to you to choose where.'

'Great,' I said. Two kids, a germaphobe who hated eating inside, an insectophobe who hated eating outside, Noleen's unshakable dedication to 'no nonsense' and extreme view of what constituted nonsense, Devin's allergies and avoidances, Della's scorn for American cuisine, Roger's healthy habits, my mum and dad's problem with avocados, and only twenty-four hours to make the reservation.

'Oh and she's included Meera and Arif,' Noleen said. 'And José and Maria. She was sorry not to get more time with them at the wedding that wasn't.'

Superb. An observant Muslim, a pregnant vegan and two elderly Mexicans with teeth of chalk. 'Are Meera and Arif bringing the kids?'

'Of course,' said Noleen.

I was sorely tempted to book one of those bossy-arse pop-ups where you have to eat whatever they've made and like it. But then *I* might have to choke down red cabbage or squid. I'd work something out, I told myself. Then I had a brainwave! I would shunt this task off on to Taylor to punish him for whatever I was going to find out when he came home and I winkled out whatever it was Todd and Kathi weren't telling me.

Meanwhile, I went to my boat to stew in solitude.

* * *

They intercepted him and warned him, the treacherous toerags. All three of them arrived on deck together and they had clearly told him something was up. He tried his usual hilarious 'Honey! I'm home!', but his eyes were wary and he had his phone in his hands as if to call for help or start filming me to put on Twitter and ruin my life.

'Tay,' I said. 'Oh hi, you two, by the way.' He sat down on the porch floor and started removing his boots. 'Remember way, way back at the start of this case and the start of our wedding planning, when we went to the cemetery that night and I told you about Linda Magic saying they held weddings there, and you went into that crypt and you called me in there too and said you thought it was a lovely venue?'

Taylor peeled off one of his socks and dropped it over the side of the boat into the slough. 'You mean when I went back in to get that guy's attaché case after Todd left it behind?' he said.

'That's right,' I said. 'Excellent. We've homed in on which night running about a cemetery we're discussing.'

He peeled off the other sock and lobbed it over the side too, then he went down the steps to the one he could dangle his feet in the water from. 'I told you what abou—' he began.

'Yeah, you did,' I said. In my sessions, I'm always really clear with couples that they should hear each other out and never interrupt. It's dead hard. 'So think of this as your lucky night,' I said. 'You get a second chance to come clean and tell me the truth instead.'

'OK,' said Taylor.

'Bad idea,' said Todd, disguising it as a dry cough.

'Disastrous,' added Kathi, disguising it as a sneeze, like she would just sneeze and cope. Like she would stay sitting next to Todd if he had just coughed.

'I had a premonition,' Taylor said. 'You had just said "my wedding" to me. Not "our wedding" and I had a clear premonition of what was coming. I suppose I just kind of lost it for a moment. I wanted to stop it all from happening. What I thought was going to happen. What *did* happen. It soon passed over and I accepted my fate, as you know. But, just for a minute there, in the dark of the crypt that night, it was like I saw a chink of light and couldn't help turning my face towards it.'

I breathed in and out. Box-breathing: in for four, hold for four, out for four, hold for four.

'Sorry,' he said.

'The thing is,' I told him, 'we think we know who killed Sister Sunshine and we think whoever it was wanted to kill me but couldn't get to me. And we think they wanted to kill me because I – we – got their cancelled wedding date. We think one of them punched me that night in the cemetery in February, and one of them torched Spence's boutique to try to burn my wedding dress in March, and then one of them came screaming at me like a banshee in April and then, in June, one of them was all set to kill me. So, looking at it all objectively, I'm not in any position to tell you you're mistaken about how bad brides and sometimes grooms can be.'

'What?' said Taylor. He swivelled round and tucked his wet feet up on the step beside him so he was facing me. 'That's insane.'

'Like you've just been telling me,' I said. 'Brides gone wild.'

'No, not that,' Taylor said. 'Well, yes that would be insane. But I mean you're insane for thinking that's what happened. This wasn't a disappointed customer, Lexy. Even you didn't go nuts enough to kill someone and you were . . . You know what? I'm going to leave that sentence unsaid. But I'm sure you're nuts to be thinking that's what happened. This was a crime of passion. Not a crime of shopping.'

'Weddings aren't purchases,' I said. 'Marriage is—'

'Tell that to Keith and his credit card,' said Kathi.

'Well, it wasn't a crime of party-planning either,' said Taylor.

'Weddings aren't parties either,' I said. 'Marriage is—'

'Yours sure wasn't,' said Todd.

'Weddings aren't marriage,' Taylor said. He put his head on one side and smiled at me, crinkling up his eyes. As the years pass that could either become the thing about him that floods me with tenderness or possibly the habit of his that makes me want to beat him with a bat. It's too soon to tell.

Kathi's phone rang before I could think up an answer.

'Well, we're just about to find out,' she said. 'This is Spence getting back to me with the name of the bride and groom. I'll put him on speaker.'

'Hey,' came Spence's voice, out of the phone. 'We found the information you were asking for. Perry, I'm on the phone! What? Can it wait till I'm done with this? *What?*'

'God almighty, it's the gay American Judith and Keith Campbell,' said Todd.

'What?' said Spence. 'Listen, Perry wants me to tell you that we put a crino-tux – oh gimme a break! – in the window right after you left today and two kids from Jesuit High came in asking if they could hire them for their senior prom.'

'The priest's going to love that,' said Todd.

'What's a crino-tux?' said Taylor.

'Billy Porter,' said Kathi.

The reply was so inevitable that we all chorused it along with him: 'Who?'

'Anyway,' said Spence. 'Do you want these names? The groom was a guy called Steve Marr. And the bride's name was Sonja Fisher.' He waited. 'Sonja with a J and no C in Fisher. So you'll take it from there?' He waited again. 'Let me know how it goes with Cuento's Finest. Bye then. I think the call dropped,' he added to Perry as he hung up. But the call hadn't dropped. It was just that none of us could speak.

Taylor broke the silence. 'Told you,' he said. 'Crime of passion. Sonja Fisher gave away her own wedding date and her jilted lover killed her.'

'But-but-but . . .' I said. 'But that first night in the cemetery it was definitely a woman who punched me. Why would Sister Sunshine have done that?'

'Got him,' Kathi said, looking up from her phone. She's got a reverse address book on account of being a licensed PI. 'He lives in Cuento.'

'Yes, but Kathi,' said Todd. 'We don't need to tell Molly his address when we phone her to give her his name, because the cops can do that looking-people-up thing too.'

'Uh-huh, uh-huh,' Kathi said, 'and I absolutely will phone Molly. Of course I will. But does anyone feel like a moonlit drive?'

'You can't be serious,' Taylor said. 'He's a killer. You're not going to confront him. Lexy, tell her.'

'No,' I said. 'I'll tell you. We're just going to go to his house and park on the street so that, after we've called Molly and she's arrived too, we can watch the fun. Maybe take a few pics. For the archive.'

'Archive,' said Kathi. 'Where do we keep that? Is it in our office?'

'Let's discuss it en route,' Todd said. 'Taylor, please move those spongy trotters so Kathi can get by without puking.'

'Don't go,' Taylor said, as I passed him. 'Or, you know, be careful.'

'Brilliant advice,' I said. 'What would I do without you?' I was still pissed off with him but it was nice to know he cared.

'Exactly,' he said, and fell into step. We three were four, for tonight anyway.

Steve Marr lived in the newest sub-division in north Cuento, a carbon-capturing, sustainable, affordable maze of a place where eco-housing was laid out in a rough circle, which – along with the yellow colour and crispy texture of the un-irrigated communal grass – had led to it being known as The Tortilla. Marr's place was one of a staggered row of townhouses, with enormous solar-sucking windows right along the south side. Unfortunately, all the blinds were closed. We parked across the street and up a bit, waiting to see if he might come home from being out or come out from being in. If it had been bin night, the complex system of recycling would have meant he was out front for long enough to let us get a good look at him, but no such luck. Kathi was just about to dial the number for the cop shop, when the front door opened.

Todd grabbed her arm. I grabbed Taylor's arm. Kathi flicked Todd to make him let go of her arm. Todd grabbed his throbbing finger. And we were all sitting there, frozen in place like the world's least imaginative diorama, as Sergeant Molly Rankinson emerged on to the doorstep.

'Shit!' said Kathi and dived for the footwell.

I thought then, and maintain to this day, that if we had all stayed still she wouldn't have noticed us. As it was, she tramped over squeaking and crackling from her sturdy shoes and her shoulder walkie-talkie.

'Well, well, well,' she said.

'It's a public highway and I'm sober and this vehicle is taxed and insured,' said Todd.

He needn't have worried. Molly was too euphoric about her collar to bother reading us the riot act. 'We've got him,' she said. 'He's in a cell. He's denying everything but we've got him.'

'What about Linda Magic and the rest of them?' said Kathi. 'Have you still got them too?'

'The cemetery shenanigans were nothing to do with the Fisher murder,' Molly said. 'Like I kept telling you. I knew all along those four bozos were only trying for a little free PR that one and only time they called me. Cuento PD has better things to do.'

'You couldn't have told us that?' said Kathi.

Molly ignored her.

'Well, can you tell us this at least?' I said. 'How'd you catch him?'

'He left a thumbprint on one of the parts of the fairy lights that's not a bulb or a wire,' Molly said.

'A petal surely,' said Kathi. 'If it's *flower* fairy lights. Right, Lexy? He left a thumbprint on one of only three petals included in the design.'

'How did you match the print?' I said. Molly wasn't the only one who could ignore people.

'He was in the system from an incident on Earth Day when he tried to free a herd of dairy cows from the veterinary science department at UCC,' Molly said, her voice dripping with scorn. Molly was a red meat kind of gal. 'We have no motive,' she went on, 'and no theory – sorry to disappoint you all; I know how much you love a little Masterpiece Theatre – but we have solid physical evidence and an airtight case. You turning up here has actually saved me a trip. I was going to swing by and tell you.'

'It was a crime of passion,' said Taylor.

'Caused by a poor business decision,' I said.

'Well, an excellent business decision to be fair,' said Kathi. 'A poor life decision.'

'What are you all talking about?' said Molly.

'The motive,' said Todd. 'We can help you out there, Molly. Mr Marr was engaged to Ms Fisher and she dumped him.'

'I am not going to ask you how you know that, when I expressly forbade you from meddling in my case,' Molly said. 'I don't want to hear another word, OK?'

'Can I say two more words?' I asked her. 'Short ones.'

'No.'

'Can I say one?'

Molly groaned.

'One each?' said Todd.

Molly groaned again.

'You're,' I said.

'Very,' said Todd.

'Welcome,' said Kathi.

Molly, with a thunderous expression on her face, turned to Taylor.

'Again,' he said.

Which even I thought was a bit much. I didn't blame her for the way she stalked off. And, besides, I was glad she was gone. When it was just the four of us again, we all sank back and breathed as if we'd been underwater for a week.

'Right then,' Taylor said after a while. 'What do you do when a case is finished and all the loose ends are tied up?'

'Book a table for sixteen,' I said. 'Make my parents' last night a good one.'

But his words were bothering me. Were all the loose ends tied up? I fingered my cheek where the scratch of that engagement ring had long since healed.

'I'm going to try calling the Sex Volunteers,' Todd said. 'If they're still in jail, will their phones be off or will a cop answer to find ou— Oh, hello, Bob. Where are you?' He listened for a while, nodding. 'They're out,' he mouthed at us. 'Of course,' he said, into the phone. 'We should get together for a debrief— Oh they did? Are you? OK, well, until tomorrow then.' He hung up.

'Your parents invited them to dinner,' he said.

'How do my parents even know them?'

'Because they came to the motel straight from jail to speak to us, and Judith and Keith were back and apparently your dad thinks the cemetery tours sound very interesting and he's ashamed of not being better informed about those tiny coffins and . . . you know your mom. Lexy. Table for twenty it is.'

Of course we ended up in the forecourt. Of course we did. A table for twenty at a day's notice was only ever going to be a possibility in the kind of place you'd never want to eat. Devin set up a gluten-free grill. Noleen set up what she insisted on calling a 'normal' grill. We cleaned Odie's Ovens out of extra-large pizzas and my mum made five pavlovas.

'I can see why you're so happy here,' she said, looking down the length of the trestle table. Diego was thrilled to see Meera's kids again. The three of them had all had a wonderful lockdown together and the boys still missed each other, especially when the girls got too much. Noleen looked as content as was compatible with this many people bugging her. Kathi was just about coping with the communal food and close quarters; mostly because the majority of the group knew her ways and fell back into them without being asked. It helped that the Sex Volunteers were down the other end in deep talks with my dad about history and public access to records and how to start a viral trend in a small town. 'As long as he doesn't think he's getting off with the work of the B&B,' my mum said, pointing a chicken drumstick at him. 'I can write him pages of instructions too.'

I looked where she was pointing and noticed Juni Park making copious notes with that slim silver pen of hers. I found myself staring at her.

'I still can't believe they did all that,' my mum said. 'Your dad better not get any ideas in that direction.'

'Nah,' I said. 'Dad's too normal. He would never set hoaxes and pranks and then hire detectives to solve the riddles hoping they wouldn't.'

'That was bonkers,' said my mum.

'Mitch called it beta-testing.'

'It's strange that you never saw them,' my mum said. 'All those months, they were lurking around and you were lurking around and you never caught them at it.'

I turned to face her, finding her closer than I'd thought she was when we'd been side by side both looking forward. 'Mum,' I said. 'You're a genius.'

'I really am,' she said. 'You're so lucky to have me. What are you talking about?'

'We *did* overlap,' I said. 'One night. Just the once. Juni was there when we went to look at some slanderous crocus bulbs. She had a mask on but it was definitely her. She leapt out to punch me in the face and she probably forgot she was holding that bloody pen.'

'Well, we'll just see about that!' said my mum pushing her chair back.

I put my hand on her arm. 'No, leave it. It's water under the bridge now. And look how happy everyone is.'

Roger and Todd were sitting with arms around each other, as were Della and Devin. I might have joined in if Taylor had been close enough, but he was miles away, staring up the table at me with terror in his eyes, gauging the right time for his big announcement.

'Oh, all right then,' my mum said. 'Love not war. Speaking of: when's the re-match, Lexy? You going for here again or can we persuade you to come home for a ceilidh?'

Frantically, I signalled down the table to Taylor: the moment had come.

He stood up and tinged his fork against his wine glass.

'Ladies and gentlemen,' he said. 'You all dodged a speech from me a few days ago, so you're going to have to sit through one now. Keith? Judith? I know I can't be what you expected in a son-in-law, but I'm determined to make sure Lexy never regrets springing me on you. Thank you for bringing up such a . . . feisty and . . . entertaining daughter. Friends, I would like you all to raise your glasses and juice cups and join me in toasting her health—'

'Eh, son?' said my dad. 'You've skipped a bit. That sounds like a wedding speech and if you cast your mind back, you didn't have a wedding.'

'Eh, Tay?' I said. 'You *have* skipped a bit. Do you want me to do it?'

Taylor swallowed hard and shook his head. 'On the twenty-first of June,' he said. 'On our wedding day. After the M-U-R-D-E-R—'

'Murder,' said Diego.

'—before the police got us all put in order for processing, Lexy and I slipped away for a minute and did the deed.'

'Ew,' said Noleen. 'TMI.'

'Not *that* deed,' I said. 'The other deed. The relevant admin.'

'What?' said my mum.

'Hallelujah!' said Kathi.

'What's going on?' said my dad, finally forgetting about the gravestones of Midlothian and how to recreate all the fun of the Cuento Sex Volunteers.

'We got married,' Taylor said. 'Since that's what we were there for.'

'No!' said Todd. 'You mean there's not going to be another wedding? Lexy! How could you?'

'Halle-fricking-lujah!' said Kathi. 'I'm never going to have to put that muck on my face again. And Todd, are you off your meds? Lexy isn't going to be a bride again.'

'Oh,' said Todd. 'Yeah. I forgot about that part. That's a relief.'

'I wasn't that bad,' I said.

It took a long time for all of them to stop shouting me down and setting me straight, but when they finally quieted my dad cleared his throat and spoke. 'Who married you, Lex?'

'Bertrand,' I said. 'That minister mum kidnapped off the plane.'

'See?' said my mum. 'See? I told you it would be legal.'

'Well, no,' said Taylor. 'I had to lend him my phone because he hadn't paid for data roaming. He went online and got ordained while we waited.'

'What?' said my mum. 'You got married by a Church of Scotland minister but he might as well have been a dog in the street? Oh, Lexy!'

'Mum,' I said. 'You came over because I was getting married. And I'm married. You wanted a party and here we are, having a party. Bit of a long gap between the two bits, I'll grant you.'

'There always is,' said my dad. 'Those wedding photographers are out of control these days.'

'So you're not angry?' I asked him.

'Weddings are one thing,' said my dad. 'Marriage is another thing. Only one of those two things really matters.'

'Marriage is *lots* of other things,' said Roger, dropping a kiss on Todd's head.

'And even more on a Saturday night,' Todd said.

'Marriage is like running a three-legged race with a coked-up racoon,' said Noleen. 'No offence, Kathi.'

'Fair,' Kathi said.

'Marriage,' said Devin, 'is a miracle. Everyone says it's work, but it's not.'

'Oh, it's work,' said Della.

'Marriage is worth getting right,' said Meera.

'And when it's right, you know it's right,' Arif agreed.

'Marriage is looooooong,' said José.

Maria batted him with the back of her hand. 'Marriage,' she said, 'is the blink of an eye. You see a boy in the street and smile. Then poof! You are cutting his horny toenails because his back is bad now.'

'You up for that, Lexy?' said Taylor. 'I have a set of talon clippers that'll make it easier.'

'Marriage,' I said, 'is OK so far. It'll do me.'

FACTS AND FICTIONS

I've given up denying that Cuento in Beteo County is Davis in Yolo County. Apart from anything else, there are Easter eggs in every book. The egg-hunt clues for *Scotzilla* are on its page at www.catrionamcpherson.com.

Cuento's cemetery and Davis's are in roughly the same place in the respective towns but the similarities end there and, despite the fact that I attended a wedding at a hop garden and micro-brewery in 2023, my fictional venue is not Rusthaller and that sweet dream of a real-life bride was nothing like Lexy. Also, Sister Sunshine's curated collection is not based on any Davis gift shop and, unfortunately, Spence's bridal boutique is made up too.

As to the Sex Volunteers' inspirations for their doomed project, I heartily recommend checking them out: John Berendt's *Midnight in the Garden of Good and Evil*; Kit Williams's *Masquerade*; the tiny coffins, now on display in the National Museum of Scotland in Edinburgh; and Steven Moffat's brilliant *Dr Who* episode, 'Blink'.

Finally, the true inventor of the nasal cannula was a man called Wilfred Jones. I am happy to believe he was Mitchell Verducci's grandpa.

ACKNOWLEDGEMENTS

I would like to thank: Lisa Moylett, Zoe Apostolides, Elena Langtry and Jamie Maclean at Coombs, Moylett, Maclean; everyone at Severn House, especially Sara Porter, Jo Grant, Martin Brown, Anna Harrisson and Jem Butcher; the booksellers, librarians, bloggers, reviewers, and fellow readers and writers who somehow make a community out of this band of awkward loners and assorted misfits; and my family and friends around the world, most especially this time, the McPhersons. I started this book showing early chapters to someone I love to distract her from chemo. I finished the final edit in between taking care of 'sadmin' after the death of my father. Two thoughts: one, thank God the jokes were already written; two, cancer can do one. Finally, I'm indebted to anyone who has ever invited me to a wedding. Neil and I sloped off to Gretna Green. Neil – thank you. Everyone else – you're welcome.